LILAC MILLS

Love in the
City by the Sea

DCANELO

First published in the United Kingdom in 2018 by Canelo

This edition published in the United Kingdom in 2022 by

Canelo
Unit 9, 5th Floor
Cargo Works, 1–2 Hatfields
London, SE1 9PG
United Kingdom

A CIP catalogue record for this book is available from the British Library.

Print ISBN 978 1 80436 188 7
Ebook ISBN 978 1 78863 272 0

Look for more great books at www.canelo.co

Printed and bound in Great Britain by Clays Ltd, Elcograf S.p.A.

1

To my mother – who gave me her love of reading.

There is no greater gift. Thank you.

Thank you also to Nati Hurtado for making sure I didn't make a complete fool of myself in Spanish and correcting my terrible grammar.

Your help was both generous and very welcome.

October

Weight: Really?? The scales must be broken!

Tess bent over, her hands on her knees, and sucked in a great lungful of air, feeling slightly sick. Her nose was running, her chest hurt, she had a stitch in her side, her knees ached, her calves were cramping, she had shin splints, and her feet felt as though they'd been repeatedly pounded by a sadistic chef wielding a pair of steak mallets. Oh, and she thought she might have a blister on her left heel.

'Why are you stopping, you big baby?' Her sister's voice held no hint of breathlessness.

Tess lifted her head enough to snarl at Emma, who was dancing around on the balls of her feet, looking as fresh as when they'd left the house.

'We've only been out five minutes,' Emma pointed out.

Was that all? It felt more like half an hour. Tess continued to gasp for breath, wondering if she was about to pass out on the pavement.

'We've got two miles to go yet.' Emma glanced over her shoulder at their parents' house, which was all of 500 yards down the road and had been the starting point for their run.

Tess followed her gaze. The house was far too close. Someone must have moved it, because there was no way she'd only run to the end of the road. It felt like she'd run those two miles already.

'You go on, I'm done,' she said, and even those few words were an effort.

Emma stopped bouncing and planted her hands firmly on her hips. 'You promised!'

Had she? Surely she hadn't *promised*…? Vaguely agreed, maybe, but not *promised*. Tess thought back to the conversation last night. The pair of them had been snuggled up on Tess's sofa, enjoying a girly night of watching *Strictly Come Dancing* with nibbles and a bottle of wine, when Emma had asked for a favour.

Emma had always been the sister with more get-up-and-go, so it was no surprise to Tess to hear her say that she wanted to run a marathon for charity and was looking for some support.

'Of course I'm in.' Tess dipped her fingers into the bag of popcorn and stuffed a handful in her mouth. 'What do you need? Someone to chart your progress? A wake-up call every morning? What?'

It would be a pain having to get up early for the sole purpose of ensuring that her sister was out of bed but she'd do it, and anyway, she could always go back to sleep afterwards.

'I want someone to run with me,' Emma said.

Tess hastily swallowed her mouthful and almost choked on it. 'Sorry, for a second there I thought you said *run* with you.'

'I did.'

'You do know who you're talking to, right? Tess? Your sister? The one who's allergic to exercise?'

'You'll enjoy exercising once you start, honest. Besides, I want to do this for Ella.'

'Ella,' Tess repeated flatly, the lingering taste of popcorn like ashes in her mouth. Ella's memory always lay between them, haunting all the family. It had been hard for their parents to lose a child and just as hard, but in a different way, for Emma to lose her twin, her other half.

'I want to raise money for cancer research.' Emma squirmed around on the sofa to look Tess in the eye. 'It's not fair! Ella should be at my wedding, Tess, standing next to you and hating me for making her wear a hideous dress. If we can raise some money for charity, even a just a little, it'll go some way to preventing another family going through what we have.'

Tess bit her lip. Yes, Ella should still be here, but she wasn't, though Tess wished with all her heart that things were different. It hurt too much to talk about her, especially with what should be such a joyous occasion on the horizon, so she took the conversation in a slightly different direction, not wanting to visualize the Ella-shaped hole in the bridesmaid line-up.

'You've not actually said what sort of dress you've got planned for us,' Tess pointed out, knowing that talk of dresses would take Emma's mind off Ella for a while. Emma usually had good taste, but Tess could see signs of Bridezilla-esque tendencies in her sister's slightly manic expression whenever wedding stuff was mentioned, and she feared what Emma might force her poor bridesmaids to wear. There were going to be three of them: Tess, and two of Emma's forever-friends. If Ella had been alive, Tess suspected that Emma would have just had her sisters for bridesmaids, but with Ella gone the image of Tess walking a solitary path behind Emma was simply too upsetting.

'I haven't decided yet,' Emma said. 'I quite like taupe, or maybe mulberry, but that's a bit too Christmas-weddingy. The wedding shop suggested damson because it's a bit richer in colour, but I'm thinking maybe something lighter, more in keeping with the season, like shell pink, or...' Emma began.

Taupe? What sort of a colour was taupe for a wedding, Tess wondered. Yuck. It was a something of nothing colour. At least shell pink was a proper colour and quite a nice one, too. And she hoped Emma didn't pick satin, either. Satin showed every lump and bump. Please God, not satin.

Tess zoned out, letting Emma drone on. She found herself doing it more often lately, usually when weddings were mentioned. It seemed like every man and his dog were getting hitched. Not to their dog, obviously, though Dee, who owned the tanning salon across the street, did have a face like a Jack Russell terrier, sort of narrow with black beady eyes. She had a temperament to match, too.

'...which is why I want to do something in Ella's memory,' Emma was saying.

'Eh?' It looked like her sister had moved away from hideous colours and was back on the subject of charity work.

Tess didn't have anything against raising money for charity, as long as all she had to do was put her hand in her pocket and donate. She didn't actually want to *participate*.

'Haven't you been listening?' Emma demanded.

'Of course I have,' Tess said. 'But couldn't you do something else, like cut your hair off?' Tess might, just *might*, consider having her own locks chopped off if it meant not having to wear Lycra. She was well aware that she didn't look her best in tight-fitting sportswear.

Then there was the problem of getting a bra with enough scaffolding to prevent her boobs from knocking her out whenever she attempted anything more than a swift walk.

Emma gasped. 'I'm getting married and you want me to *cut my hair!*' she shrieked. 'Don't you *know* that everyone says not to do anything drastic with your hair just before you get married?'

'The wedding is eight months away,' Tess shot back at her. 'It's not as if you're walking down the aisle tomorrow.'

'Do you *know* how slowly hair grows?' Emma's voice rose another octave.

Tess shrugged. She was still thinking about enormous bras. Boobs like hers weren't made for running. Even a fast walk had the tendency to make her chest look like she had two water-filled balloons strapped to her front.

'A half an inch a month!' Emma yelled. 'That's only *four inches* by the wedding.' She held up four fingers to demonstrate. 'I would still be bald walking down the aisle!'

Maybe not head-shaving then and, thinking about it, Tess wasn't too keen on losing her own mass of long, fair hair either.

'How about a bungee jump?' she suggested. Even better, because then the whole thing would be over in a morning. Bungee jumping didn't particularly appeal to her, either – she hated heights – but it had to be better than jogging around the block once a week with her mad sister.

'No, I want to run a marathon.' Emma had her mouth set into an I'm-not-changing-my-mind line. Tess hated that line. She'd been on the receiving end of it at least once a day since Emma was old enough to realize that she could usually get her own way if she tried hard enough.

Tess stared at her sister as the enormity of what Emma actually wanted to do sunk in. 'A *marathon*. How far *is* that, exactly?' Her hand was back in the bag of popcorn and she was shovelling it into her mouth faster than a hungry dog hoovered up its dinner.

'Twenty-six miles,' Emma said.

'And you're going to run all of them? In one go?'

Emma smiled sarcastically. 'That's the general idea.'

'What do Mum and Dad think?' Surely they'd talk Emma out of it. Neither of her parents had done a scrap of exercise in their lives. They weren't exercise people. They didn't believe in it. Dad gardened and played bowls (which even he agreed couldn't really be regarded as exerting himself) and Mum did the housework and the DIY (she was considerably better at putting up shelves than their father was), which, she claimed, was exercise enough, whenever gym-mad Emma suggested they all went to aerobics together. Their parents had always argued they had all the activity they needed in work – they owned a laundry service – and they deserved a sit-down at the end of the day.

'They're fully behind me,' Emma said. 'They think it'll be a great experience.'

For whom, Tess wondered? Certainly not for *her*. She wasn't the athletic one, and Emma hadn't really been either, until Declan had popped the question. Since then, the woman had become diet- and gym-mad.

Tess couldn't see what all the fuss was about – the wedding was months away. Emma had plenty of time to drop a couple of pounds, and it wasn't as if her sister had any weight to actually lose.

Tess dipped her hand back into the popcorn bag. Mmm, toffee was definitely her favourite.

'Make the most of it,' Emma announced, nodding at the almost empty bag. 'You'll have to eat healthily from now on. You can't run a marathon on takeaways and cakes.'

'It's good that I'm not the one running it, then,' Tess replied, tipping her head back to let the remnants of the bag fall into her waiting mouth.

'You said you'd run with me.' Emma had such a good line in pouting, Tess thought her sister should do a marathon pout, instead of a marathon run. She'd raise thousands. Her pouting was nearly as good as the 'I'm-not-changing-my-mind' line.

'I said I'll help,' Tess agreed, 'and I will, but I'm not going to do any running.'

'You said, "I'm in",' Emma persisted.

'Ah, but that was before I knew what you wanted me to do,' Tess shot back at her.

'Too late!' her sister crowed. 'You already said yes. It's not my fault that you didn't ask first. You can't go back on your word now.'

Which was why Tess was pounding the streets (OK – half a street) at eight-thirty on a Sunday morning when she should still be in bed. But she wasn't actually pounding anything right now, was she? She was bending over, with her hands on her knees, trying not to be sick.

'You most certainly *did* promise,' her sister insisted. 'So stop being a wuss and get moving.'

Emma was like a kid who wanted their mother's attention – she kept on and on when she got an idea in her head, and she wouldn't let up until she got what she wanted. This was shaping up to be one of those times.

'I honestly don't think I can,' Tess admitted.

Emma took her phone out; Tess hoped her sister was going to ring for a taxi to take her back to Mum and Dad's. The sisters had agreed to meet at their parents' house, because there were woods at the end of the road and Emma said it was a good place for a beginner to start running, rather than through the streets.

'Smile,' Emma said.

'What?' Tess looked up.

'That's one for my fundraising page.'

'Don't you bloody well dare!' With an unexpected burst of energy, Tess lunged forward and made an ineffectual grab for the mobile.

Emma danced away, a couple of feet out of reach. 'Come and get it,' she taunted.

'Give it to me!' Tess shrieked.

'I will when you've completed the two miles.'

'Do you know how much I hate you?'

'Enough not to want to go to Barcelona?'

Tess paused. 'Who is going to Barcelona?' she asked.

'We are.'

'Why?'

'Because that's where the marathon is taking place.'

Tess opened and closed her mouth, trying to suck air into her beleaguered lungs once more – this time as a result of shock, and not physical exhaustion. '*Really?*'

'Really.'

Tess's face split into a huge grin. 'Why didn't you say so?' she demanded. But when she chased after Emma with renewed vigour, her sister wasn't fooled: Emma shot off across the road into the park like a mouse being chased by a cat, waving the phone above her head and with Tess's yells of 'I hate you, Emma-bloody-Barton' following behind her.

But with every step that Tess took as she staggered after her sister's annoyingly pert backside, it wasn't the threatened Facebook posting she was thinking of – it was Gaudi.

Picasso, Van Gogh, Matisse, Monet, Da Vinci, Turner, Michelangelo – the list was endless. She loved them all (OK, maybe not the Cubists, so much), but she adored the Impressionists and her favourite was Monet. His series of paintings of lilies was to die for, and she wished she had just a fraction of his talent. Her own style was less impressionistic and more detailed, but when she'd first started becoming serious about painting when she was taking her A-levels, she'd tried to emulate his style – and had failed miserably.

And then there was Gaudi. When she thought of his architecture shivers of delight travelled up and down her spine. It was magical, surreal (but in a good way – not in a "Is that a piece of art, or did someone leave a crate in the middle of the room and forget about it" kind of way), and although she'd only seen photographs of his work from having studied him as part of her fine art course, his vision and creativity took her breath away.

And where could Gaudi's most famous work be found? Barcelona, of course!

Architecture wasn't really her thing, in that she'd never considered doing a degree in it (too much focus on modern stuff, like steel and glass, and buildings made out of weird materials like car tyres or spaghetti), but that didn't stop her from enjoying and appreciating beautiful buildings and painting them. Worcester Cathedral, its spire dominating the skyline of the city where she lived, had served as inspiration for many of her paintings in the past, and she loved the magnificence of it: the carved stone, the stained glass, the sense of history.

But, in Tess's eyes, Gaudi was the king of designing beautiful buildings. They didn't have any great age about them, nor did many of them have the grandeur of buildings such as the cathedral in her hometown, but what they did have was imagination, quirkiness, flowing lines, and an organic feel, as if the stone had moulded itself into those glorious shapes without any human intervention. And she understood all this without ever setting foot in Barcelona, her knowledge gleaned from photos and other people's paintings of his architecture. Imagine what it would be like to see it all in person!

She'd attempted to paint the Sagrada Familia once, but without actually being there in front of it, she clearly hadn't been able to do it justice. What had happened to that piece? she wondered, as she puffed and panted after her annoyingly composed sister, guessing it was probably in a box in their parents' attic, with the rest of her student paraphernalia.

She'd tried painting still lifes, portraits, landscapes, abstract art, scenes of everyday life, and even a religious piece or two, but her favourite thing, and the thing she was best at, was bringing other people's imagination to life. Lately she'd become a dab hand at fairies…

Darn it – Tess's legs were refusing to work, so she sat down in the mud. Random thoughts ran through her mind, like why wasn't Lycra waterproof (her bum was uncomfortably wet), and surely trainers were meant for strolling around the supermarket in, not for slipping and sliding along muddy woodland trails, and why was it so soggy underfoot when it hadn't rained for at least a couple of days?

'Another bend, then we're into the field and almost home,' Emma called from a few feet further along the track. 'You can do this.'

I can't, and I don't want to, Tess thought. 'Just leave me here and pick me up on your run around this hellhole next week.' She stared dully at a tree trunk directly ahead. Even her eyeballs were exhausted.

'Come on, you can't stay here all day.' Emma grabbed Tess's arm and heaved.

Tess's bottom made an undignified squelching noise as it was pulled free of the mud.

With every inch of her hurting, she clambered to her feet and promptly burst into tears. 'I can't, Em, I just can't. My body isn't made for running. Look at it.'

Both the sisters looked. From Tess's angle, directly above the body in question, all she could see was boobs. She thought her legs and feet might be somewhere underneath, but she couldn't be certain, because she hadn't felt them for the past half hour. However, she knew what the mirrors showed, and though some were kinder than others, they all painted a similar picture. Tess was plump; curvy if you wanted to be tactful. The only problem was, she had little idea where one curve ended and another began. They all seemed to merge into one roly-poly, barrel shape. Emma, on the other hand, was tall and lanky. If her sister had a body shape like a stick of celery, then Tess was definitely an apple. Or perhaps 'watermelon' was a more accurate description.

Emma gave her an up-and-down scrutiny. 'You've got all the right bits in all the right places, and a damn good figure to boot. There's nothing stopping you from running.'

'But I'm all fat and wobbly,' Tess wailed, clutching hold of a handful of belly and squidging it. It wasn't fair that one sister carried enough weight for the both of them, and why did it have to be her?

'That's got more to do with lack of muscle tone than with fat. If you keep running with me, you'll be toned and honed by Christmas,' Emma promised.

Tess glared at her; the witch wasn't even out of breath.

'Look, I'll do you a deal.' Tess was feeling desperate. 'I'll help you train, I'll come out with you every day if you want, and cheer you on from the sidelines. I'll even come with you to Barcelona.' (That last one wasn't exactly a hardship, though Tess tried to make it sound as though it were). 'But please don't make me run. You're perfectly capable of running all by yourself.'

Emma took Tess's mud-covered hands in her own relatively clean ones (how had she stayed so mud-free, considering Tess was coated in the stuff from head to foot, and who knew running could be so dirty anyway?) and said, 'I don't want you to just train with me, Tessy.' Emma's expression was pitying. 'I want you to run the marathon with me. The two of us, sisters together.'

'Nooo,' Tess wailed.

'It'll be fun, you'll see, and you'll get to visit a city you've always wanted to go to, at the end of it.'

'I'll be too tired to appreciate any of it,' Tess predicted, sourly.

'Tess, this will probably be the last time we'll do anything together.'

'Hen weekend,' Tess retorted. They'd be together then all right, for two whole nights and days, hopefully in a spa, being treated to facials and prosecco, preferably at the same time.

'I don't want a hen weekend, and even if I did, it wouldn't just be *us*, would it? It would be my friends, too. I want you to come to Barcelona with me. I want you to run the marathon with me. For Ella. For *us*.'

'We'll have plenty of other times when we're together – you're getting married, not going to prison, or moving to Australia. And you've bought a house less than a mile away from Mum and Dad's.'

'It won't be the same.'

No, Tess acknowledged, it wouldn't. 'It hasn't been the same since you met Declan,' she pointed out, wanting Emma to realize that this was a natural progression, and the way it should be. They would always be sisters, but they couldn't live in each other's pockets forever.

Emma's eyes began to fill with unshed tears. 'I don't mean to push you out, but—'

'I get it, Em!' Tess was quick to reassure her sister – that hadn't been what she was getting at. 'Three's a crowd. And it would be too weird for words if you invited me along every time you saw your fiancé. I don't feel left out, pushed out, sidelined, or whatever you want to call it.' She linked arms with her sister and the two girls walked slowly out of the woods and across the field. 'I'm really very happy for you. We'll still see each other, and spend time together, honest. But I don't understand why you need to spoil a perfectly good trip to a fascinating city by running a marathon in the middle of it.'

'Nice day,' a passing jogger called, and Tess gave Emma a nudge in the ribs.

'You could always run with him,' she suggested. 'He's fit. In more ways than one.' Tess watched his backside move rhythmically away from them. 'Do you see him here often?'

'Every Sunday.' Emma's lips twitched. 'And you're forgetting that I'm engaged.'

'You might be, but I'm not. Maybe I *will* come running with you again next week,' Tess said.

'Does that mean you'll run the marathon?'

'I'll try, OK?' Tess wasn't promising anything, but if it meant so much to Emma, she'd give it her best shot. Besides, she wanted to do it in Ella's memory, too. Ella deserved to be remembered and if they could raise money for cancer research at the same time, then that would be great.

She just prayed she had the willpower and stamina to do all the training that needed to be done.

Tess regretted the decision later, when she had to crawl on her hands and knees up the stairs leading to her flat, because her ankles didn't seem to want to flex any more.

The drive from their parents' house had taken all of ten minutes, and Tess's body had used every second of the journey to decide to let her know just how upset it was with her. Her back ached, her knees ached, and her ankles had seized up. To top it all off, she was covered in mud (bits of it were flaking off onto the stairs, like a trail of dirty breadcrumbs), and she was so tired she felt she might sleep for a week. Coupled with this, the pain-au-chocolat that she'd been looking forward to as a treat for after the run now held all the appeal of a piece of cardboard. In fact, the very thought of eating made her feel slightly nauseous.

Tess came to the conclusion that she had done some serious damage to her body. It might even be permanent.

She heaved herself to her feet by hanging onto the wooden doorframe for support, and rammed her key into the lock. At least her hands and arms worked OK, so she had something to be grateful for. Then she fell in through the front door and commando-crawled to the bedroom, shedding excess items as she went. Once there, she scaled the mighty heights of Mount Bed and flopped up onto it, pretending the drying mud that she was covered in didn't exist. She'd deal with it later.

Later happened rather sooner than she anticipated.

Her mobile, which she'd dropped in the hall along with her coat and trainers, began to ring incessantly. She resisted the insistent calls for half an hour before giving in and levering her very reluctant body off the bed (it took several attempts). Standing upright was a major achievement, she thought, and possibly the most significant thing she'd do for the rest of the day.

How was she going to manage to do any work, when everything below the waist was such a mess and everything above it was in only slightly better condition? She had a series of illustrations for a book to finish and a deadline to meet, and here she was with barely enough strength to take her disgusting running kit off.

Running kit? Ha ha! The only running that particular kit had done was the two-mile stagger/lurch/stumble today. She'd only ever worn the trainers to the supermarket, and the shorts and top had been bought during a half-hearted attempt at gym-joining a couple of years ago. She had attended once, decided she hated it, and the clothes had spent the time between then and now in a bag at the back of her wardrobe.

'Coming,' she shouted, as if the person on the other end of the phone could hear her. She started to peel the sodden Lycra shorts down her legs. It took a great deal of persuasion to get them to roll down over her thighs but, finally naked, she padded to the door and grabbed her dressing gown off the hook, refusing to even look at the mess she'd made on her lovely bed. Sheet-changing would have to wait until she'd given whoever was on the other end of the phone a piece of her mind. A shower might be a good idea, too.

She snatched up her mobile, wincing at the twanging pains the sudden action caused. 'Hello,' she snarled.

'Did I wake you?' The voice belonged to the editor who had commissioned Tess to do the illustrations she was currently working on.

What was the woman doing, phoning her on a Sunday? Didn't she have a life?

'No, I've been out for a run,' Tess said sanctimoniously, liking the impression the words gave – fit, slim, active, in control, busy.

'About *Away with the Fairies*,' Carol said, without preamble. 'How far have you got with it?'

Tess hobbled over to her workstation, jammed the phone in between her ear and her shoulder, and gently lifted the paper separating each delicately painted illustration.

'The cover is done, and so is the frontispiece, all the line drawings for the start of each section are complete, as are the first three interior illustrations that you've signed off on. I've started work on the fourth, and the fifth is ready to go straight afterwards. I just need the author to approve the rest before I can go any further with them.'

'Good. Publication day has been brought forward.'

Tess wasn't sure whether to laugh or cry. 'To when?'

'The end of March.'

'Oh, bother.' Five months to publication meant the illustrations needed to be done yesterday.

'Exactly.' There was a sigh from Carol. 'Can you do them in time?'

'I'll have to, won't I?' If Tess didn't fulfil the contract, she wouldn't get paid.

'I've spoken to the author and she's happy with the others, except for a few minor changes,' Carol said, and for the next few minutes they discussed the amendments.

'Right,' Tess said, finally. 'I'll have them done by the end of next week.'

Tess loved that she sounded professional and confident, when she was feeling anything but. To get them all done on time, she'd have to start now and not eat or sleep for the next ten days or so. Tess had some organising to do.

With a sigh, she ended one conversation and began another, pressing a preset key on her phone.

'Mum? I'm not going to be able to work this week,' she said, holding the phone away from her ear as she waited for her mother to explode.

'Never mind,' her mother replied calmly. 'Angela was just saying yesterday that she needed some extra shifts. Anyway, why can't you do this week? Is it this marathon training? Has it worn you out?'

'Cheeky!' Tess was relieved her mum wasn't giving her grief over being let down at the last minute. 'You know that commission I'm working on?'

'The book about fairies?'

'That's the one. They want all the illustrations completed by next week.'

'Is that a good thing, or a bad thing?' Her mother sounded as if she had a mouthful of marbles.

'What are you eating?'

'A sherbet lemon.'

'Ooh, nice. Anyway, it's a bit of both, really. The sooner I get it done, then the sooner I can move on to the next commission. But it does mean that I'll be really pushed for time for a couple of weeks.'

'Your dad and I can manage,' her mum replied. 'We managed when you were in university, didn't we?'

Hmm, her parents most certainly had, which made her wonder, and not for the first time either, if the only reason she was given regular shifts in the laundry was because they knew she needed the money.

'—will he?' Tess heard her mother say, as her attention came back to the present.

'Sorry, what?' Tess asked, wincing as her mum crunched loudly on the sweet she was eating.

'I was saying, Brian won't like you bailing on him.'

No, Brian wouldn't. Tess doubted the pub's owner would be as understanding as her parents, so she'd still have to work tonight and any of the other afternoons or evenings he'd scheduled her in for. Therefore, along with no eating and no sleeping, she could forget showering, putting on make-up, and straightening her hair, too. Oh, and the running – that would definitely have to go. She simply wouldn't have time for it.

—

'Come on, Tess, some of us have work to go to!' Emma yelled through the door to Tess's flat.

'Go away.' Tess burrowed deeper into her bed and pulled the duvet over her head. Surely it couldn't be morning already? She'd only just gone to bed.

'If I can manage to do this before work, then you can too,' Emma shouted, and pounded on the door yet again.

Thank goodness next door on the right belonged to a funeral director; Tess doubted anyone alive would be there at seven in the morning, and the dead ones were in no position to complain about the amount of noise her sister was making.

Another bang. 'I'll tell Mum,' Emma yelled.

How old was she? Three? Tess didn't care who Emma told, she just wanted to go back to sleep.

'Right, I'm coming in,' her sister announced, and Tess heard the turn of a key in the lock.

Before Tess had a chance to crawl out of bed, the duvet was dragged off her, and Emma was pulling at her arm. 'If you get a move on, we can be out of here in ten minutes,' Emma urged.

'You'll be out of here in ten seconds, if you don't let go of my arm,' Tess growled. 'I didn't get to sleep until four.'

'Partying?'

'Grrr. No! Working. It's all right for you with your nine-to-five job, smart suits and bloody meetings. Some of us were working in a pub, fending off drunks, then coming home and painting sodding pictures of sodding fairies!'

'Then a run is just the thing you need to help you relax,' Emma retorted chirpily.

'I was relaxed enough, until you barged into my flat.' Tess paused. 'That's a point – how have you got a key?'

'Mum gave it to me.'

'Remind me to have a word with our mother,' Tess grumbled.

'Well?'

'Well, what?'

'You're awake now, so you might as well come with me.'

Sighing, Tess stood up, ignoring her sister's amused stare: Tess liked her cow onesie, and it was perfect for sleeping in; she didn't care what Emma thought.

'Do you mind? I want to get dressed,' Tess said, crossing her arms.

Emma retreated to the living room, bouncing on the balls of her feet as she went.

After dragging on her still-damp running kit (yuck), Tess shuffled painfully after her. 'I can't even walk. How do you expect me to run?' Every bit of her ached. It would take at least a week, if not two, to recover from yesterday's pathetic attempt.

Emma put her arm around her and gave her a squeeze. 'I know it hurts, but if you wait for everything to stop aching, you'll be back to square one the next time you train.'

Train? Is that what they were doing? It was more like a medieval form of torture. Tess felt as though she'd been pummelled, racked, hung, drawn, and maybe even quartered to boot. The only bit of her that wasn't aching was her hair.

'Please don't tell me we're going to be doing this every morning until March,' she begged.

'Of course not,' Emma said.

Tess breathed a sigh of relief.

'In a few weeks' time, the runs will be too long to do in the morning, so we'll have to train after work,' Emma added.

'When you say "too long", what exactly do you mean?'

'By the end of November, we should be running at least five miles, four times a week, with a longer one on Sunday.'

Oh God, her sister was a sadist!

November

Weight: Step on scales, stare at them, shake head in disbelief, step off and repeat. No change — these scales must be wrong.

'Looking good, girl, I could almost fancy you myself.' The speaker slurped his pint, a foam moustache coating his real one.

Tess grimaced. 'In your dreams, Kev.'

Kev was at least fifteen years older than Tess's twenty-seven, skinny as a spade handle, and looked like he needed a good wash. He usually smelled as if he need one too, though Tess tried to never get close enough for a sniff.

'He's right. You do look fit,' his sidekick, Dale, chimed in. 'Have your boobs got bigger?'

Tess stuck her nose in the air and stalked to the other end of the bar. She really should look around for another job, but the pub was right on her doorstep and the pay was OK. And sometimes the miserable gits on the other side of the bar gave her a tip. Besides, the kind of people who frequented this sort of place liked normal drinks such as pints of bitter and halves of lager, and not the cocktails they served in the more upmarket bars in the city centre. The Spit and Sawdust was aptly named. It suited her fine, and the owner, Brian, treated her well enough. As long as she kept the booze flowing and the punters happy, he let her get on with it.

'Hey, Brian, your barmaid there has gone and had a boob job,' Dale shouted. 'Look at 'em.'

'Shut up, man, you'll get me done for sexual harassment,' Brian said in a disinterested voice, without looking up from his newspaper.

Not just sexual harassment, Tess thought, remembering some of the conversations the regulars had. It made her cross just thinking about them.

'How much did that cost, Tess? It must have set you back a bob or two. You're paying her too much, mate.' This last was directed at Brian.

'If you tipped her more often, I wouldn't have to pay her at all,' Brian quipped back.

Tess tried to ignore them, and concentrated on scrubbing a greasy lipstick mark from the rim of a pint glass, whilst wondering why she put up with it. Oh, yes, because she needed the money, that was why.

But maybe, not too far into the future, she'd be able to pack this shitty job in. The last commission had been well received, and she'd gained another off the back of it. The only problem was, the work wasn't quite yet steady enough or reliable enough.

She stretched up to slip the freshly washed and dried glasses into the overhead racks, felt her jeans slipping down yet again, and yanked them up crossly. Wasn't denim supposed to shrink, not grow, when it was washed? But then she'd had this pair since university, so the fabric had probably lost all its cohesion by now.

Then something the decidedly rude Kev and his sidekick had said registered. Her waist *was* actually smaller. She hadn't really noticed until now, what with being so busy working three jobs (two and a half really, because she weaselled out of more shifts in the laundry than she actually took on), and all that training her sister was forcing her to do. The healthy eating must have helped too, though she felt as though she was eating more now than before, but then wasn't it a well-known fact that you used more calories chewing salad stuff than you gained? She'd not eaten any chocolate for weeks, (OK, maybe a square or two) and she'd eaten more salads than a hutchful of rabbits (she still preferred pizza to lettuce, and she had a feeling that was never going to change). Surely that would go some way towards explaining it.

She *must* have lost weight, despite what her scales said. Tess couldn't believe it! All that hard work and healthy eating was actually paying off. Suddenly, she found she didn't resent all those hours she'd put in running. She didn't feel quite so peeved about missing all those episodes of Corrie either, or any of the other programmes she liked to watch. She'd toned up and slimmed down, and she found she was feeling really rather good about it.

Most of it seemed to have come off her waist, giving the impression that her boobs were larger than they actually were. When she ran her hands down her sides, for the first time in a long time she noticed that her boobs and her waist were actually separate entities. Plus, she was wearing a bra she didn't often wear, because it was of the push-'em-up-and-stick-'em-out variety (actually, it was the only clean one left in her underwear drawer, which was ironic considering the business her parents owned), and the bra served to accentuate the difference between her boobs and her waist.

She vowed to buy a new set of scales.

Lost weight. Jeans too big.

23

She sent the text to Emma, doing a mental fist pump of satisfaction.

Well done. But don't forget, it's not about the weight, it's about the fitness, came the reply.

> Scales don't say I've lost any. They must
> be broken.

Tess gave a mental 'harrumph'.

> They might be right.

Emma's reply was depressingly swift.

What! This time Tess's harrumph was quite verbal. Impossible!

> ????

Tess typed, and pressed 'Send'.

Muscle weighs more than fat, her sister responded.

Her sister might have a point — Tess' remembered hearing something like that on the TV, and she'd noticed that her thighs weren't quite as wobbly. Curious, she poked one of them, discovering her finger didn't sink in the way it used to. Not that she usually made a habit of poking her wobbly bits. Then she ran her hands over her hips and down the tops of her legs, feeling muscles there that she hadn't had since puberty.

There was no doubt about it, she was getting a leg pack — or whatever the defined muscles in one's legs were called.

OK, they weren't *defined*, and probably no one else would notice, but a smirk of satisfaction spread across her face and for once she actually felt quite magnanimous towards the two blokes propping up the other end of the bar, and she turned to give them a delighted smile.

'Kev, mate, our Tess fancies you,' Dale crowed, nudging his pal, and Tess's grin was hastily replaced with a repulsed frown.

'Not on your life!' she retorted, turning her back on the obnoxious duo, thankful that it was nearly time for her shift to end and she could go on the run she'd promised Emma she'd do.

Emma was away for a few days on a course, but before she left she'd made Tess swear to do a five-miler in her absence, and though Tess had whined about it, she found she was actually looking forward to stretching her legs.

Ooh, get me, she thought. Barely a month ago she'd almost collapsed before she'd got to the end of the street, but now she could manage five miles. Just. And she found that she felt so much better for it too: had more energy, more fizz. Maybe, just maybe, she'd keep up the running when the marathon was over. She still wasn't too keen on the gym, but jogging in the fresh air was completely different.

She knew the run that evening wasn't going to be easy: it would only be the third time she'd attempted the distance, but she vowed she'd try to make it all the way around without stopping.

To while away the half-hour until she could leave, she fished her phone out from underneath the bar, plugged an earbud in and let her hair fall about her face, then she half-turned away from Brian, and pressed "Begin". With any luck her boss wouldn't notice what she was doing, and she could get a sneaky ten minutes of Spanish practice in. She'd downloaded the app a week ago, and she had already ploughed through several modules. Admittedly, they were only ten minutes long, but at least she felt as though she was achieving something.

'*Buenas noches,*' she called happily, when she finally disappeared out of the door at the end of her shift and headed home to change.

She was still reciting Spanish words and phrases in her head as she set off on the five-mile circuit that Emma had worked out with meticulous care by driving various routes until she had found one which she was happy with and which was the correct mileage.

Tess was perfectly happy to let Emma take care of the race stuff, whilst she filled her head with the romance of Barcelona. As she ran, her breath clouding behind her in the chill of a dank November evening, all Tess could think about was warm spring sunshine, and a city filled to bursting with wonderful art.

'How long do you think it'll take?' Tess asked.

Emma was lounging on the floor with her back against the sofa and a selection of almost identical wedding invitation cards scattered around her. Tess peered over her sister's shoulder at them, trying to appear enthusiastic but really not seeing how the slight difference in font affected the look of the particular card Emma was thrusting under her nose. It was much the same as the previous 20 white-and-silver embossed cards she'd already been shown. She knew she was supposed to be the arty one of the family, but come on! There were more differences between the blades of grass in a field than there were between this lot.

'How long will what take?' Emma asked, twisting a card this way and that to catch the light. 'Do you think the silver on this one is a bit dull?'

Tess really wanted to say that her sister was the dull one for spending so much time, money and energy on a bit of cardboard which most people would have a quick glance at in order to check the where and the when, and would then throw in the bin. Who knew weddings could be so time-consuming and so *spendy*?

'The marathon,' Tess explained.

'Hmm? Or what about this one? I really like this one. It says elegant but not too overstated.'

'It says, "I've got more money than sense", that's what it says. How much are they charging you?' Tess demanded.

'For the invitations, the RSVP cards, the menus, and the seating place cards, altogether... three hundred and twenty-six pounds.'

'*How much?* I hope it's real silver on that embossing.'

Emma's expression hardened. 'I thought it was quite reasonable. That's for two hundred guests.'

Tess didn't think she even knew 200 people; or rather, not ones she would want to invite to her own wedding, were she ever to have one.

'Anyway, back to the marathon,' Tess continued, eager to avoid any further confrontation with the slightly demonic bride-to-be. 'Because I've been Googling it and it's going to take forever to run twenty-six miles.'

'No, it's not!' Emma scoffed. 'We should do it in about four, four and a half hours, tops.'

'Really?' Tess was astounded. She had been thinking more in terms of eight. Maybe ten. Four hours didn't sound too bad at all, though she had a sneaking suspicion that Emma might be a bit on the optimistic side. All Tess was praying for was to finish the darned thing. 'Good, more time for sightseeing, then,' she said, hoping her sister's estimate was accurate.

'And the beach – if it's warm enough.' Emma picked up yet another card, held it up to the light, and put it down again.

'Barcelona has a beach? Surely not…?'

'They call it "the city by the sea",' Emma replied, absently. 'I think it's got a couple of beaches, actually.'

'I don't know whether it's by the sea or not,' Tess said. 'All I'm interested in is Gaudi and Picasso.'

Ah, yes, Gaudi. The back of her neck tingled at the thought of seeing his architecture, and she marvelled at the artist's ability to create the most fantastic designs using stone and glass and ceramic. But what she really loved about his work was the sheer wackiness of it, and she couldn't wait to see his creations in real life.

Emma finally stopped fiddling with the invitations, and said, 'I've booked the flights and the hotel. Here.' She brought the details up on her phone. 'See, it's near to the start of the race, so we don't have to trek from one end of the city to the other on the morning of the marathon, and there's a metro stop within walking distance – from there we can get to every part of the city.'

'Including the Sagrada Familia? Can we visit it? And Casa Batlló?'

'Tess, as long as you run all twenty-six miles, I don't care if you want to climb to the top of Everest. I'll happily visit whatever you want, but please, please, please, can I go shopping instead when you go to the Picasso museum? I hate his stuff.'

'Philistine,' Tess snorted. But, she had to admit, Picasso could be an acquired taste, and the pair of them had all week together so it wouldn't hurt if they split up now and again to do their own thing.

'Now, back to the important stuff,' Emma said. 'What do you think of these two?'

Tess sighed and squinted at the invitation cards her sister held aloft, seeing absolutely no difference between the two. 'I like that one,' she said, pointing at the one in Emma's left hand, hoping that was the one Emma wanted her to choose.

'Call yourself an artist? It's the worst one there!' her sister cried.

'Why did you show it to me, if you hate it?' Tess protested.

'I was showing you the difference between the worst one and the best.' Emma huffed out an aggrieved sigh. 'But if you're not going to take it seriously, then I'll ask Mum.'

Good idea, Tess thought, with a twinge of guilt at putting their mother through the same torture, but her guilt was short-lived as her mind turned to Barcelona once more.

December

Weight: Not looking. Nope. No way. Not after all those mince pies and chocolates.

'You want me to go for a run? Now? After everything I've just eaten?' Tess was appalled. She felt like a walrus who had swallowed a huge shoal of fish all by itself, and she probably looked like one, too.

'Exactly!' Emma said. 'Pop home and change, and I'll meet you back here.'

"Here" was their parents' house. It was her parents (and her mother in particular) who Tess blamed for her current predicament of not being able to walk without barrel-rolling from side to side, because her cooking was simply so good, and so very, very plentiful.

Who in their right minds went for a run on Christmas Day? Christmas afternoon was meant for sprawling on the sofa, feeling too full to move, watching rubbish on TV, and wondering which chocolate to have next. She had no intention of going out into the almost-dark of a midwinter afternoon, wearing nothing but a vest and shorts, with the sole intention of getting damp, muddy and sweaty. So far, Christmas Day had displayed typical non-festive weather – it was overcast and dank, with a hint of drizzle, and Tess was happy where she was, thank you very much.

She glanced around the living room for help, but her dad had his head in yesterday's paper, Declan was pretending to be asleep and her mother was staring fixedly at the telly.

She frantically thought of an excuse. 'I've not got my running kit with me.' (Why would she – this was Christmas Day, for goodness' sake!) 'And I can't drive back to my flat because I've had a couple of glasses of wine.'

'That's OK,' Emma said. 'I'll drive you.'

'Didn't *you* have anything to drink at lunch?' Tess prayed that her sister had downed half a bottle of red and a couple of Baileys Irish Creams.

Emma looked horrified. 'Do you know how many calories there are in alcohol?'

Tess shrugged. She didn't care.

'Come on, Tess,' Emma urged. 'You've been doing so well. You can't give up now.'

'Who said anything about giving up? It's Christmas and I'm taking a break, that's all.'

'You took a break yesterday, too, and the day before. You do realize it'll be that much harder to get back into the routine again?'

Tess thought her sister sounded like a naggy teacher and she gave another shrug. She would deal with getting back into a routine when Christmas was over.

'Please, Tess, I don't want to go on my own.' Emma changed tactics.

'Take Declan,' Tess suggested.

Emma cocked an eyebrow at her fiancé. *Or perhaps not,* Tess thought, looking at him. He was in a worse state than she was and at the mention of accompanying his wife-to-be, he gave a little grunt and started snoring with gusto.

'It's not Declan who needs the training,' Emma retorted. 'It's you.'

With a deep sigh, Tess reluctantly gave in. Her sister would just keep on and on until she got her own way. Besides, if Tess did some exercise now and burned off some of the humungous number of calories she'd consumed over the past couple of days, she could justify the turkey sandwiches, mince pies and eggnog that she was planning on enjoying later.

'Go on, then,' she said reluctantly, and Emma did a little whoop of joy.

Once Tess had changed into her kit, she found it was actually a relief to be out in the fresh air and getting her body moving. Much to her surprise, she had recently discovered that on the days when she didn't run, she actually missed it. Running seemed to sharpen her mind and clear it of rubbish, so when she returned to her painting it was with greater intensity and concentration.

She was now managing to run three times a week: eight miles on a weekday and fourteen on a Sunday. She did this religiously, with or without her sister. Today would be a short one, though, in recognition of the amount of food she had eaten, and the fact that there was a certain film being shown on TV in an hour or so which she didn't want to miss. Watching *The Wizard of Oz* was a tradition and Tess intended to uphold it.

As they pounded the roads on the outskirts of the city, Tess wasn't at all surprised to find that they seemed to be the only idiots who were running, though plenty of people were out and about, walking dogs, or accompanying small children on their Christmas-present bikes, or in cars, probably visiting relatives. But no one else was daft enough to jog.

It looked like they really were taking this marathon thing seriously, and for the first time since she'd agreed to her sister's madcap idea, Tess was actually beginning to enjoy the running.

Mostly.

January

*Weight: Not too bad, considering… but more importantly,
feeling absolutely wonderful.*

The dismal overcast days of December had given way to
snow in the first month of the new year. The white stuff
had been forecast to fall by the end of the week, and
Tess was looking forward to painting it, but first she had
promised herself new clothes, and the January sales were
just the thing for finding a bargain or two. So, later that
day, she found herself clutching several large bags and with
her bank account rather the worse for wear after hitting
the shops with enthusiasm.

High on a shopping buzz and delighted to find she
had dropped two whole dress sizes, she sauntered into the
restaurant where she had arranged to meet Faye for lunch.
They didn't meet that often – Faye had a husband, two
children, and a job to work around – but when they did,
it was as though the two friends had only seen each other
yesterday.

'Oh my God, look at you!' Faye exclaimed.

Tess dropped her bags by the table and did a twirl.

'You look fabulous. Not that you didn't before,' Faye
hastened to add, 'but you're absolutely stunning now.
Who's the lucky man?'

Tess gave a smug smile as she sat down. 'There is no man.'

Faye's eyes widened in surprise. 'Not even a hint of one?'

'Nope.'

'No?'

'No,' Tess replied firmly. 'I'm happy on my own.'

She wasn't lying – she really didn't feel the need to have a man in her life. Yes, it would be nice, but she hadn't met anyone that she was prepared to give up her independence for. And so far, no one had touched her heart with more than a fleeting stroke of a fingertip. Tess was waiting for someone to come along, grab it with both hands, and never let it go.

Of course she'd had boyfriends, especially during the time between leaving school and before going to university to get a degree in fine art. She had been undecided what she wanted to do after finishing sixth form and she had flitted from job to job for four years, before taking the plunge and going to university. She looked back on that time with fondness. It had given her the chance to sow a few wild oats, go on several holidays, and kiss more than a few frogs.

She was still waiting for her prince, but it wasn't a priority in her life right now. At the moment all she wanted to do was to concentrate on building her career and making a name for herself, and she felt very lucky that she loved what she did. During those carefree years when Tess had lurched from one job to another, she had slowly come to realize that what she had been searching for all along wasn't Mr Right (unlike her younger sister, who had found her soulmate before she was twenty and was now all set to marry him). She had been looking for an outlet for her latent creativity. Once she had registered for the fine art course everything suddenly became much clearer, and although she had dated occasionally during the three years of her degree, it was always casual because she never wanted to let anything come before her painting.

Now, two years out of university, all her hard work was beginning to pay off and she wasn't prepared to jeopardize that for the sake of some guy.

A couple of times her sister had tried to convince her the two weren't mutually exclusive and that Tess could have both the man and the career, like Emma did. And yes, Tess wanted it all too, but the time wasn't quite right yet. She had a fledgling business to nurture, and she couldn't afford any distractions.

'So, what is it, then?' Faye demanded.

'I'm training for a marathon,' Tess said.

'Really? Good for you!'

'It's in Barcelona in March, and I'm really looking forward to it,' she added. Then clarified the statement by saying, 'Visiting Barcelona, that is, not the race itself.'

'What made you decide to run a marathon? You were never particularly sporty at school.'

'That's the understatement of the year! Remember when you pretended to have a sprained ankle to get out of PE, and while I was trying to help you hobble to the school office, I fell and sprained mine for real? I managed to avoid having to do games for two whole months. It was bliss!' Both friends laughed at the memory. 'As for the marathon, blame Emma. She blackmailed me into it. We're running it in memory of Ella, to raise money for cancer research.'

Faye was still chuckling at the sprained ankle incident. 'That's wonderful. I really admire you. Remind me to give you a donation. Ella would have been so proud.'

Faye and Tess had been friends long before Ella's diagnosis, when the twins were only nine years old, and Faye had lived through Tess's grief, supporting her all the way, bearing her up when life threatened to beat her down.

'She would have,' Tess said wistfully. 'Anyway, how are hubby and the kidlets?'

'They're all fine. I can't believe Sky will be starting nursery soon. It's scary how they grow up so fast.' Faye looked away, and Tess noticed tears gathering in the corners of her friend's eyes.

'Hugh still won't budge?' Tess asked. She hadn't seen Faye for a while, but the last time they'd met, her friend had confided that she was desperate for another baby but Hugh wasn't so keen. Faye and her husband had been 'discussing' it for the past year or so, with ever-increasing animosity between them.

'No. He's adamant he doesn't want any more children,' Faye said.

Tess didn't know what to say. Faye was another woman who seemed to have it all – an attentive husband, two children, a nice house, and a job which she could mostly do from home, to fit in around her family. Yet she wasn't happy, and the arguments over having a third child were clearly taking their toll. She looked tired, with fine lines showing on her immaculately made-up face, and her eyes were full of sorrow, and... what?

'There's something else, isn't there?' Tess asked. 'Do you want to talk about it?'

Faye let out a deep sigh and tears welled in her eyes. 'I found a condom in his trouser pocket the other day.'

'I don't follow.'

'Hugh has no need to buy condoms. I'm on the pill.'

'Oh.'

Faye laughed bitterly. 'At least I should be grateful that he's not trying to get anyone else pregnant.'

'Could there be another explanation?'

'Like what? He was hanging on to it for a friend? I don't think so, Tess. He's having an affair. No wonder he doesn't want another baby with me. I'm not sure if he even wants *me* any more... I can't even remember the last time we had sex.'

Why would anyone not want Faye? She was gorgeous inside and out, smart, funny, and everything Tess wished she herself could be.

It just shows, doesn't it? Tess thought. You never really knew what somebody else's life was like.

February

Weight: Have I really lost that much? Yay!

Tess had been aiming for a leaf–framing effect, but she couldn't quite get the angle she wanted. In fact, for the past couple of days she'd had an urge to paint something dark and angry, with swirling black and greys, her painting matching the mood of the dull and dreary winter days. But today was different. She'd woken up to a cold, crisp, snow–covered morning, a break between the storms which had swept in from the west, one after the other, so she'd decided to take advantage of the sun and snap off some photos of nearby Strathcombe Park. Tess wanted to replenish some of her stock after the Christmas rush (such as it was). The online sales for her paintings had been steady, with a peak in December as expected, and even though she had a new book to illustrate (and by a deadline that she refused to think about right now), she needed to get out of the flat. There was only so much of being cooped up she could take, and not for the first time she bemoaned the lack of a studio, if only to get her out of the house.

Hastily, eager for some fresh air, she cleared her paints away and washed her brushes meticulously: no matter how rushed she was, she took care of the tools of her trade (good brushes were alarmingly expensive). Thick leggings, a large jumper-dress, fur-lined boots, hat, scarf, mittens, a quick squirt of perfume, and she was ready to go. Her hair was in a loose bun, piled on top of her head, ready to be stuffed under a hat, and she grabbed her camera, a sketch pad and a couple of pencils, and hurried to her car. Tess had work to do.

When left to her own devices, Tess enjoyed painting landscapes, mostly, with the odd building or two thrown in for good measure, and she preferred using gouache, though she used both watercolour and oils when the occasion warranted it. Gouache was her favourite, however, because it was a bit like watercolour, but opaque, and she thought it produced the most brilliant colour. The medium had certainly worked well on the book of fairy tales she had recently finished illustrating.

She took the drive out to the park with care. The roads were treacherous, and Strathcombe wasn't exactly on a main road, but when she arrived she knew that the slightly hair-raising journey had been worth it. The gardens covered a massive area and she could immediately see why they were called 'gardens', in the plural. Strathcombe Park wasn't simply a country house, either; it was a stately home, and her attention was once again arrested by the view of the house as she drove in through the impressive wrought-iron gates and up the long, sweeping drive to the car park. From the outside it appeared magnificent, with its turrets, wings, and floor-length mullioned windows.

Today wasn't a day for exploring the interior, though she did make a promise to herself to come back another time. Today was about the gardens and all they entailed, and there were acres of them, from the expertly managed parkland which lay to the rear of the manor house to the elegantly crafted, well-manicured maze at the front. In between the two lay all sorts of hidden gems, like the pretty walled cottage garden, and sweeping terraces, each with their own theme.

'Where do I start?' she breathed, itching to get out her sketchbook and start drawing. A snowy, bright day was perfect for painting. The sky was clear, and the sun had driven the clouds away for now. Though Tess preferred the summer, there was something magical about snow. Everything was still and calm, as if nature was holding its breath, waiting for the days to lengthen and the sun to warm the soil once more.

The snow lay in three-foot drifts in places and the gardens were blanketed in shades of white and glitter. An occasional set of birdy footprints marred its perfection in places, but the hints of any wildlife which were still active at this time of year only made the whole scene more interesting. A deeper, more substantial set of prints trailed from underneath a bush and led down to a small stream, and Tess thought they could possibly belong to a fox.

She knelt and took a photo. The painting she intended to produce from it would make a wonderful, thoughtful piece, almost better than seeing the animal itself. It was the spirit of the fox, and she couldn't wait to begin work on it. Watercolour, she decided, her mind already picking out the colours she wanted to use. She would have dearly loved to have started painting right then and there, but she realized just how cold she was starting to feel when she became conscious of her wet knees, so she hastily scrambled to her feet. She'd simply have to make do with the photos.

When she thought she'd got enough material to make a start, she made her way back to the car but, on a whim, instead of heading home, Tess aimed for the entrance to the large house and was delighted to find that the doors were open.

'Do you want a guided tour?' the woman who took her money asked.

'A tour?' Tess was thrilled. She'd love a tour.

'Or have you seen the house already?' the woman enquired.

Tess shook her head. 'It's not shut up for the winter?'

'We're only shut on Christmas Day and New Year's Day,' the woman said, then leaned closer and whispered, 'but if I had my way, we'd close on Boxing Day, too. We don't get many visitors on Boxing Day.'

Tess wasn't surprised. She'd spent her own Boxing Day slumped on the sofa – she had needed to after that run her sister had dragged her on. 'Yes, please, I'd love to,' she said.

'Okey-doke. Now,' her guide began, leading her into a vast hallway, 'if you were alive when the house was in its heyday, the servants' entrance would be the only entrance you would have been allowed to use.'

'Thanks,' Tess said, dryly.

'It's true!' The woman laughed at the expression on Tess's face. 'You would have to have been a member of the aristocracy to use the grand front door, so unless you've got a duchess or two in your ancestry…?'

'The nearest I can get to a title is "Duke" – the name of my Great-Aunt Nelly's dog,' Tess joked, following the guide as she climbed the huge sweeping staircase. The woman began pointing out features, like the six-foot chandelier hanging from the domed ceiling.

'It is fashioned on the famous chandelier in the Dolma-bahçe palace in Istanbul, which was a gift from Queen

Victoria and had seven hundred and fifty lamps. This one is slightly less impressive with only three hundred and seventy-six, but it's still beautiful,' the woman explained.

'I can just imagine it glittering in the candlelight,' Tess said.

'Ah, sorry to disappoint, but it's electric.'

Tess gasped with mock disappointment. 'Don't spoil this for me,' she warned. 'I'm pretending I'm a princess in a palace, where men wear swords and fight duels to protect a lady's honour.'

'I don't think past events were quite so romantic. See that young woman?' Her guide pointed to one of the many portraits.

Tess looked and nodded.

'She threw herself off the balustrades. Unrequited love,' the other woman said. 'And that one?'

Tess looked again, this time at the image of a whiskery older gentleman.

'Rumour has it that his wife poisoned him. Apparently, his ghost still haunts one of the landings.'

'Have you seen it?' Tess gaped at her.

'No, thank goodness! Anyway, I'm never here during the night. I love working here, but living in such a big place with all this history around?' The woman shuddered. 'No thanks!' Then her attention was caught by another painting. 'Ah, see that fella there?' She indicated a portrait of a rather stern gentleman also sporting an impressive set of whiskers. 'The story goes that in 1789 he challenged a man to a duel and stabbed him through the heart with his rapier, just because he had the cheek to speak to his daughter.'

'I can't imagine my dad getting even the slightest bit flustered if a whole army were to talk to me. All he would do is ask for a show of hands from anyone who wanted to take me on a date,' Tess joked. 'He can't wait to get rid of me. I live on my own, but there's nothing like your dad for when the washing machine breaks down, or your car starts to rattle. He's looking forward to the day when I phone him just for a chat, and not to ask him how to retune the TV.'

The guide was biting her lip, and Tess could see she was trying to hold back a grin. 'You're not that helpless, surely?' the woman asked.

'No, I'm not, but I must admit, dads do come in handy now and again. Especially mine – he's really practical and he *knows* stuff.'

'You two must be close.'

'We are, I suppose.'

They carried on up the staircase and the guide continued to talk about the house and its former inhabitants. Tess was fascinated, and she wondered if she would be allowed to sketch any of it. She couldn't help enthusing over the fireplaces, and the silk carpets from the Middle East, and the pieces of dark wood furniture, and the paintings, and everything else she set eyes on.

When the tour was done, Tess headed home, eager to start work, reinvigorated by her visit. As soon as she took off her coat she downloaded the photos onto her computer and began to sift through them. Unable to help herself – the book she was working on would just have to wait a while – she drooled over the beautiful landscapes as she began to sketch. The first drafts were very rough, with only a hint of colour where she wanted it, and she worked well into the night until she was happy that she had at least four draft sketches, showing a flavour of what the finished paintings would look like.

By the time midnight arrived, Tess was tired but happy. She'd thoroughly enjoyed the evening, losing herself in her work and doing what she loved. It was the only thing that mattered to her.

March

Weight: It's too late to worry about it now.

Ten Days to Race Day

'You look awful,' Tess said to her sister.

'Thanks.'

'But you do,' Tess insisted.

'No need to rub it in. I feel awful, too.'

Emma was running at a snail's pace. A tired toddler would have a better turn of speed than her sister, Tess thought. She looked really pale and was a bit clammy and sweaty, though they'd only run a couple of miles, which was hardly far enough or fast enough to work up a sweat. Emma's face was also suffering from a major breakout attack of spots, a sure sign that her sister must be a bit run down. Tess smiled at her marathon-themed joke – 'run down'? Ha, ha!

'We've got to keep going,' Emma insisted, panting hard. 'This is the last proper run before Barcelona.'

'Is it really necessary? We did twenty-two miles last week.' Tess felt really fit. She couldn't believe how far she'd come since October, when she'd hardly been able to summon the energy to get off the couch and stagger to the fridge. Now she was full of beans and had more get-up-and-go than she knew what to do with. Unlike her sister right now. Poor love, she clearly wasn't well.

'I'm not saying we run that far,' Emma puffed. 'About eighteen miles today, then thirteen the day before we fly – just to keep the fitness levels up.'

'You don't look as though you could run one mile, let alone eighteen,' Tess pointed out. 'And we're both fit enough now, thank you very much. It's not as though the next week is going to make a great deal of difference.' Tess felt the familiar twinge of apprehension at the thought of actually taking part in the marathon. The twenty-two miles had been gruelling enough, and it had taken her the whole week to recover, despite her all-time-best fitness levels.

'Can we stop?' Emma gasped. She really did look unwell.

'You need to take it easy,' Tess advised. 'I know what you're like – burning the candle at both ends. Promise me you won't do any more running until the day of the race.' She gave her sister a hug, then looked at her in alarm. 'You're shaking,' she said.

'I feel awful.' Emma looked even worse than she had earlier.

'I'm calling a taxi,' Tess said, firmly, praying that her sister was going to be OK. She couldn't face any more heartache.

Eight Days to Race Day

'You're not going to believe this.' Emma sounded rather strange on the phone, not worried, or alarmed, just a bit off, and for a moment Tess wondered if her sister was pregnant. If she was, it might explain her exhaustion during their last training run.

'Hi, Em, how are you feeling?' Tess held her breath, waiting for Emma to say the words that would make Tess an auntie.

'I've been to the doctors, and it's not the flu.' Emma paused. 'It's chickenpox.'

'Say that again?'

'Chickenpox.'

'Oh, dear.' Tess was quite disappointed. She'd been looking forward to bouncing a niece or nephew on her knee.

Tess had already had chickenpox, having caught the virus during a school trip to the Lake District. When she'd come out in spots the day before they were due to return home Dad hadn't even allowed her to step foot in the house, but had taken her straight to Grandma's and she'd had to stay there until she was no longer infectious. Tess recalled how miserable she had been, wondering what was going on at home and how Ella was doing. The overriding memories of that time was of being so covered from head to foot in calamine lotion that she had looked like some kind of weird, pale pink ghost, and insisting on ringing home every half hour to check on Ella.

'No wonder you felt so ill the other day,' Tess said, pushing the memories to the back of her mind.

'I'm feeling much better now – my temperature is down, I'm not so achey, and the awful headache I've had for the past two days has gone. But I've come out in horrid little spots and they're driving me mad. The doctor said they'll blister in a day or so, then scab over before they dry up. And he warned me not to scratch them, or they might leave a scar. When I told Declan what he said, Declan threatened to tie my hands behind my back to stop me.'

'Poor thing. Is there anything I can do? Tell Declan to go to the chemist and get you some calamine lotion,' Tess advised. She couldn't remember if the stuff had helped, but it certainly couldn't hurt. Tess recalled how terribly irritating the itching had been, and she totally sympathized. Declan would have a fight on his hands to get his fiancée to behave herself.

Emma sighed. 'No, but thanks anyway. Declan's got it all under control, though I will ask him to pop to the chemist on the way home from work.' There was pause, then Emma said, 'I'm so sorry, Tess.'

'Sorry about what? It can't be helped. It's not as if you asked to be ill. Just hurry up and get better. At least you've done all the training you need to do, and there's over a week to go before the race. I'll go for that thirteen-miler tomorrow night, but you should rest. Conserve your energy for the big day.' A horrible thought hit her. 'Do you think you'll be well enough to run by then?'

'It doesn't matter if I am or not,' Emma said in a flat voice. 'I can't go.'

'Of course you can!' Tess's mind reeled at Emma's words. 'We might do a worse time than we wanted, but you said yourself that you feel better today.'

Emma interrupted her. 'I'm not allowed to fly, Tess.'

'Wait, *what?*'

'It's an infectious disease, remember? The airline won't allow me to fly. I'm so sorry.' The last word turned into a sob.

Tess was stunned into silence.

'Say something,' Emma urged, sniffing.

'At least I can run a mile without fainting and I can touch my toes again – more or less – so the training isn't wasted,' was all Tess could think of to say. Disappointment flooded through her. No marathon, no Gaudi, no Picasso, no Barcelona. She might have been coerced into running the race in the first place, but as she'd become fitter and more confident, she had found herself looking forward to it more and more.

'*You're* still going,' Emma said. It wasn't a question, it was a statement.

Once more, Tess was put on the back foot. 'Say again?'

'You are still going. On your own.'

'On my own?' Tess repeated. She heard the incredulity in her own voice.

'Why not?'

'Because…' Tess was dismayed. 'I'll be *on my own*, that's why.'

'Yes, you will, but you can do it. It's not like you've never gone anywhere by yourself before, is it?'

Tess detected an undertone of scorn in her sister's tone. 'I'm not worried about going to Barcelona on my *own*,' she countered, although that was one of her concerns. 'What do you take me for? It's running the race alone that scares me.'

'You'll be fine. You've done the training, you're as fit as you can be. Hell, you've even done a virtual walk of the course courtesy of Google. What is there to be scared of?'

'Failing,' Tess wanted to say. She'd never done anything like this in her life. What if she had to stop halfway round? How embarrassing would *that* be after all the sponsor money Emma had raised (Tess had raised some, but it was

Emma who'd done most of the begging) – if Tess didn't complete the race?

Emma continued, 'I can track you in real time as you go around, and if you keep your phone on I can yell encouragement to you at every step if you need it. Besides,' she said, and Tess waited for the clincher which she guessed was coming, 'I've gone and had a couple of T-shirts made with Ella's photo on.'

Yep, that was it, that was the reason Tess was going to do this on her own, whether she wanted to or not. In memory of Ella.

'You owe me one, Ell,' Tess mouthed at the ceiling, imagining her sister's little face peering down at her, with her dimpled cheeks and that impish sparkle in her eyes. Emma and Ella had been identical, but from the moment Mum had brought them home, Tess had seen the differences more than the similarities, and Ella's innate mischievousness had been one of them.

'OK, I'll do it,' she said in a rush, before she had a chance to change her mind.

But she had an awful feeling she would regret her decision.

'So, will you come with me?' Tess asked, holding the phone in one hand, and crossing her fingers with the other. She wasn't expecting her mother to run the course with her (God forbid!) but it would be nice to have someone there, cheering her on.

'Oh, darling, I'd love to, but Grandma is having her cataracts done, and I can't leave her,' her mother replied.

Damn. Tess had forgotten about that. Grandma was having the procedure tomorrow, then she was staying with Mum and Dad for a few days until she recovered.

'You'll be fine,' her mother added. 'What can possibly go wrong?'

Tess wondered where to start: she could miss her flight, her suitcase might end up in Moscow, the hotel might be really awful, her money or her passport might be stolen (both, even, because Barcelona was well known for its pickpocket problems). She might get lost, or abducted, or worse… she might not get to the finish line.

'I know I'll be OK, but it would be nice to share the experience with someone, that's all,' Tess said, in a small voice.

'I'll pop over later,' her mother promised, as if that was going to make everything all right.

Tess tried Faye.

'I'd love to, God how I'd love to, but it's a bit short notice. I don't think I can get a babysitter, and Hugh is away on business *again*. Ha! As if I believe that old chestnut. What does he take me for? I'm not stupid, I know what he's up to.'

'You still think he's having an affair?'

'Too bloody right. Charles, stop that. Your sister doesn't need peanut butter in her hair. No, you can't have a biscuit. Sorry, it's mayhem here. A typical calm lunch at the Mayor household. Do yourself a favour – don't have kids, and certainly don't get married. *Charles!*'

'I'll let you get on. You sound like you've got your hands full.'

'I envy you, I really do. What I wouldn't give to be footloose and fancy-free. Go and enjoy yourself, you deserve it. Make the most of being single and childless. I wish I had.'

The last comment was laced with such bitterness that Tess was left quite concerned after the call ended. Faye used to be so fun-loving and upbeat. Now she just sounded harassed and despondent, and Tess vowed to be there for her more often when she got back from Barcelona.

As she put the phone down on her final begging call, one thing became perfectly clear to Tess: despite dangling a trip in front of her friends and family, it looked like she was going to Barcelona on her own.

Six Days to Race Day

Landed safely. Wish me luck!

Tess pressed 'Send' and took a deep breath. She was here, really here! Emma, the organizer, had written down exactly what Tess needed to do next, so after she'd cleared immigration and had collected her case, she queued at the desk at the airport to buy a *Hola!* ticket which would allow her unlimited travel on both the underground and buses (and the funicular railway – whatever that was). Afterwards, clutching the ticket in her sweaty hand, it was time for the scariest part of her journey: making her way from the airport to her hotel without getting lost.

It was a long, slightly confusing walk from the terminal to the train station, but a nice woman showed her the coloured guide painted onto the floor, and she followed it religiously until she found the train platform she needed.

That wasn't so hard, was it? she thought, her confidence growing with each successfully completed stage of the journey.

She even managed to change from the normal rail line to the metro without any difficulty, though she did keep her eyes glued to the overhead map to make sure she got off at the correct stop.

A section of underground tunnels later, and she popped up from the depths and into the open air, at exactly the right spot, blinking in the unaccustomed spring sunshine.

Lordy, the Plaça Espanya was busy! A massive round-about with cars, vans, lorries, and taxis swirling around it in a never-ending stream, like water down a plughole, and Tess had the horrible feeling she was on the wrong side of it. Her hotel, she realized, after studying the map on which Emma had placed a large red cross to highlight the relevant road, *was* on the other side, and she certainly wasn't looking forward to playing chicken while trying to cross.

She took a moment to get her bearings, feeling for the little wallet she had tucked into one side of her bra, and her mobile phone, which she had tucked into the other – no pickpockets were going to get anywhere near *her* valuables! Reassured that everything was where she had put it, she glanced behind her, already knowing what she was going to see.

Two massive, pointed, red-brick columns reached into the sky, gleaming in the midday sun. Beyond them, at the end of a fountain-lined avenue, was a sight to take her breath away.

Shimmering in the distance was the magnificent Museu Nacional d'Art de Catalunya. Not only did the marathon start on the road below its impressive terraces, but the museum itself was on Tess's 'must-see' list. It held a vast collection of art from the medieval to the modern, and she couldn't wait to get inside it. From the outside, it looked like a fairy-tale palace, and she stared at its cream-stoned beauty with her mouth open in awe. She'd only been in the city for a few minutes and she was already half in love with it. Fancy having something like this on your doorstep!

Well done, Emma, for booking a hotel within walking distance of this magnificent building, Tess thought, though she was aware that Emma had actually chosen the Sant Jeroni hotel because of its proximity to the start of the race, and not because of Tess's fascination with art. To be fair, Emma had agreed to accompany her to most of the places Tess wanted to see, even if her sister thought Picasso painted with as much finesse as a three-year-old. Emma, Tess decided, was a heathen and in dire need of being educated about art.

When Tess finally managed to close her mouth and drag her eyes away, she looked around for a less dangerous method of crossing to the other side of the busy round-about. Happily, she discovered that she could go under it, rather than across it.

Mission accomplished, she dragged her case along yet another frenetically busy road, once again thankful that her sister had made her do a virtual walk of the route beforehand. Las Arenas de Barcelona should be on her right——? Check. It was once used for bullfighting but was now a shopping centre, and the place where Emma had planned to spend a considerable amount of time – apparently her sister hadn't found a veil she liked in England, and had wanted to explore Barcelona's shops in the hope of finding one in Spanish lace. A park, also on her right——?

Check. Relieved that she was heading the right way, Tess walked to the end of the park, turned right, and saw her hotel.

Tess gave herself a pat on the back: from her flat to the hotel in one smooth operation. She'd not got lost once, and – she surreptitiously felt her boobs – she'd not had anything stolen either.

The hotel, situated on a wide, tree-lined road, was a brown stone building. All the windows facing the road were full-length and had tiny little wrought-iron Juliet balconies. It looked really sweet and old-fashioned, although when she entered the foyer, the inside was ultra-modern, with polished wooden floors and tasteful grey and white décor. It looked exactly like the photos, which Emma had also made her look at.

She walked up to the reception desk, her case trundling behind her, and checked in. Thankfully, the staff spoke English reasonably well, so she wasn't forced to try out her rather dire Spanish, and very soon Tess was given a key card and directed to her room. Not that she intended to be in it for long – she was starving and she also couldn't wait to go exploring – but a quick unpack and a freshen up wouldn't go amiss.

Her room was lovely and Tess smiled in delight as she stared around it. There were two large beds, a big, marble-tiled bathroom (with a selection of complimentary shampoos and scented soaps), a TV, and a mini-fridge. Although she didn't have a view of the park, she had a view of a pretty interior courtyard, with plants and a seating area. It looked very Mediterranean, with its flag-stones and terracotta pots, and the occasional mosaic on the walls.

Eek, she was here! She was really here!

She opened the window and leaned out, breathing in a heady scent of jasmine, and gazed at the view. She dearly wanted to sketch the scene and was desperate to paint the way the shadows deepened the blues and aquamarine colours of tiny coloured tiles on one side of the courtyard, while the yellow and white on the other side shone and gleamed in the sparkling sunlight. And those pots with their dark green foliage, and bright crimson and fuchsia flowers tumbling down the side…

She could happily spend the next week just in this one spot! But there was so much to see and her time was limited, so she forced herself to turn her back on the window and its lovely, secluded secret. She wished her flat in Worcester looked onto something as nice, and not onto the private car park where the funeral director's hearses were kept, and she sighed with longing.

Unpacking quickly, she washed her face and hands, ran a brush through her hair, and checked her bra again. Satisfied that her boobs were still keeping everything safe, she pinged off another text to her poorly sister.

> Hotel in fab location. Well done, you! Nice
> room. Will post photos later. Off out for
> some lunch. Need carbs xx

As she grabbed her bag and slipped her sketchbook, a few pencils, and some assorted arty essentials into the side pocket along with her map, her phone bleeped.

> Have fun. Wish I was with you. Have a
> salad – something healthy x

Tess wished that her sister was here, too. It would have been so much more fun to have someone to share all this with; not to mention having someone to run by her side. Resolutely, she put all thoughts of the marathon out of her mind. It might spoil the rest of the day if she dwelled on the horror to come – she had no doubt the experience was going to be awful. There was time enough to worry about the race when the day actually arrived. Right now, she wanted to explore.

Tess retraced her steps to the manic roundabout and dived into the underground once more. Today (what was left of it) was more of an orienteering day, and she came out of the metro station and into the sunlight at the other end like a cork bobbing up from the bottom of the washing-up bowl. Once again, she marvelled at the unaccustomed sunlight illuminating a small square with cafes and shops around its perimeter, the metro station entrance in the middle. It was really strange to think there were swarms of people under her feet, and trains whizzing through tunnels, yet up here on the edge of the Gothic Quarter, she could almost imagine herself in a long-ago century as she peered down the narrow winding streets radiating out from the square.

Ignoring the tantalizing smell of coffee, she consulted her map, then picked a tiny side street hardly wide enough for people to walk two abreast, before plunging into the shadows cast by the cliff-like buildings that towered above her head. She craned her neck, staring upwards at the tiny balconies above, and she noticed that a sliver of bright cobalt sky was visible. It was almost like being in a tunnel where the roof had caved in, and she guessed that the original residents had built up rather than out. Had that been because of the price of land, she wondered, or because the Gothic Quarter had been surrounded by ancient walls?

Tess wandered on, making a note to pick up a good guidebook. She hadn't really thought to buy one before, thinking she'd be concentrating mostly on Gaudi and the multitude of museums that the city boasted, but from what she'd seen of Barcelona so far (and she admittedly hadn't seen a great deal of it yet), there was much more to this city than art.

Little doorways on either side of the street revealed quaint shops, bars and restaurants, while fairy lights were strung at intervals overhead, like tiny glittering stars twinkling in the upper reaches. *I bet they look fabulous at night*, Tess thought, vowing to come back after dark. With each step, she was more and more entranced by the narrowness of the streets and the way the little balconies overhead seemed to be closing in on her. It was all very medieval, and she could imagine it looking exactly the same now as it had 500 years ago.

She halted at the entrance to one such street, which looked more like a passageway than a thoroughfare, admiring the way it took a sharp turn to the left, so all that could be seen from where she stood was a wall and a hint of something beyond it, just out of view. It was dark and mysterious, and so inviting. She was dying to dart down it and discover its secrets.

But first, she simply had to draw it.

Using charcoal pencils, with a few deft strokes she soon had the contours of the street outlined, scribbling frantically to capture the shadows, the rough stone, the flattened cobbles, and the way a shaft of sunlight pierced the gloom like a lance, straight and true, illuminating one small patch of ancient stone wall. She worked hastily and with complete concentration, blocking out everyone and everything as she poured her soul into the task.

When she was finally done and could do no more, she held the sketch at arm's length, eyeing it critically, pleased with the way it had turned out. Sometimes, it was right to spend hours on a piece, while for others a swift rendering was all that was needed to capture the mood and emotion of the scene.

She gently blew away the excess charcoal dust, then rooted around in her bag for a small can of fixative spray to stop the charcoal from smudging. Some women carried make-up bags, hairbrushes, or a spare pair of tights in their handbags – Tess carried her faithful sketch pad, assorted pencils in graphite, charcoal and pastel, and a can of fixative in hers. And a pack of wet-wipes for occasions like this one. The fixative dried quickly, and she slipped the sheet of paper back into the pad before wiping her charcoal-covered hands clean.

Artistic talent appeased for a moment, Tess was suddenly, sharply aware that she needed to eat. There certainly wasn't any shortage of places to choose from. Enticing smells wafted across her nose as she wandered deeper into the stone maze, and as she peered through various doors and windows, she realized she was spoilt for choice.

Wanting to try something Spanish, she kept an eye out for a tapas bar. She'd been reading up on those lovely little restaurants and was anxious to try out some of the local delicacies.

Ooh, look, an ice cream parlour. Her mouth watered, but she stopped herself from going in. Tempting as the array of multi-coloured ice creams was, she knew she had to eat properly first; there was no point in undoing all her hard work of the last few months by blowing it all on ice cream and pastries now. If she was still hungry after her meal, she could treat herself to one then.

A narrow wooden doorway with a sign above it, 'Las Tapas Picantes', caught her eye. Like many other shops and restaurants in the Gothic Quarter, it was half hidden, with only a tiny window next to the door revealing what was going on inside. She peered through it, relieved to see tables and a long counter. The smell wafting through the slightly open door made her stomach rumble in anticipation.

A couple pushed past her and went inside, chattering in rapid Spanish, and her mind was made up. If it was good enough for the locals, it was good enough for her. She didn't want food aimed at tourists; she wanted to eat the food the locals ate. Besides, the aromas coming from its rather dark depths were absolutely mouth-watering, so she stepped through the doorway into the gloom.

As her eyes adjusted she realized the place was actually quite full. Finding a free table, she sat down, soaking up the atmosphere, her mind on the drawing she'd just done and thinking that she'd add some colour to it when she got home.

Home. Emma. She would have loved this – not the standing around when Tess was sketching, but the secluded little restaurant behind an old wooden door – and Tess was hit by sudden loneliness. Poor Emma, she should have been here enjoying the experience, not stuck at home with horrid spots and a bottle of the pink stuff (and she didn't mean rosé wine, either). She blinked back some tears, putting her emotion down to hunger and the after-effects of the solitary journey, and took a steadying breath.

'English?' a waiter said, appearing at her elbow.

Was it that obvious?

Wondering what to order, and not seeing a menu on the table, she looked up with a smile, hoping the waiter spoke more English than she spoke Spanish.

A pair of concerned eyes stared back at her.

Good lord! Were those lashes real?

Snapped out of her silly melancholy, she squinted up at the man standing by her table. Oh my! If she'd already had a menu in her hand, she'd be fanning herself with it. That face was to die for. Was he really a waiter, or was he a film star doing some hands-on research?

He was gorgeous. Not her usual type – though she had been without a boyfriend for so long, she wasn't exactly sure what her type was any more. His skin was lightly tanned and he had a hint of stubble. With black hair, dark-chocolate eyes and a sensuous mouth, he also had that chiselled-jaw thing going on. A white shirt, the top button undone, did a good job of outlining a broad chest and a flat stomach, while a pair of black trousers showed off his legs. Tess simply itched to get her sketch pad out and draw him. She could just imagine him standing on a parapet somewhere, staring moodily out to sea.

He gave a small cough.

Oh, yes, he'd asked if she was English, Tess realized, as he waited patiently for an answer, and she gulped and nodded. Falling for a Spanish waiter was such a cliché, but she could see how it could easily happen if they all looked as good as this one did!

'You want a drink, perhaps something to eat?' he asked.

Ooh, that accent!

Tess found her voice, though the words that came out of her mouth were a bit breathier than normal. 'Yes, please.'

'Wine?'

'Er, no thanks. It's a bit too early for me.'

His eyes widened. 'It is never too early for wine,' he protested, clutching a hand to his chest in pretend shock. 'Food is no good without a fine wine to complement it. Have you learned nothing since you have been in Spain?'

'I only landed a couple of hours ago,' she replied, trying not to laugh. 'I'll just have a mineral water, please. And the menu.'

'We don't have a menu,' he said. 'The selection changes daily. It is always a surprise. It is what makes us famous.'

Tess blinked. 'How do I know what to order?' she asked.

'Have you ever eaten tapas?' he enquired, and when she shook her head, he smiled. 'Do you trust me?'

Trust him? She'd never met him before in her life, and she wasn't in the habit of trusting strange men, however handsome they might be.

'Yes,' she replied, and almost clapped a hand to her mouth. That wasn't what she had intended to say, at all. *Sod it, live a little*, she told herself. After all, if a waiter in the restaurant she was eating in couldn't recommend a dish, then who could? She was sure it would be lovely. Whatever it was.

'I will bring you a selection of the finest tapas in Barcelona,' he said theatrically. '"Las Tapas" bars are famous all over Catalonia, all over Spain. Once you taste our food, you will never want to eat anything else.'

I'll be the judge of that, Tess thought, as she watched him saunter over to the bar to place her order. Tapas might be nice, but she had a secret passion for pizza, and she had already decided that for dinner that evening she would look for a pizzeria. If she had a salad with it, she could honestly tell Emma that she had eaten healthily.

She hoped she'd like what her waiter chose. Besides, she knew that tapas wasn't exactly one dish; it was more a series of snacks, and although she was quite apprehensive about what she was going to be presented with, if she didn't like one of the dishes he brought out, she may very well enjoy another.

She watched as her waiter disappeared into the kitchen, only to reappear quickly, followed by a man who Tess could only assume was the chef, who narrowed his eyes at her and shook his head. The waiter waved his hands around and shook his head several times, and every so often turned to her and smiled reassuringly. Finally, the chef shrugged and returned to his kitchen.

Tess got her phone out.

> In a tapas bar. Not sure what I've ordered.
> Hope it's not sheep's eyeballs, lol.

She smiled as she pressed 'Send', then jumped as the waiter placed a jug of water and a couple of glasses on the table, before pulling out a chair and sitting down. Tess raised her eyebrows. Did he intend to join her? And, more to the point, did she want him to?

'What was all that about with the chef?' she asked, when he made no move to leave, watching him as he poured water into both glasses.

'*Salud!*' He took a sip of his drink and shuddered. '*Dios mío!* To drink this with tapas is *sacrelegio*. I will fetch the wine.'

Before Tess could protest, he'd snatched up both the glasses and the jug of water and returned to the bar. He had his back to her, but she heard the pop of a cork and she sighed. Getting tipsy was not on her agenda and, after the early morning she'd had and all the travelling, it wouldn't take much to make her merry.

'This is better,' he announced, pouring the wine and putting the bottle in the centre of the table. He sat down again, picked up his glass and sniffed. The red liquid swirled darkly.

Tess took a tentative sip. It was full-bodied but not too rich, the flavour bursting over her tongue. 'Mmm.'

'Water is for exercise or on the beach,' he said. 'Not for food. Wine will clear your... how do I say... *paladar*...?'

'Palate?' Tess guessed.

'Yes, of course, "palate", so each mouthful is fresh and new, and not tainted by the one before.'

'Your English is very good,' she said, wishing her Spanish was better. She could hardly remember a word of her online lessons now that she was here.

'Thank you. I practise a lot,' he replied.

Tess wondered if he intended to sit there and watch her eat, and was just about to ask him when the first dishes arrived. Plate after plate of steaming food was placed on their table, with one or two cold, salady ones too. How on earth was she expected to eat all that? Or pay for it? She stared at them with a mixture of greed and dismay.

'It is on the house,' the waiter said, accurately reading her expression. 'Do you mind if I eat with you? It's too much for one, and it's a pity to waste it.'

Tess thought for a moment. Would it be so bad? A lovely meal and a handsome man to help her eat it? It wasn't as if he'd asked her out on a date, was it? And at the end of the meal she would walk out of there and never see him again. Besides, she could just imagine Emma's expression when she told her sister about it! What the heck, let him join her. But there was no way she wasn't going to pay her share: now Tess wasn't so bothered about what was on the table, she was more bothered about the cost and the fact that this man seemed to want to feed her for nothing. It was a little strange, to say the least.

'I can pay,' she said, feeling a little alarmed. She didn't want to be beholden to anyone, least of all a waiter who probably earned less than she did. A suspicion that he might expect payment in other ways sneaked into her mind.

'I don't say you can't pay. I say I don't want you to. I want to show you good food, and perhaps you will tell your friends about Las Tapas Picantes, and they will come here.'

'Look, I'm sorry...' She halted. 'I don't even know your name.'

'Roberto, Roberto Pérez Montero.'

'Well, Roberto, I'm here on my own so I won't be bringing any friends along.'

'No matter. You will visit Barcelona again. Everyone does. They fall in love with her.' He sounded so confident that Tess had to smile. He was also right; she was already half in love with the city, and she'd only seen a fraction of it so far.

'What is your name?' he asked.

'Tess Barton.'

'Hello, Tess Barton. Please accept this' – he waved a hand over the table with its numerous dishes – 'as a welcome to Barcelona.'

'I still want to pay.'

'If you must,' he relented with a sigh. 'But for the tapas of the day only. The rest is gratis, and the wine is for me to buy.'

'Do you mean free? How much are they and which ones are the tapas of the day?' Tess stared at the assortment before her, confused.

'There is a set price for five dishes,' he said, pointing to the chalk board above the bar. 'And the tapas change every day. Some of these dishes here are not on the menu today, but they will be again tomorrow, or the day after that. I asked Mateo to cook them for you especially. I think you'll like them.'

'If that's the case, then I don't blame him for frowning,' Tess mused. 'Please tell him I'm sorry for the extra work I've caused him.' Now that she knew how much the meal was going to cost, she relaxed a little. The price was around what she'd budgeted for and it meant she could stick to her daily allowance – she was scared of running out of euros before the end of the holiday.

'Don't take any notice of Mateo,' Roberto was saying. 'He often frowns. He frowns over the quality of the shrimp, the mussels, the chicken, or if the rice is not right, the flour is old… He frowns every day, all day.' He shrugged. 'Chefs like to complain, and Mateo is a chef. I think he believes he isn't a true chef unless he's frowning.' Roberto drew his eyebrows down and glared out from underneath them. Tess giggled.

'Shall we eat before the tapas is cold, or do you want to talk about Mateo some more?' he added.

Tess decided to go with the flow and just enjoy the meal. 'Eat, please. I'm starving.'

Roberto spooned a couple of deep-fried balls of something onto her plate. 'Try these. They're very good.' He popped one in his mouth and chewed, as if to demonstrate how tasty they were.

'What are they?' Tess watched him chew.

'*Buñuelos de bacalao*, cod balls with salt. Eat,' he urged.

So she did, and when Tess put one of the cod balls in her own mouth, she found it was very good indeed, so she had another. And another. Then it was time to try the pan-fried squid with hot chorizo. As soon as she declared it was lovely, Roberto insisted she have a bread-stick wrapped in ham and a fig to go with it.

'Wait,' she said, before any more dishes could be decimated. 'I forgot to take a photo.'

'Why do you take photos of your food?' he asked, as Tess scrabbled around down the front of her top, took out her phone and snapped away. 'And why do you keep your phone down there?'

'For my sister.'

Roberto looked puzzled. 'You keep your phone in your' – he waved a hand in the direction of her chest – 'for your sister?'

'No, silly, I put my money and my phone in my bra, so they won't be stolen. And I'm taking a photo of all this scrummy food because my sister, Emma, was supposed to be here with me, but she caught chickenpox and can't fly, so I'm here on my own.'

'It is sad that you are here alone. Couldn't you have changed your flights? Sometimes hotels will let you book for another time.'

'You don't understand – we're supposed to be running the marathon together. That's why I'm here. There was no point in changing to another weekend.'

71

'*La maratón?*' Roberto looked at Tess. 'I'm impressed. I run too, but I've never run a marathon. But what is this chicken's socks?'

Tess giggled. 'Chickenpox. It's a nasty little bug that brings you out in a rash, which then develops into blisters.'

'I am not sure what bleesters are, but they don't sound nice.'

'They're not. Anyway, she's still infectious so the airline won't allow her to fly.'

Roberto recoiled ever so slightly.

'Don't worry, I had it when I was a child, and you can't catch it again,' Tess said, though she wasn't entirely certain that was true.

Roberto leaned forward and put his elbows on the table, as if to say he hadn't really been bothered about catching it himself and coming out in "bleesters".

'So, here you are, in my beautiful city, all on your own. I will not have it!' he declared. 'I intend to make it my business to show you Barcelona and keep you company.'

When Tess didn't reply, his confident mask slipped a little. 'If this is OK with you?' he added. 'I promise you I'm not a bad man. You'll be safe with me. I was right about the tapas, wasn't I?'

Letting him choose her lunch was hardly the same as letting him show her around. He might take her anywhere! She knew absolutely nothing about the bloke. He could be a mad serial killer for all she knew, and everyone knew you could never tell just by looking. It wasn't as if they wore signs. For instance, take that film where the guy worked in a shop which developed photos – he turned out to be a serial killer. The film might be an oldie, but it just went to show that you never could tell.

'Eat first, then I'll show you my city,' he instructed. 'I want you to try everything. Have some of this.' He pointed to a dish brimming with slices of chicken in a rich sauce.

'Thank you for the offer,' Tess said, 'but I'm fine exploring on my own.' She began to tuck in with gusto. She had no intention of being escorted around Barcelona by a complete stranger.

When Tess was finally full and unable to eat another mouthful, Roberto brought two tiny cups of strong black coffee to the table, and two small glasses of reddish-brown liquid, hardly larger than a thimble.

'*Pacharán*. A digestif, to help your meal settle,' he said, seeing her dubious expression.

It was sweet and strong. No wonder it was served in such small glasses, because Tess realized you couldn't drink too much of it. Still, she finished her drink and her coffee, then wondered how she was going to extricate herself from the situation.

Yes, she had enjoyed the meal, and the company as well, if she was honest, but she felt very uncomfortable at the thought of not paying for it all (even though she suspected that the full cost of this meal might blow her food budget for today in one go), and even more uncomfortable at Roberto's suggestion of accompanying her. As lovely as he was – and he was very lovely indeed to look at, and lovely to talk to – she wanted a chance to take stock of the city by herself, so she was glad she had refused his offer.

'Please, put your money away,' Roberto said, seeing her discreetly fishing around down the front of her top. 'I'm not going to let you pay.' He turned to shout something to the staff behind the bar. One of them grinned back at him and winked.

Tess felt distinctly uncomfortable, wondering how she'd managed to get herself into this mess when she'd only been in the country a few hours. There was no way she was going to sleep with him, if that was what he was expecting.

Roberto put a hand on Tess's arm. She was shocked to feel a small frisson go through her. She had to concentrate very hard on not letting it show in her face. 'Please, I want to do this. There is no *obligación*.'

'You said I can pay for the tapas of the day,' she protested, pulling out some notes and counting them.

The waiter sighed. 'Yes, I did,' he said, and took the proffered money.

Feeling better about things, Tess put the rest of the notes back where they came from and made to rise, but Roberto beat her to it, getting out of his seat and walking around behind her. Tess stiffened, wondering if her drink had been spiked and he was getting ready to catch her when she toppled off her chair. Maybe he had a racket going, where he preyed on young blonde women for the slave market. She had seen *Taken*, but unfortunately there was no Liam Neeson to rescue her, only her dad, and she couldn't see him chasing over rooftops to save her. Complaining to the British Embassy was more his style.

Tess lurched to her feet, only to find that Roberto had pulled her chair out for her and was holding her jacket. 'You will want to put this on,' he advised. 'March in Barcelona can be quite cool in the late afternoon.'

She thanked him and he said, 'It's my pleasure', as he studiously ignored the catcalls that were suddenly coming from behind the bar.

'What are they saying?' she asked, as he helped her shrug into her jacket.

'They are making fun of me for falling for a beautiful woman. They say I'll never see you again.'

'I bet you do this all the time,' she joked, yanking the strap of her bag onto her shoulder.

The expression on his face surprised her. 'No, I don't. This is the first time.'

The way he said it made Tess think it might also be the last, and a frisson of guilt shot through her. He looked both serious and a little sad.

'Goodbye, Tess Barton. It was nice meeting you,' he said, a soft smile playing about his lips.

Was that it? He wasn't going to insist on accompanying her?

'Thank you,' she said again, smiling and nodding at the restaurant in general to encompass the rest of the staff in her appreciation. Even though the place was still very busy and they had customers to serve, they were lined up against the bar like a trio of old ladies ready for a good gossip to watch Tess's departure – though the grumpy chef remained in his kitchen, Tess noticed.

She stepped out into the narrow street, seeing that the sky high above had lost some of its brilliance as the colour leached out of it, and she glanced at her watch. Two hours had gone by since she'd entered the restaurant, and she had no idea where they had flown.

She stood there for a minute, thinking. Then she turned on her heel and marched right back in. Roberto was nowhere to be seen.

'You want *jefe*?' one of the waiters asked.

'No, Roberto,' she replied, wondering who Jefe was.

'*Sí, es* Roberto. I call him,' was the reply.

75

Maybe 'Jefe' was a nickname, or it meant 'headwaiter', or something.

Roberto reappeared within seconds, a questioning smile on his face, his eyes wary. 'I didn't think I'd see you again,' he said.

Tess blushed. 'I'd like to take you up on your offer of showing me around, if that's all right with you—?' What was the worst that could happen? OK, she'd already been over that in her mind, but it was unlikely, and she didn't want undue caution preventing her from seeing things other tourists might miss.

The huge smile that lit up Roberto's face made her heart melt. He seemed genuinely delighted.

'Wait while I get my coat?' he asked, as if he expected her to change her mind and make a dash for the door.

'You can show me around right now?' she asked, surprised that he could leave. Or maybe he had offered because his shift was about to end? Either way, she was pleased she didn't have to wait, otherwise it might have given her time to change her mind again.

She nodded and he disappeared, but was back in a trice, wearing a black leather jacket. It made him look less waiterish and more roguish. She liked it. She liked *him*.

'Do you want to start with the tourist stuff?' he asked. 'La Catedral de la Santa Cruz y Santa Eulalia is not far, but everyone goes there and it can get very crowded. I know another church, just as beautiful and not so many people. Santa Maria del Mar is nearby, three or four streets away from *la catedral*. I'll take you there, if you want.'

'I really want to see Gaudi's work,' she said, laughing at his enthusiasm. 'And Picasso's.'

'Ah, you love art but not religion?'

'Yes, I love art, but I do like churches, too. The Sagrada Familia is on my must-see list.'

'*Bien*, it is on everyone's list. But if you want to see Gaudi, we'll start with *la exposición* Paseando con Gaudi, I think. This isn't far also. Come.'

He led her through the maze of streets for a few minutes, and though she desperately wanted to peer into doorways and linger at shop windows, she trotted along beside him.

'What is the... *exposición* Paseando con Gaudi?' she asked.

'A museum for Gaudi. Look, we're here.'

They emerged from a tiny street into a large square. Tess turned to where Roberto pointed, but something else caught her eye first. The building on her right soared into the sky, its intricately carved stone and arched windows rising into decorated spires towering over the open space, and she gasped. The carving was impressive, but even more breathtaking was the entrance: two massive wooden doors were flanked by a series of statues, and above the doors a succession of arches had been carved, each one higher than the last, almost as tall as the main frontage. Above that were those spectacular spires. Her intention to visit the Gaudi museum was all but forgotten as she stared open-mouthed at the sight in front of her.

'What is it?' she asked, craning her neck to peer at the topmost turrets.

'That is La Catedral de Barcelona,' he said, catching her arm when she threatened to topple backwards.

'No wonder it attracts so many people. I want to go up *there*,' she breathed, pointing skywards.

'I don't think it's allowed,' he said. 'But I can ask and maybe...'

He still had hold of her, and without thinking she leaned back against him. 'It's beautiful,' she said.

'Yes, it is,' he agreed, but when she swivelled around it wasn't the cathedral he was gazing at – it was her.

Hastily she shuffled away, not wanting to give him any ideas.

'Come, the exhibition is this way.' He gestured to one side of the busy square.

People were milling about, some clearly tourists with their cameras and phones out, whilst others appeared to be locals. Vendors selling everything, from lucky heather to fruit, dotted the main street which ran along one side of the open space, and people sat outside bars and cafes, drinking coffee, chatting and watching the world go by.

Tess wanted to see beyond all the modern activity, and she narrowed her eyes as she tried to imagine how it would have looked centuries ago. 'I bet this place hasn't changed a great deal,' she said.

Roberto laughed. 'I don't think it has, though a thousand years ago the exhibition building was once a place for the poor and for pilgrims. A Roman wall stood here, and part of it can still be seen. I will show you later.'

'Wait,' she cried, as he began to walk across the square, and he stopped obediently as she snapped away on her phone.

Thinking she was ready when she replaced her phone down the front of her T-shirt, he started to walk away, but when she failed to follow he turned back, his eyebrows rising when he saw what she was doing.

Tess was seated on the warm stone ground, balancing her sketchbook on her knee, drawing furiously, this time in pencil. There was so much colour here, each block of stone a different shade of blond and cream and pale dove-grey, and so many other tones, that a line drawing wouldn't do it justice. This building cried out for the delicacy of watercolour or the bolder statement of oils. She couldn't decide, and maybe she didn't have to. She could do both!

Excitement coursed through her, and it was only when Roberto eventually sat down beside her that she remembered he was there at all. He'd been so quiet, not saying anything, simply letting her do what she was doing as if he understood her burning need to let the image flow from her eyes, through her heart and out of her fingers onto the page.

She was conscious of him glancing at her from time to time, but her attention was on her work as the cathedral came to life.

When she was done, she straightened her back to ease out the kinks, revelling in the wonderful feeling of creating something out of nothing flooding through her. She was both exhilarated and exhausted at the same time. And her bottom was numb from sitting on the hard stone.

Coming back to herself, she became conscious of people staring at her, some going so far as to peer over her shoulder to see what she'd drawn, and making noises of appreciation.

Self-consciously, she put everything away, not meeting Roberto's eye. Did he think her slightly strange, plonking herself down in the middle of a square and drawing away as if the very devil himself was threatening to confiscate her pencil if she didn't hurry up?

But when she tried to stand, her legs tingling from being in the same position for so long, he was already on his feet and holding out a helping hand. She took it gratefully, and as she did so, a bolt of... *something*... shot through her.

Shocked, all she could do was clamber to her feet, and let go of his hand as soon as she was upright.

'That was amazing,' he said, gazing at her, and she heard awe and respect in his voice. 'You are an *artista*, an artist, yes?'

'Yes.' Tess dusted off the back of her jeans and smiled up at him. It was almost true, in the sense that she was an artist, though she didn't solely make her living from her work. *Give it time*, she thought, crossing her fingers. 'I illustrate books, mostly, but I also do my own stuff.'

'I'm impressed. I wish I was like you. I couldn't draw a straight line with a...' He held out his hands to indicate a ruler, and she laughed.

'Gaudi now?' he asked, 'or would you like to draw some more?'

'Gaudi,' she replied firmly and he nodded, leading her across the square.

Tess didn't know what she'd been expecting, but the entrance to the museum was quite disappointing, just a door with a small sign on it which could be easily missed if you didn't know where to look, and she realized how lucky she was to have met Roberto. There was nothing like a local to show you around, and Tess was grateful for his company.

Thankfully, there wasn't a queue to get in (she had read somewhere that the queues to enter some of the more popular places could be horrendous), but there was a sticky moment when Roberto tried to insist on paying.

'No, absolutely not,' Tess argued, folding her arms and pursing her lips. 'You kindly offered to show me your city, and I won't have you out of pocket because of it.'

'It's fifteen euros,' he said, shrugging, as if the money was inconsequential.

'That's *each*,' Tess pointed out, firmly. 'You're not paying for me to go in. In fact, I want to pay for *your* ticket.'

It was Roberto's turn to look stubborn, and Tess wondered if it was a macho thing, but even if it was, she still intended to stand her ground. 'You bought me most of my lunch and the wine, so this is the least I can do,' she persisted.

Roberto opened his mouth, and Tess suspected he was going to continue the argument, but he shrugged again and said, '*Vale*, OK, but next time I'll pay.'

What next time? Tess wondered, though with the matter settled, she paid the entrance fee and darted inside, Roberto hot on her heels. Victory was hers!

'"*Paseando con Gaudi*" means "walking with Gaudi",' Roberto explained, as Tess bought a guidebook, and wandered into the depths of the building, Roberto close behind her.

'This might be a silly question, but have you been here before?' Tess asked, thinking about her own dire lack of knowledge regarding her own home city – unless you counted where to get the best pizza as vital information.

Roberto laughed. 'Yes, many times. I feel I know Gaudi very well. It's rumoured he was an irritable man, rather unpleasant and arrogant, but those who were close to him tell a different story. They say he was friendly and polite. I hope when I am gone, those who love me won't just say I was "polite".' He shook his head ruefully. 'Perhaps his mind was too full of his creations for people to have much of an impact on him. Such is the price of genius, no?'

The following two hours were enthralling for Tess, and her companion seemed to enjoy it as much as she did, even though he'd been there before.

Open-mouthed – she seemed to be doing a lot of jaw-dropping since she'd landed at the airport – Tess came to a stop next to a giant sculpture of the famous Gaudi lizard. She had already noticed there were images and trinkets of this beast everywhere.

Roberto nodded at it. 'He is called "*El Drac*", or "the dragon", and you will find him and his brothers all over the city. We have taken him as a symbol of both Gaudi and of Barcelona, though there are over four hundred dragons in the city and many of them date from before Gaudi. You can see dragons with wings, snake-like dragons, some who are terrifying, others who look more like this – a lizard. But Gaudi took the dragon and made it his own, and this is the scale model of a much bigger one which is found in Park Güell.' Roberto looked at Tess, to check she was following him. Reassured, he continued: 'His name is Python, for the snake of the temple of Delphi. In Greek mythology, this dragon was killed by Apollo, and he buried it underneath the temple. There are many other Gaudi dragons in Park Güell, though,' he added.

Tess nodded – the park was on her must-see list – but was then captivated by the many glass cases displaying old books on architecture, instruments the great man had used (it was amazing to think Gaudi himself had touched these things), and shards of pottery and ceramics.

Roberto pointed to one of the cases. 'Gaudi was responsible for the new technique called *trencadís*, a type of mosaic made from broken pieces of pottery and ceramic. He preferred glazed, fired clay, though glass, and even

82

buttons and shells were sometimes used. You'll see this effect on a lot of his work.'

Tess was astonished at his knowledge. Roberto was such a great guide, he should take it up professionally! There was so much to see and absorb, and although Tess had a grounding in Gaudi, as she wandered around the museum she realized just how little she actually knew. It was one thing looking at books and the internet, but it was a different thing altogether being here, almost inside the mind of the great man himself. And as she stared at the many photos, and circled the glass cases which housed gleaming white scale models of his famous buildings, she was so glad that Roberto had brought her here. Now, when she explored Gaudi's architecture over the next few days, she'd have a better understanding of the thought processes behind the structures and the artwork.

After being entranced by a series of interactive screens and informative videos, they finally reached the end of the museum; when they emerged into the fresh air, Tess shivered a little at the chill.

When she checked her watch – nearly seven o'clock – she wondered what had happened to the afternoon.

'I would like you to see the Roman walls. I did promise,' Roberto said. 'Then how about dinner afterwards?'

She eyed him warily. Dinner sounded good, but not if he was going to take her back to his restaurant and insist he paid. 'Not tapas?' she asked.

He threw his head back and let out a laugh. 'Only if you want to. Personally, I have eaten enough tapas for one day.'

Tess breathed a sigh of relief. 'Roman walls and dinner,' she agreed, and they set off down the side of the cathedral, diving immediately into the tiny, narrow passages again.

'Barcelona was originally a Roman city, Barcino, and was founded by Emperor Augustus around 10 BC,' Roberto told her. 'Walls encased the city, and some of them can still be seen today. There were four gates, one on each side of a rectangle, connected to two main streets. It is quite a walk around it, and will take about an hour,' he warned, 'so we'll only look at this part.' Seeing her disappointed face, he added, 'There is plenty to see, and I suspect you'll be stopping often.'

Tess already had her phone in her hand, but she was surprised when he continued, 'I expect you will want to draw, too.'

Not even Emma was this tolerant of Tess's often obsessive need to sketch, even though her sister understood how important it was for her. Tess took her sketchbook out and grinned at him.

She grinned even wider when they halted almost immediately.

'This is the entrance to the Carrer del Bisbe, meaning "Bishop's Street",' Roberto explained. 'And this is the "Pont del Bisbe" or "Bishop's Bridge", which crosses the street uniting buildings on either side. You must not be fooled by its look, though, because the bridge isn't that old – it was built in 1928 by Joan Rubió i Bellver. He wanted to construct a series of Gothic buildings which would blend in with the medieval, but the government refused permission, allowing only this bridge to be built. It's rumoured that in revenge, he secretly hid a skull with a dagger somewhere inside the construction, and legend says that anyone who crosses the bridge and sees the skull will fall prey to an evil spell.'

Thrilled with the story, Tess sank to the ground and balanced her pad in her lap, glancing at Roberto as she did so. He nodded, leaned back against a wall, and proceeded to check his phone, leaving her free to draw to her heart's content. Captivated by the ornate stonework with its arches and scrolls and intricate lattice work, her pencil flew over the page.

When she could finally do no more, she sat up, realising that the shadows had crept up on them. She smiled apologetically at Roberto. He simply smiled back, his eyes crinkling at the corners, and helped her to her feet. Another bolt of electricity shot through her at his touch, and her gaze darted to his face – had he felt it, too?

Using the excuse of needing both hands to carefully put her drawing away, she eased herself a step or two away from him and prayed that her equilibrium could be restored by the time she had to face him again.

'It's better to see the rest of this in daylight,' Roberto said, gesturing down the street. 'So shall we have dinner now?'

'Yes, please.' Lunch seemed a very long time ago, indeed. In fact, she had packed so much into the past few hours, and Roberto had been so knowledgeable and easy to be around, that she felt like she'd known him for a week.

–

'That was wonderful.' Tess pushed her plate away, replete. 'I've had paella before but nothing like this.'

The dish had been served on a sizzling skillet, accompanied by chunks of fresh bread and a simple salad – oh, and wine. *Mustn't forget that!* It seemed that Roberto couldn't eat a meal without drinking wine. Was that typical of the Spanish, or did he have a problem?

The restaurant was in a backstreet, and one that she wouldn't have looked at twice. Nondescript from the outside, the inside wasn't much better, but the food had been positively delicious. Roberto had reassured her it would be, and she had taken him at his word, letting him guide her through a series of ever more scruffy streets, and hoping they weren't going to end up in a sleazy part of the city.

She checked her watch. Now for the awkward part. It was ten o'clock, she'd had a busy, exciting day, and she was really very tired. The overriding problem, though, was that she had absolutely no idea where she was or how to get back to the hotel.

'It's time I went back to my hotel,' she said, trying to stifle a yawn. 'I'm beat.'

Roberto looked at his own wrist, and a chunky, gold-coloured watch flashed in the candlelight. Tess stared at it. It looked expensive, very expensive. She guessed it was probably a fake, just like the handbag that her mum had bought for her last summer when she went to Turkey. Her mum swore no one would be able to tell the difference, though her mother wouldn't recognize a real Hermès bag from a Tesco's own brand.

She yawned again. It had been one of the most exciting and busiest days of her life, but she could hardly keep her eyes open.

'I'll make sure you get back safely,' he offered, taking his wallet out of his trouser pocket and signalling to a hovering waiter that he wanted the bill.

'You are not paying,' Tess said, and she had to laugh when he rolled his eyes. 'I insist we go Dutch.'

Roberto frowned. 'What is this "Dutch"?'

She laughed again. He really was very cute, in a rugged kind of way. 'We split the bill,' she explained.

He didn't look happy about it, but he must have seen the determination on her face, for he agreed without any further argument.

Thankfully, and to Tess's surprise, the meal didn't cost as much as she thought it was going to. She ferreted around in her bra for her stash of euros.

'You really don't have to keep your money down there,' Roberto pointed out. 'Barcelona is no more dangerous than any other city.'

Maybe he was right – and it couldn't look very good to shove her hand into her bra every time she wanted to pay for something. Blushing, Tess transferred most of the money to her purse, though she left some notes where they were, just in case.

Outside the restaurant, the night had turned chilly, with a cool breeze blowing straight into their faces, and Tess shivered.

'The wind comes from the sea,' Roberto explained, taking off the leather jacket he had only a second ago put on. 'Wear this.' He held it out to her.

'I couldn't possibly,' she protested.

'I insist, and I'm bigger than you.' He thumped his chest. 'I don't feel the cold as much as a little person.'

Tess hardly considered herself little, though she did feel quite small and delicate next to Roberto, but it was only when she took the proffered jacket and slipped her arms into the sleeves that she realized how much bigger than her he actually was. The jacket dwarfed her!

It also smelled nice, and she inhaled deeply, taking in the scent of leather, aftershave and man. It was the man part which intrigued her the most. He smelled divine, and it was enough to make her mouth water. She snuggled into the jacket, the leather buttery-soft against her cheek, and she wished she owned something as nice. Though in Britain, any jacket needed to come with a hood as standard to keep off the infernal, ever-present rain!

As they strolled down the street, Roberto kept glancing behind them, and when he raised his hand and she realized he intended to hail a cab, she was horrified.

'No need,' she protested, as one of the waspy, black-and-yellow cars began to pull in towards the pavement. 'I've got a *Hola!* card. It seems silly not to use it.' *And let's not mention how much a taxi ride would cost*, Tess thought, which was why she intended to do all her travelling by public transport.

Roberto glanced down at her and, when she nodded emphatically, he waved the cab away with an apologetic smile.

The metro was becoming almost familiar as they trotted down the steps and into the underground. Because it was much warmer down there, Tess made to return his jacket.

'Keep it. You'll need it for sure when we get off the train,' he said, and he was right. Emerging once more onto the Plaça Espanya, Tess was glad of its warmth. This time she was on the correct side of the roundabout, and they walked in companionable silence until they reached the street where her hotel was located. It was then that a thought occurred to her.

Would he expect to come in for coffee? Should she invite him? But she had a fair idea that "Would you like to come up for a coffee" meant the same thing in most languages, and she really didn't want to give him the wrong idea.

Worrying about it, she grew more tense the closer they got to the hotel, until she was thrumming with anxiety by the time they reached the entrance.

'This is it, no?' Roberto said, coming to a halt outside the hotel's glass doors.

Tess nodded and slipped the beautiful jacket off her shoulders. 'Thank you,' she said simply. 'I've really enjoyed today.'

'I have, too,' he said, taking it from her.

An awkward pause ensued.

Roberto ended it when he stepped closer and took her face in his hands. His skin was warm, his touch firm, and it sent shockwaves through her.

Without thinking, she raised her chin, closed her eyes, and waited for the kiss she knew he was about to give her. But kiss or no kiss, she still wasn't going to invite him into her room, no matter how nice the next few minutes might be.

Soft breath fanned her skin, then his lips made contact… and she opened her eyes in shock.

He'd kissed her on the forehead. That wasn't what she'd been expecting at all!

'Put my number in your phone,' he said, and waited for her to get her mobile out. 'If you need anything, call me,' he continued, after she had keyed the number in.

Was that it? Wasn't he going to ask to see her again?

Apparently not, she realized, as he stepped away and began walking down the street.

'Thank you,' she called, feeling disheartened. She hadn't even considered that this might be the end of it, and she watched him go, his long legs eating up the pavement, his stride jaunty.

'I'll phone you,' he shouted, from halfway down the street.

'How?' she called back. She definitely hadn't given him her number.

'I know where you are staying,' he countered with a cheeky grin, and blew her a kiss as he disappeared around the corner.

Tess went to bed, hugging the thought that he may want to see her again as she lay in the dark, waiting for sleep to take her. Suddenly she sat up. Bugger! In all the excitement she'd forgotten to text her sister!

Five Days to Race Day

The bus was bright red and open-topped. Tess, having got up early and wolfed down her breakfast of coffee and a pastry, made sure she was in prime position at the hop-on, hop-off bus stop. She had been determined to get a seat on the top floor right at the front, and she'd succeeded. Complimentary headphones in, she listened to the commentator's tinny voice as it pointed out things of interest.

It was another beautiful day, the sun shining in a cloudless sky, and though it was a little cool both the weather and the temperature were far removed from a damp and cloudy English March.

Tess had her phone in her hand and was taking photos at a rate of one every ten seconds, then pinging them off to Emma.

> You're still alive, then?

Emma texted back.

> Sorry. I forgot to text last night.

> You forgot to text yesterday afternoon, too.

Oh dear, so she had. Her sister hadn't crossed her mind since Tess had sent her the photo of all those lovely tapas dishes, even though she'd taken loads of snaps.

She texted again:

> Sorry!

> Are you OK?

Tess sensed a softening in her sister's tone.

> Great. Was a bit busy.

> What with? Sightseeing?

You could say that, Tess thought, though she'd spent quite a lot of that time sneaking glances at the man she was with. And drawing, of course.

What did you do yesterday? And what was
all that food about? I hope you didn't eat it
all yourself!! Lol

Emma wanted to know.

Tess most certainly hadn't, but she wasn't going to say so. She wanted to keep Roberto to herself for now. Besides, she'd only be on the receiving end of a lecture from Emma if she mentioned him.

Ooh! Look! Casa Batlló was on her left, another definite destination on her must-see list, and she peered up at it in awe. It was one of the most other-worldly buildings she'd ever seen: it wouldn't have looked out of place in *The Hobbit*. Everything about it was organic, as if the stone had flowed into the weird and wonderful shapes of its own volition, and now that she knew more about the origins of the building and the man responsible for its conception, she felt more connected to it, somehow.

She took a photo and sent it to Emma, thinking that fairies or elves would love to live in a house like this (of course, it wasn't a house any longer but a museum, the disembodied voice in her headphones informed her, but she could pretend). This was exactly the sort of look she'd been trying to achieve in the book on fairies she'd recently illustrated.

Emma texted back:

Pretty.

Was that all her sister had to say about such a magical building? The woman had no soul. Everything about it called to Tess, and she was envious of the residents who had once lived in those apartments. This was definitely a place she'd return to, but for now the sole purpose of the open-top tour was to get a feel for the city, and to work out which places she wanted to spend more time visiting.

The bus left the Passeig de Gràcia and turned left onto the Avinguda Diagonal, a broad, tree-lined avenue which, according to her headphones, stretched from one side of the city to the other. This was one of the wealthier parts, apparently, with million-dollar apartments and high-end shops, banks and car dealerships like Ferrari and Porsche along its length.

Although Tess was interested, and despite some of the buildings being quite old indeed, they didn't hold the same appeal for her as the ones Gaudi had designed, and she found her mind wandering to Roberto. Yesterday had been so exciting and romantic. Fancy her meeting a gorgeous man on her first day in Barcelona, being taken to both lunch and dinner by him, then being escorted home in the most gentlemanly fashion imaginable!

The whole time they had been together they had talked and talked. Roberto had been delighted to show off his city, and she had been impressed by how very knowledgeable he was. It put Tess to shame. If the shoe had been on the other foot and Roberto was visiting Worcester, Tess couldn't have said much about her hometown at all. Yes, she could take him to the cathedral, but she had no idea who had built it or when. It was old, she knew that much, but the details escaped her. There had been a famous battle somewhere nearby (she'd learned about it in school), but again, she lacked those all-important details. She couldn't even remember who had been fighting whom! She was fairly sure it occurred in the seventeenth century, though. Or was she?

She shrugged, her gaze turning to the people on the pavements, most of them striding purposefully, but a few dawdled and Tess guessed they were probably tourists, too.

Her stomach rumbled and she checked her watch. Breakfast had been three hours ago, and she was hungry once again. The tour lasted two and a half hours altogether, but it was one of those where people could join and leave at any time. Her ticket was valid for the whole day, so now might be the right time to get off and find a cafe. She decided to wait until the bus turned off the Avinguda Diagonal, though, because everything around there looked mighty pricey.

The headphones had just instructed her to look at a building on her right, which apparently housed some of the most expensive apartments in Barcelona, when a dark-haired man around thirty years old caught her eye. He had his head down and was looking at his phone as he walked out of the foyer of one of those expensive apartment buildings. Tess peered at him, thinking he looked familiar, before telling herself not to be so silly. Many men in Barcelona were tall and had dark hair – what were the odds of seeing Roberto in a city of thousands? Anyway, he was probably a couple of miles away, slaving over hot tapas or polishing cutlery.

Actually, she could really eat some tapas right now...

Her gaze fell on the pedestrian again, and she watched him idly as the bus driver waited for the lights to change, imagining it really was Roberto. That certainly would be a coincidence, wouldn't it?

Hang on a sec! The guy looked up briefly as he approached a smart black car, aiming a key fob at it. The car flashed an acknowledgment.

The stranger did look remarkably like Roberto, and when he opened the car door and prepared to slide into its depths, Tess was convinced it *was* him. He wasn't dressed like a waiter, though – he was wearing a suit, but the shirt was open at the neck and the suit was dark navy – but if she squinted she could just imagine the suit jacket was a leather one, and…

Darn it! He'd climbed into the car, and now all she could see were tinted windows. She usually didn't take much notice of cars, but this one was large and sleek, all elegant lines and shiny chrome. It reminded her of a big cat, and she bet the engine purred like one, too.

Abruptly, she lurched from her seat and ran down the stairs. If she got off here, she might be able to catch this elusive man and double check.

'No,' was the only word Tess understood, as the conductor refused to let her off, wagging a finger at her, and no matter how nicely Tess asked (in English, of course, because she couldn't remember a word of her self-taught Spanish) the doors stayed stubbornly closed. Slumping into a free seat on the right side of the bus to stare out of the window at this might-be-Roberto, she was frustrated to see that the car was already pulling away from the kerb, preparing to join the rest of the traffic. Just then, the lights changed, and the bus chugged off, taking her further away from her goal.

By the time the tour reached the next legitimate stop, Tess realized, the car carrying the Roberto-lookalike would be well on its way to wherever it was going. And there was also the fact that it almost certainly wasn't him, and she was simply letting her imagination run away with her.

Shrugging (the action reminded her of Roberto), she skipped off the bus at its next stop, wondering where exactly she was. The city was huge, much larger than she'd anticipated, and the sheer size of it momentarily overwhelmed her. It hadn't been so easy to visualize how large it was when travelling by metro, or how much traffic there was, or the thronging crowds. All of yesterday had been spent in and around the Gothic Quarter, and she'd thought that had been busy enough, but it was nothing compared to the size of this enormous square, nor the activity going on both around it and in it. To regain her equilibrium, Tess made her way into its pedestrianized middle, scattering pigeons in her wake, and found a bench.

Dropping down thankfully onto the wooden seat, she pulled her map out of her bag and tried to get her bearings. After squinting at it and turning it upside down, looking around her, then turning it the right way again, she decided she must be in the Plaça de Catalunya. If she was right, then El Corte Inglés should be around here somewhere.

Ah, there it was. Emma would love to be let loose in such a large department store, and Tess decided she'd pay it a little visit at some point during her stay. But, right then, her stomach rumbled loudly enough to scare those pigeons who had plucked up the courage to land once more, and she scared them further when she got to her feet to scan the edges of the square.

There didn't appear to be many cafes or restaurants on the square itself from what she could see, but the nearest side street looked promising, and so she set off in search of lunch.

A board outside the first place she came to tempted her in – all she could eat for eight euros? That would do nicely, and when she saw that most of the tables were occupied by what she assumed to be a mixture of office and shop workers, with the occasional family thrown in, she stepped inside.

Spotlessly clean, bright and airy, the place had a salad bar, a pasta bar, soup tureens, and several hot dishes which looked like stews or casseroles, plus a huge pot of rice. Tess was spoilt for choice. She helped herself to some salad, piling her plate high with delicious healthiness, took a piece of bread, then found a table and tucked in. The variety and quality of the food astonished her, and she couldn't resist trying a sample of each dish on offer, topping it off with some jelly and ice cream. She ate the dessert with a huge smile on her face – she couldn't remember the last time she'd had jelly, and she felt like a kid again. With a couple of cups of strong coffee to finish, Tess was stuffed. She'd be lucky if she managed to walk out of the restaurant, let alone do any more sightseeing. But once she was on her feet and moving, walking back towards El Corte Inglés, she was captivated by the city once more.

Although magnificent and impressive, the Plaça de Catalunya didn't inspire her to whip out her sketch pad, so she was happy to let another one of the hop-on, hop-off buses take her the short distance to Casa Batlló.

She jumped off right outside and stared up at it in amazement. It was even more impressive down here than it had been from the top deck of the bus. At this angle, the topmost semicircular balconies reminded her of parts of a skeleton – the jawbones, maybe? Nearer the ground, the long windows, which were decorated with many beautiful circles of blue stained glass, had been gracefully caged by slim pillars of stone, which were carved in the middle, reminding her of the joints of some exotic and long-extinct animal. There were no straight lines that she could see – everything ebbed and flowed, curved and coiled around the building and its windows and entrance. Even the roof was uneven, and sported a spire in which she imagined Rapunzel lived, letting down her hair. The roof tiles shone purple and blue and silver, or green, depending on the angle and the light, and reminded her of the scales of a dragon. Even the very top of the roof, the apex, was studded with tiles to resemble the backbone of some ancient great beast.

The whole facade of the building was painted white, with what looked like thousands of stylized leaves and blossoms in vibrant shades of lavender, purple and blue, and greens and yellow. It was as if Gaudi had wanted a perpetual bloom of wisteria and lilac, but as she drew nearer she realized that what she had assumed was paint was in fact thousands of tiny pieces of glazed ceramic tiles. Tess had never seen anything so beautiful in her entire life; it looked like something out of a fairy tale, and she longed to live there, to experience this magic every day.

Hastily she made her way inside, eager to see what else Gaudi had in store for her.

It was like being inside the body of a great animal – when she looked through the windows, it was as if she was peering through the beast's ribcage. Undulating walls, wood so finely polished that it resembled weathered bones, and yawning open spaces: the ceilings swirled above her head, a vortex drawing the eye to the incredible lights. Soft music played through the rooms, filling her ears with the same beauty that delighted her eyes.

She wandered from room to room, each one flowing into the other, like the arteries and chambers of a massive heart. Even the floor was on different levels in the same room, so that sometimes she was reminded of the inside of a church; at other times she felt the air flow around her and could imagine she was inside the living, breathing heart of Gaudi's sensational creation.

Sweeping, curved staircases, the handrails like branches of a tree, took her up to the roof, and her eyes filled with tears at the sheer magnificence of it.

But the pièce de résistance was the interior of the spire itself. Hollow, with light shafting down through its depths to illuminate her face as she bent her head back to stare at the heavens, her face was bathed in a soft glow, reflected off the blue tiles. It was like being underwater, with the surface just out of reach.

Organic and fluid, and with so much detail that everywhere she looked there was something new and wonderful to see, Tess felt sure no mere mortal could have designed this spectacular building, and that it must have been born and not built, its design a result of millions of years of fantastical evolution, and not the creativity of one man alone.

When she finally emerged, she felt cleansed and drained, uplifted and exhausted, all at the same time, and the images swirling in her mind made her want to both paint like a woman possessed and filled her with despair of ever being able to come anywhere near to Gaudi's brilliance and vision.

'*Señorita?*' Tess had her key card in her hand and was heading towards the lifts when the receptionist called her back.

'There is something for you.'

'Oh?' Tess took the folded piece of paper with excitement. Anyone who needed to get in touch with her had her mobile number. 'Who is it from?'

It was a daft question – she knew exactly who. Roberto. It couldn't possibly be anyone else.

But it wasn't from him: it was a note reminding her to order the early breakfast she had requested for the day of the race, and she was hit with a feeling of disappointment.

How silly, when it was clear he wasn't going to make contact.

Stop it, Tess, she admonished herself, as the lift took her up to her floor. But she couldn't help how she felt. There had definitely been something between them, some connection. But though they'd talked the whole time they were together yesterday, Tess realized she actually knew very little about the man, apart from his name. When she thought back to their conversation, it had been mostly about Barcelona (he had been a perfect guide in that sense) and about her. There had been nothing about Roberto whatsoever, really.

Her room phone rang, from the nightstand next to the bed.

Expecting it to be reception, she picked up the receiver. 'Buenos días?' she said, hoping she wasn't making a fool of herself with her pigeon Spanish.

'Tess?'

It was Roberto, and somehow there was an inevitability about it all, as if deep in her heart she'd known he would call, despite what her brain was telling her. And she knew what was coming next. The question was, should she agree to see him? She wanted to, but was it wise? She'd known him just over twenty-four hours and already he was having an effect on her.

'Tess?' He sounded uncertain.

'I'm here.'

'What are you doing this evening?'

'I have to go for a run,' she said.

'You will need to eat later. Let me take you to dinner,' Roberto suggested.

Tess hesitated.

'You haven't answered my question,' he said, when she didn't reply. 'Was lunch yesterday so bad?'

He sounded worried and, despite her intention to not get involved, she couldn't help saying, 'It was lovely. The whole day was lovely. But,' she added, 'it's probably not a good idea.'

'Why?'

If she told him the truth – that she was only here for a short time and she didn't want to risk getting hurt, she'd sound a bit crazy. After all, they'd only just met yesterday, and it wasn't as if he'd proposed or anything. All he was doing was asking to take her to dinner.

On the other hand, what harm can it do? she argued, as long as she maintained some perspective and kept her heart firmly under control. She had really enjoyed his company, and he was so knowledgeable about his city (she'd missed his company today for that very reason – or so she told herself) that it would be worth seeing him for that alone. Besides, what woman could resist an invitation to dinner with a gorgeous man?

'OK,' she said, suddenly. 'I'd love to have dinner with you, but I really must go for a run, first.'

'I will take you somewhere nice, not tapas. I think we've both had enough of the tapas.' She loved the way his English could become a little erratic at times, though usually his grasp of her language was excellent. It made him seem a little more vulnerable.

Roberto might have had enough of tapas (not surprising, considering he worked in a tapas restaurant), but Tess could go another round without any difficulty at all, despite her enormous lunch. It must be all the walking she was doing that was making her so hungry, she decided.

'It's five o'clock. How about I pick you up at eight? Do you go for your run now?' he asked.

'In about half an hour. I want to get back before it gets dark.' She also wanted to relax for a while and check her emails, as well as sorting out her sketches. She didn't want to risk any of them getting crumpled in her bag.

After she got off the phone she took out the few she'd done that day and added them to yesterday's haul. The way she was going, she'd have enough projects to keep her occupied for the next ten years, and she was spoilt for choice about which one to start on first. Anyway, she didn't have to make a decision now – she would probably have many more to choose from by the time she returned home.

Finally ready to face her run, though she did feel a little apprehensive about jogging around a strange city without her trusty map, she did a few warm-up stretches, zipped her mobile phone and room key into the little pocket at the back of her running top, grabbed a bottle of water from the well-stocked minibar, and was off.

She'd only got as far as the kerb outside the hotel, when she stopped.

Leaning against a rather battered, brown hatchback, his arms folded and legs crossed at the ankle, was Roberto. He was wearing shorts, vest and trainers.

Black was clearly his colour. He looked lean and very athletic, and really quite scrummy.

'What are you doing here?' she asked, coming to a comedy halt like the Roadrunner when the bird spotted some of the grain he loved so much.

'Waiting for you.' He straightened up and took a step towards her. 'I thought I could show you Montjuïc.'

'But I'm just about to go for a run!' she protested.

'So am I.' His smile was so gorgeous, she thought she'd dissolve into a puddle on the pavement. 'I don't like you to run alone, so I will come with you,' he added.

Tess considered his suggestion. She wasn't used to running with anyone else except her sister, and she wasn't sure how she felt about his offer. Then she realized how ridiculous that was – in a few days' time she would be running with thousands of other people, all of them total strangers, and here she was worrying about running with Roberto. She had no qualms on the fitness front – she'd come an awful long way over the course of the last few months, she was in the best shape she'd ever been in and was feeling race-ready and healthy, so there was no doubt she'd be able to keep up with him. Besides, it would be better if she was accompanied by someone who knew the city, otherwise there was a strong possibility she might get lost. She was actually quite relieved he was there, if she was honest, and not because he made her all fluttery inside whenever he looked at her, either!

'What's Montjuïc?' she asked, falling in beside him when he straightened up.

'You'll see.'

Setting off at a relatively slow pace to allow time for their muscles to warm up, Roberto led her back to the enormous roundabout, through the underpass and onto the wide road lined with fountains with the Museu Nacional d'Art de Catalunya rising up in front of them.

'Montjuïc is the hill the museum is built on,' Roberto said. He wasn't at all out of breath and he ran with the even, steady strides of an accustomed runner.

Tess stared up at the building, and the artist in her went into overdrive. She was planning on spending either the Friday or the Saturday morning around this area, as she had to register for the marathon in the exposition centre on one of those days, but right then she was about to get a close-up of the museum just as the sun was setting. How magical!

As they drew closer to the building, Tess saw a series of terraces and fountains with cascading water, and steps, lots and lots of steps, rising up either side of the misting water. Every so often, as the breeze eddied, the fine spray blew in their direction and cooled Tess's rapidly warming face.

Darn it, but those steps were gruelling. She could feel the strain in her thighs and buttocks, and when they finally reached the top, Tess was gasping.

'We'll stop a minute,' Roberto suggested, but Tess shook her head. All those steps were really good fitness training, even though it was a bit late to do any more, what with the race being so close.

'Please,' he insisted. 'I want to show you something.'

She followed him around to the left of the museum, and the sight took her breath away. Barcelona was laid out before them, the city glowing in the evening sun, framed by mountains all around, and the sea in the distance. She'd forgotten the city was right on the coast, having been too wrapped up in the narrow streets of the Gothic Quarter and the city's cafe culture. And, of course, Gaudi had commandeered her attention quite a bit, too.

'There, can you see la Sagrada Familia?' Roberto pointed to the spires reaching up into the sky, gold in the setting sun.

'It's beautiful,' she breathed, and for a few minutes the pair of them stood side by side, admiring the view.

'OK, enough. Let's carry on,' he suggested, but Tess found she didn't want to move from that spot.

She was mesmerized, awed, and excited all at once. Barcelona was at her feet waiting to be explored, and right then there was no other place on earth she wanted to be, and no one else she wanted to be there with. Not even Emma.

Guiltily, she turned her back on the view, remembering the purpose of the trip, and allowed Roberto to lead her further up the mountain.

'Montjuïc is the mountain on which the stadium for the 1992 Olympics was built,' he informed her, panting slightly as they continued to climb steadily. At least they were running on tarmacked roads and not up those hellish steps, but the gradient was still taxing.

Tess hadn't realized just how green the city was as now the heady smell of pine and flowers filled her nose, while birds chirped from the trees and bushes. She felt as though she was miles away from the city centre, with all its hustle and bustle. Even the passing traffic couldn't subdue her mood.

The road became narrower the higher they climbed until, without warning, Roberto darted to the right, up a dirt track. Branches arched overhead, and Tess breathed deeply. She loved running through woodland and Barcelona seemed to have a surprising amount of it.

Bursting out into the open, they crossed a main road then once more plunged into greenery, but this time there was a paved path – lots of them in fact, all going off in different directions, but at each fork in the road Roberto didn't hesitate.

'Where are we?' Tess panted.

'This is the Jardí Botànic, the botanical gardens. It is beautiful here in the summer, so cool, but I want to show you something else.'

Another road to cross and more steps, and all around them were landscaped gardens and the feel of being somewhere far removed from the metropolis below. *How much higher could they possibly go?* Tess wondered, her lungs and legs burning with the effort of the steady, unrelenting climb.

Tess sensed they were near the top, and she glanced over her shoulder at the view. The city was visible through the trees and she wanted to stop again to admire it, but suddenly, after a few more steps, they were in an enormous paved area, and beyond it was a huge wall encircling what looked like a fort. But it was the vista below that captured her attention once more. The city was spread over the landscape like a multicoloured blanket, with the grey of the distant mountains beyond, and the sun setting behind them. To the right was the sea, darkly blue, stretching to the horizon. She had an urge to paint it, but the whole thing was too large, too grand. Her eyes caught some of the details, but she felt a painting would lack the majesty of the experience. Nevertheless, she wanted to try, and decided to return with her pad on another day.

'This is my city,' Roberto said proudly, as Tess dug around in her pocket and brought out her phone. 'For your sister, yes?'

'For me, too, but mainly for Emma. I wish she could be here.'

'I am happy she isn't.'

'Excuse me?'

'If she had been with you yesterday, then we wouldn't have met.'

'I don't understand.'

'You looked worried and nervous,' Roberto explained, 'as if you were scared to be on your own.'

'Is that why you insisted on joining me for lunch and being my guide?'

'Yes, and because you are beautiful, and what man can resist a beautiful woman?'

'Aw…' She nudged him with her elbow, blushing furiously, but enjoying the flattery all the same. 'No, seriously, what made you do what you did?'

She was still staring out to sea, but Roberto had turned to face her. 'You looked lonely,' he said, 'a little sad also, and nervous. I thought you might be in trouble.'

Goodness, had she really looked like that? She needed to do some serious work on her resting face. 'If I had been middle-aged and frumpy, would you still have offered to buy me lunch?' she asked, lightly.

Roberto smiled wryly. 'Actually, I would have,' he admitted, a little sheepishly, as if he expected her to make fun of him.

But Tess thought that was one of the sweetest things she'd ever heard. 'Your boss must be very understanding,' she said, and her eyes widened when he gave a derisive snort.

'My boss thinks I am mad, or an idiot.'

Tess noticed the way he emphasized "boss", and gathered there was no love lost for this man on Roberto's behalf.

'Why do you work there? Surely there are loads of other jobs?' Tess waved her arm at the city. From what she had seen of it so far, bars, tavernas and restaurants seemed to make up about half of the businesses.

Roberto lifted his head and his dark eyes stared into the distance. 'It pays well, and it is expected.' He hesitated. 'I mean to say, I am used to it,' he added. He was silent for a moment, then said, 'I am sorry, I didn't bring you up here to tell you my troubles. Look.' He turned his back on the view and Tess turned with him.

'Montjuïc Castle stands over one hundred and fifty metres above the port,' he said, in guide mode once more. 'It was constructed in the seventeenth century, but it is said there was a building on this site long before then. Just think, during the Spanish Civil War prisoners were tortured and executed here. Now, thankfully, it's a museum. You should come back when it's open.'

Goodness, not another place she needed to see! She'd have to stay for a month, if she was to visit all the places on her steadily growing list.

He led her to another viewpoint and Tess followed, glad of the additional rest, even though the return journey was all downhill. From this vantage point, the city had disappeared and below them lay the port of Barcelona.

'This is the working port,' Roberto explained, 'where container ships dock. If those trees weren't there, we'd be able to see the harbour and the cruise ships. My city has everything,' he boasted. She had to admit, though, it was well deserved. Barcelona *did* seem to have everything, and she was totally in love with it already. This run up to the top of Montjuïc had simply confirmed it.

They set off back down the hill, taking a slightly different route from the one they had run up, because Roberto wanted to take her past the Olympic Stadium, which she agreed was impressive, although it didn't rock her boat in the same way the view from the top had. By the time they were back on more-or-less flat ground again, it was starting to get dark.

When they came to a stop outside Tess's hotel, Roberto checked his watch. She noticed the muscles in his arm flexing, and the fine coating of dark hairs on his skin, and for a fleeting second she wondered how it would feel to have those arms wrapped around her.

Tess asked, 'Do you have to be in work soon?'

'No. I was thinking of coming back for you in an hour. If that's OK?'

It certainly was, and she was surprisingly relieved that he was coming back.

Tess hurried to get ready whilst sending off another text to her sister, and by the time the hour was up she was ready and waiting in reception, her hair freshly washed and dried, and wearing her favourite jeans, a pretty blouse and a warm cardigan.

'Are you hungry?' Roberto asked, taking her elbow and guiding her through the doors.

'Starving!' she replied. There was nothing like a good run to sharpen the appetite.

'Good. I know just the place.'

He tucked her arm under his and they set off, taking a right-hand road, and strolling along it, before turning again, and walking down another, the sights and sounds of the busy city for once unable to distract her from the man by her side. When he stopped outside a restaurant and let go of her, she felt a tiny pang; she'd enjoyed the warmth of his skin through her light sleeve, and when he placed a hand on the small of her back, she shivered, and her heart beat a little faster at his touch.

'Italian,' she said, surprised. 'I expected Spanish.'

'And you shall have more Spanish – I guarantee it. But tonight, I thought Italian would be nice, and this restaurant is close by and is very good...' He hesitated. 'We can go somewhere else, if you like?'

'No, this is fine.'

And it was. The food was excellent and the company even better.

'So, tell me more about your painting,' Roberto suggested as they waited for dessert. Tess had wanted something sweet but was unsure whether she could manage one all by herself, so Roberto had ordered a tiramisu for them both to share.

'What do you want to know?' she asked.

'Everything! Like, do you work for a company, or for yourself? What do you enjoy painting most? When did you start painting? Who is your favourite artist? What—'

'Slow down!' she cried, laughing. 'I'll start at the beginning, shall I?' Tess took a deep breath and began. 'I've always loved drawing, painting and making things. One of my earliest memories is making a card for Dad's birthday, using a potato sliced in half and with shapes cut into it, and then we'd dip it into a tray of paint and squash it onto some paper. Mum had to cut the shapes out for my sisters, Ella and Emma, but she let me have a go myself – until I almost sliced my finger open, that is.' Tess smiled sadly at the bittersweet memory.

'You don't seem very happy,' Roberto pointed out, astutely.

'Oh, I was, but whenever I remember something about Ella, the realisation that she's gone always follows after it.'

'Gone? You mean...?'

'Yeah.' Tess sighed. 'She died when I was twelve. Ella and Emma were twins. They were only nine. She had cancer and—' Tess swallowed.

Roberto reached across the table and covered her hand with his own. 'I am sorry. It must have been hard for you, for all your family.'

She blinked back tears. She would have thought that she was beyond crying after all these years, but every so often grief would rear its head and bite her.

'It was,' she agreed, then gave herself a mental shake. 'Anyway, back to my painting. I started becoming more serious about it after Ella died. It was my escape, I suppose, the one place where I could be myself, and not have to think about anyone else. Then I did my GCSEs and A-levels – the high school exams we take in Britain – and got an A grade in art for both, and after that I sort of lost my way a bit. I didn't know what I wanted to do, so I did whatever I could – shop work, cleaning, a stint in a warehouse, reception work.' She paused. 'I even tried my hand at clearing the canal that runs through the city where I live, until I fell in – not once, either, but twice!' she said, giggling. 'That mud on the bottom doesn't half stink, and the slimy weed isn't much better.'

Roberto leaned back when the waiter arrived with one dessert and two forks, and as he took his hand away from hers, Tess felt another little pang.

Taking a fork each, they dived in, as Roberto asked, 'Didn't you paint then?'

'Yes, I did. Lots. But I never thought I was good enough to do anything with it, despite everyone telling me otherwise. It was only when my friend, Faye, shoved a prospectus under my nose and forced me to apply to university, that I realized I might be good enough after all. I had to take samples of my work to the interview,' she explained, when she saw Roberto's confused expression. 'And it was during the interview I realized that if the lecturers thought my work was OK, then it must be.' She shrugged.

'Go on,' Roberto urged. The plate had only one bite of tiramisu remaining, and he nudged it towards her.

'I did all right,' she said modestly, failing to mention that she had come out of uni with a first-class honours degree. 'I graduated, and since then I've been doing illustrations mainly, and some commissions – I'm in the middle of doing a series of paintings of the garden of a country house. And I sell some stuff sometimes.'

'How do you sell it? The internet?'

'Yes, I've got a website,' she said, 'and I've been in a couple of exhibitions.'

'Where is your studio?'

'I… er…' She hated it when people asked her that, and she vowed to rent a suitable space as soon as she could afford it. 'I work in my living room,' she said.

'I would like to see it,' Roberto said.

'My living room?'

'Your website. Can you show me?'

Tess nodded and took her phone out of her bag. 'There,' she said, passing it to him when the page loaded.

'I like it,' Roberto said, after a long pause as he scrolled through her paintings. 'You did all these?' Again, there was admiration and respect in his voice.

'Yes.'

'You have talent, Tess.' He looked up from the screen.

'Thank you.'

Roberto asked Tess a few more questions as they sauntered back to Tess's hotel, and she answered them readily enough.

'No! I wish I did,' she laughed, when Roberto told her that he imagined her living in a house in the countryside, with lots of light and beautiful views. 'I live in a flat above a second-hand shop, with a funeral director on one side, a kebab shop on the corner, and a sleazy pub within spitting distance. The view isn't great and the only green I can see is the reflection from the traffic lights down the road. Where do you live?' she asked, suddenly realising that she'd hogged the conversation once again, and had done nothing but talk about herself all evening.

Roberto grimaced, hesitating, and Tess wished she hadn't asked. Barcelona, like most European cities, was an expensive place to live, and she didn't want to make him feel uncomfortable in any way, by asking about his domestic arrangements.

'My friend Diego has an apartment near the university,' he said, with a shrug. 'The rent is not too expensive.'

At least he didn't say that he was still living at home.

'We're here,' Tess said lightly, as she halted outside the hotel.

'So we are. Well, goodnight, Tess.' Roberto took a step towards her, then stopped. 'Where are you going tomorrow?'

'The Sagrada Familia,' she replied promptly.

'I will take you there,' he said.

Hang on a minute, she thought, *Roberto is assuming a great deal*. Who said she wanted to see him tomorrow? As if sensing her apprehension, Roberto added, 'If you would like me to.' His tone had lost a little of its arrogance. 'Please? I like your company.' He gave her puppy-dog eyes, and she laughed.

'Don't you have to go to work?' she asked.

He frowned, staring off into the distance. 'I can take some time off,' he said. 'It is of no matter. So, can I join you tomorrow?'

'That depends...'

'On what?'

'Whether you know anything about it, because you seem to know a lot about everywhere else. Or should I go on my own and buy a guidebook?' She smiled up at him to show she was teasing.

'Save your money – I shall be your guide and I promise I am more fun than any book,' he said. 'I will meet you there tomorrow at eleven, if that's OK? I have an... er, an appointment first. *Dentista*,' he added, and pointed to his mouth.

Then he kissed her on the forehead again and was off down the street before Tess had a chance to react.

She went to bed that night with butterflies in her stomach at the thought of seeing him again.

Four Days to Race Day

I could get used to this, Tess decided, as she skipped down the road and headed for the little bakery she'd found the day before, for a repeat of the pastries and coffee she'd enjoyed for her breakfast.

She sat at a table on the pavement, feeling the warmth of the sun on her face, and thought about the day ahead, interspersed with images of a pair of dark-chocolate eyes and a gorgeous smile. Roberto was too good looking by half and he was nice with it, too – a deadly combination for any woman. She couldn't help but see how considerate he was, thinking of the little peck on the forehead he'd given her, not once but twice, when he could so easily have kissed her properly... Her stomach did little flip-flops at the thought of seeing him again.

'Get a grip,' she muttered, earning herself a strange look from an elderly couple sitting on the next table, and she winced. Talking to oneself wasn't good, was it? Luckily her phone pinged with an incoming text.

When she fished it out of her bag she saw that it was from Emma.

> Where were you last night? I was worried.

Um...

> I went out for dinner.

> What did you have? Send me a photo.

> Forgot to take any. Sorry. I can send you a pic of my breakfast, if you want? ;)

115

What are you doing today?

The Sagrada Familia.

Then what?

Not sure yet. Depends.

Tess neglected to explain exactly what (or rather 'who') her plans depended on.

Her leisurely breakfast was followed by a metro ride across the city and, when she emerged at the correct stop, the Sagrada Familia was almost directly in front of her. Craning her neck and trying not to bump into anyone, she made her way to the entrance, where Roberto would be waiting for her.

Wow! Just wow! She'd viewed the cathedral from the top of the hop-on, hop-off bus and had seen it in the distance from Montjuïc, but seeing it close up in all its weird and wonderful glory was something else. Even though it had scaffolding on one side and it would be several years yet before Gaudi's dream was completed, it was still an awe-inspiring sight. It towered above its surroundings, the spires reaching into the sky. The way each tower was carved and moulded... parts of it reminded her of the palace in Disneyland, but this was real and solid, and carved out of stone. Tess hadn't seen anything like it in her life before.

'It's not easy to appreciate the Sagrada's beauty from here,' Roberto said, by way of greeting, as she approached.

'You really should stand much further back. But we can do that later if you want to draw it, because the queue is short, and now would be a good time to enter.'

'Hello to you, too,' she said, smiling.

'You wanted a guidebook, so I will be your guidebook.' He grinned down at her. 'OK,' he began, as they paid for their tickets and went through the barrier. 'Building started in 1882 and it is still under construction. When Gaudi died, only a quarter of the cathedral had been built, but hopefully it should be finished by 2026.'

'Hang on, I just want to take a minute,' she said, looking up and leaning back as far as she dared. 'Just look at those spires,' she breathed.

'You can see right to the top of the biggest spire if you stand at the bottom,' Roberto informed her. 'When they are all completed, there will be eighteen towers – twelve for each of the apostles, four for the evangelists, one for the Virgin Mary, and the last one, the highest one in the middle, will be for Jesus Christ.'

'Can you get to the top?' she wanted to know, and Roberto nodded.

With their cut-out, worked stone, the spires reminded her of the skeletons of huge, conical corals. And the imposing piece of architecture which jutted out above the entrance looked like a combination of a jawbone and a backbone with ribs, as if some giant alien being had died on earth millions of years ago and was only just now being uncovered. In fact, that was exactly what it felt like to her – not so much a building, but rather a discovery.

'There are lifts,' he explained, 'but it still can be an effort. Did you know that when La Sagrada Familia is completed, it will be tallest religious building in all of Europe? The central tower in the middle will be one hundred and seventy metres tall. But' – Roberto paused dramatically here – 'Gaudi believed that nothing man-made should ever be higher than God's work, and so when the tower is completed, it will be one metre less than Montjuïc.'

As they made their way to the entrance, Tess found it hard to believe that the intricate carvings around the entrance were actually made of stone. Heads, bodies, arms and whole figures of both people and animals pushed through the stone, as though trying to escape their rocky prisons.

'They look so real,' she said, in awe.

'All of Gaudi is dedicated to nature and attention to detail, and he designed La Sagrada Familia with pure and simple geometric forms, so that any architect could understand the drawings and continue his work after his death. Imagine, to think he knew he would not live to see it completed!'

Once inside, Tess was speechless. It was less like a place of worship and more like a museum. It had the same feel and atmosphere as Casa Batlló, seeming to lack the history and reverence that she'd experienced in other grand churches.

'It doesn't feel like a cathedral,' she said, surprised. 'I expected it to be quiet and for people to be more reserved. It's nothing like the cathedral in Worcester, for instance.'

'It's not a cathedral, but a basilica, which makes it more significant in the eyes of the church,' Roberto said. 'But I know what you mean. It is less a church, and more a place to celebrate God and nature at the same time.'

'Can we sit down?' Tess asked, her legs suddenly wobbly. She'd never been inside any building filled with so much light and colour. What a place to worship! As she took a seat in a nearby pew, she thought back to the many other churches she'd visited; buildings of an entirely different nature. Even Worcester Cathedral, which she knew quite well, appeared dark and sombre compared to this, as if religion should be grave and solemn. Instead of hushed reverence, the interior of the Sagrada Familia rang with excited chatter and laughter, and the sound of many voices. And the overriding colour was white, or ivory, or pale yellow, or dove-grey, depending on how the light fell on the stone, giving the whole interior a heavenly feel. The Sagrada Familia was all brightness and laughter, making her think that worship was to be embraced with love and a happy heart. She felt happy there, she realized.

Roberto joined her in the pew. As they sat there, a shaft of sunlight shot through a high round window, pouring a rainbow of blue, green and yellow over them both. She leaned back against the wood, letting the soothing colours wash over her face and bathing her in tranquillity, and she understood that some of this happiness was down to the man sitting silently at her side. *Enjoy this for what it is*, the light seemed to say, *as this is what the good memories are made of.* She could go back home, remembering the wonderful time she'd had, and how she'd been half in love with a handsome Spaniard during a magical visit to his city.

They took their time exploring the rest of the remarkable building, and Tess observed that she felt as though she was inside a great stone forest. When she looked at the massive columns, she thought they resembled trees. Roberto pointed out the tortoise and turtle holding up the pillars, explaining that they represented both the earth and the sea.

'Everything Gaudi did was full of symbolism,' he said, as she gazed at the upper balconies, which were lit from the inside by a soft, orange-yellow glow.

To Tess, the light inside was inspiring, and she was grateful to Roberto for giving her the time and space to sketch whatever caught her eye. She did try to ration herself, though, or else she would still be there at closing time, and besides, she could never hope to capture the incredible light pouring through the stained-glass windows, which were so reminiscent of medieval ones, yet lighter, more modern, the colours flowing into each other like so many rainbows.

Then there was the fantastic Art Nouveau chandelier with the carving of Christ on the cross hanging from it at the far end of the basilica, drawing the eye to it, acting as a focal point with two massive organs flanking it on either side. Oh, how she wanted to paint it – a few quick pencil lines scribbled on a piece of paper would in no way do it justice. She needed to spend a week here, a month…

Finally, they paid a visit to Gaudi's tomb in the crypt.

'He was hit by a tram,' Roberto explained, as they stood in front of it for some time in respectful silence.

What a waste, Tess thought. *So many ideas and designs still to be unleashed on the world – he was cut down too soon. What else could he have created had he lived another few years?* And she felt sad for humanity's loss.

–

Lunch was a quick sandwich and a long, cold drink, despite Roberto's protestations that the meal should be savoured and that they should take their time over it. Tess protested, wanting to reach the next item on her list as soon as possible. She was here for such a short time, and there were so many things she wanted to experience…

And Park Güell was one of them.

They had to walk for a while after they got off the metro, but when Roberto turned into a side street and Tess saw what was ahead, she stopped.

'An escalator in the middle of the street?' she asked, bemused.

'It is a long way up,' Roberto stated. 'Do you want to take the steps? I think you should, for the marathon. It will be good for your legs.'

Tess groaned. 'You're worse than my sister.' But she started to climb all the same.

Roberto was right – it was indeed a very long way to the top. Tess's thighs were burning by the time they got there, but the hike wasn't over yet, as they still had further to climb until they reached the park's entrance. Tess quite fancied a sit-down at this point, but Roberto ushered her inside by bribing her with the idea of cake and a coffee when they'd finished.

They had to purchase tickets for the main area – called, rather disappointingly, the 'Monument Zone' – and were given a slot in two hours' time, so they decided to wander around the free part of the park first, which involved considerably more climbing. The park was built on the side of a mountain and although there were many winding paths, Tess was breathless once more by the time they'd reached the park's highest point. But Lordy, was it worth it!

The city spread out below, stretching right to the edge of the sea, and from there she could view the monument area from above. The view of Barcelona was incredible

– even better than from the Museu Nacional d'Art de Catalunya.

'It's spectacular,' she said, taking a deep breath of fresh air, noting that it was cooler up there compared to sea level.

'It is better from Tibidabo,' Roberto said.

'What's Tibidabo?' Tess asked.

He grinned, his smile so wide and excited that he reminded her of a little boy. 'An amusement park, with some of the best rides in the world, and to get to it you can go on a funicular railway!'

Tess rolled her eyes.

'But the view from the top is fantastic!' he said, then added, when he saw her less-than-enthusiastic face, 'It is also the highest mountain in the Collserola mountain range, and there is a church called Sagrada Corazón, and on a clear day you can see Montserrat.'

'The Caribbean island?' Tess asked, amused.

'No! *Eres bien chistoso* – you are being silly,' Roberto translated when Tess raised her eyebrows at him. 'The mountain range. Your hotel is named after one of the peaks. I will take you tomorrow.'

There he goes again, Tess thought, *presuming too much* – but this time she was more than happy to let him arrange her itinerary. After all, he'd shown her some things she never would have thought about seeing on her own, and she'd so very much enjoyed the excursion to Montjuïc, despite the run.

'OK,' she agreed, already looking forward to it. 'Can I use my *Hola!* ticket?'

He smiled down at her. 'No, I will drive us there,' he said, but his smile was swiftly followed by a frown, which had no sooner appeared than it was gone again, just as quickly.

They spent the next hour or so exploring the park, with its paved, winding paths, and strange columns that were reminiscent of fossilized trees, yet were carved from stone. Nature and art were so intertwined it was difficult to determine where one ended and the other began, and the overall sense was one of peace and serenity, despite the crowds.

Tess wanted to stroke and touch everything, and her sketchbook took a bit of a hammering as she had a tendency to whip it out at the slightest opportunity. Roberto watched her with quiet indulgence, a soft smile on his face whenever she glanced up at him, which was far too often. Once, she was tempted to draw him instead, but thought he might think it a bit odd, so she stuck to outlining the weirdly organic viaduct instead.

But when they eventually entered the Monument Zone, Tess's creative juices went into overdrive, as she exclaimed over the lizard on the stairs, and drooled over every exquisite detail – from the mosaics which covered practically every surface, to the intricate carved furniture in the house where Gaudi had once lived. All the while, Roberto was able to keep up a fascinating running commentary.

By the time Tess had had her fill – although she knew she'd sell her soul to come back – and was glad of a sit-down and the promised coffee, she realized she'd learned so much from Roberto that she might otherwise have missed. It really was like being accompanied by her very own personal guide.

'I'm so impressed,' she told him. 'I can't believe you know so much.'

Roberto picked up his cup and took a sip. He looked a little embarrassed. 'Have I bored you?' he asked, somewhat apprehensively.

'Certainly not! I've loved every second, and I don't know how to thank you.'

At this, a slow smile spread across his face. 'I do,' he said. 'Have dinner with me?'

What else could Tess do but say, 'Yes'?

Three Days to Race Day

Tess's mobile woke her from a deep sleep. 'Whassit?' she slurred, trying to get her bearings. For a second, she had no idea where she was.

'Where are you?' her mother demanded.

Tess sat up, rubbing her eyes, and switched on the bedside light. 'Er… Barcelona?'

'Don't you use that tone with me, young lady!'

'Where do you think I am?'

'There you go again,' her mother cried. 'You'd better change your attitude.'

'Hang on a minute – you call me in the middle of the night, and demand to know where I am?' Tess frowned. 'Seriously, where do you *think* I am?'

'In Barcelona, but—'

'There you go then!'

'I was about to say, I don't know *where* in Barcelona you are.'

'Mum, is everything all right?'

'I don't know, Tess, you tell me.'

'Tell you what?'

'If everything's all right.' Her mother's irritated sigh floated over the airwaves.

'*You* rang *me*.'

'That's because your dad and I haven't heard from you since you arrived. I was just about to call the police.'

'Eh? I've been texting Emma every day, and several times a day at that! What do you mean "you haven't heard from me"?'

'You should have called,' her mother insisted. 'Your dad and I have been worried sick.'

Tess took a deep breath and tried to remain calm. Her mother tended to overreact when it came to her children and understandable though it was, it could sometimes be enough to try the patience of a saint.

'Couldn't this wait until the morning?' Tess asked.

'It *is* the morning – seven thirty to be precise – and that's not the middle of the night in my book. And you've been in Barcelona three days and you haven't once picked up your phone to let us know you're all right. Anything could have happened!'

'I'm fine, Mum, and I'm sorry to worry you. I just thought that Emma would have told you I am OK.'

'Oh, she did,' her mother said, 'but I wanted to hear from you myself. Right then,' her mother continued, apparently happier now that she'd spoken to her daughter in person. 'What's the weather like? Better than here, I bet.'

'It's lovely, really warm and sunny. We're in T-shirts during the day, but it does get a bit chilly in the evening,' Tess said.

'We?' Her mother dived in on the word like a kestrel after a mouse. She didn't miss a trick, and Tess could have slapped herself for letting it slip. There was no point in telling her mother anything because she would only worry, so Tess would save mentioning Roberto until she got home. In fact, she mightn't tell anyone about him even then, because she had an uneasy feeling she was going to feel more emotional at leaving him and his glorious city than she wanted to.

'I mean, there are lots of people in T-shirts and stuff,' she amended, hastily.

'Hmm.' Her mother wasn't convinced, Tess could tell, but she let it go readily enough. 'What are you doing today?'

'W... er... I'm going to Montserrat. It's a Benedictine abbey up in the mountains.'

Her mother harrumphed. 'I'd have thought there'd be enough to keep you occupied in Barcelona, without you having to traipse all over the country. You be careful, my girl. Call me when you get back safely.'

'I will,' Tess promised.

'How are you getting there?'

'Oh, it's some kind of trip,' she answered vaguely, crossing her fingers against the lie.

'I don't like the sound of that. I don't think you should go. Why don't you visit a nice museum instead?'

Because the man I'm slowly falling for wants to show me the mountains and I'm not about to say no, Tess thought. But that wasn't what she said. Instead she replied, 'I've been to plenty of museums, and seeing some of the surrounding countryside will make a nice change. Um, I've got to go – I need to have a shower. Ro... the... um... trip leaves in an hour, and I want some breakfast first.' Lying and deceit clearly didn't come easily to her, Tess realized – she'd almost slipped up three times already and she'd only been on the phone a minute. It was best if she ended the call now, even though she really didn't have to be ready until eleven.

126

'All right then, but make sure you take your mobile with you. If there's any trouble, ring your father.'

'I will,' Tess promised again, though she had no idea what her mother thought her father could do to help from a thousand miles away.

Whatever happened today – or didn't happen – Tess was on her own.

The old jalopy was held together by rust and bits of string, although Roberto had appeared to have given the interior a quick once-over, as there was a plastic bag filled with cans and fast-food detritus behind her seat, she noticed. He also couldn't get the indicators to work, and as he flicked stalks and turned dials, he muttered a stream of what she assumed were curses under his breath. Tess wondered if he'd teach her a couple (being able to swear in Spanish might come in handy one day), but she didn't think right then was the best time to ask.

'*Lo siento*,' he said, after he'd managed to switch on the headlights instead, then unintentionally turned the radio on full blast, making Tess jump out of her skin. 'I'm sorry. The car, it is temperamental.'

He waved a hand in the air as they pulled out, and Tess wished he'd put it back on the wheel, as the car did a little bunny hop to the end of the street before Roberto jammed on the breaks at the junction and the car juddered to a halt. Tess wondered if she ought to offer to drive.

'That's OK,' she said reassuringly, meaning anything but.

'See, that is what I like about you,' he said. 'You are hanging on to your seat belt with one hand and the door handle with the other, but still you are serene and calm, and saying that everything is OK.'

Serene? Her? As if! But it was nice that he thought so.

'It must be a British thing,' he said. 'I have seen it before with the English, many times. Unlike the Spanish who can be *whoosh*.' He took both hands off the wheel now, and threw them dramatically up in the air.

Please don't do that, Tess begged silently, breathing a sigh of relief when he returned his hands to the wheel.

'But you can be playful, too, and… what is the word… *entusiasta?*'

'Enthusiastic?' Tess guessed. She found it quite endearing that his command of English went to pot at times; she thought it might be when he was a bit stressed, or self-conscious.

'*Sí!*' he said. 'You love life, you are not bored or *desdeñosa*.' He effected a haughty, contemptuous expression, then he turned his head and looked at her for longer than Tess was comfortable with, considering his driving wasn't the best. 'Are you?'

She answered quickly, wishing he'd concentrate on the road and not her, as they headed out of the city and up into the surrounding hills. 'No, I'm definitely not bored, or…' She pulled the same face.

'*Bien!* It makes me happy.'

Roberto uttered another expletive as the car careered around a steep hairpin, the bend clearly more bendy than he had anticipated. He over-corrected slightly and muttered again until he had everything under control once more. Roberto might be a whizz at showing her around Barcelona, he might be a competent runner, he might also be really handsome and clearly a nice person, but his driving definitely left a great deal to be desired.

Tess gripped her seat belt with both hands and refused to think of the return, downward journey. She wasn't even sure she wanted to look at the scenery (which she would have been more than happy to do under any other circumstances), but peering out of the window was better than watching the road ahead, so she stared rigidly at the view as the car climbed higher and higher into the mountains.

Almost an hour later, and just when Tess thought her nerves couldn't take any more, Roberto eased into a parking space and switched off the engine. She breathed a huge sigh of relief and clambered out thankfully, on slightly trembly legs.

'We are here,' he announced, sounding rather relieved himself, and Tess forced all thoughts of the return journey out of her head.

'It's a bit more' – Tess struggled to find the right word – 'commercialized than I expected,' she said, gazing about with a smidge of disappointment. When Roberto had said 'Benedictine monastery', she'd naively imagined a small, secluded house of God hidden in the mountains. The reality was a large, well-planned car park, security at the barriers and too many people.

'It's a tourist attraction,' Roberto said, 'but if you want a more authentic religious experience, I can take you to a church in one of the villages.'

'Maybe later, but we're here now and the building is impressive.' Gaudi's organic flowing lines were nowhere to be seen. The monastery looked more like a prison, with its solid square tower and blocky construction. The only hint that it was a religious building was the very top of the tower where, Tess assumed, there might be bells. And the whole place was absolutely huge, she realized, once they had made their way inside those forbidding walls.

Forbidding – yes, that was a good word to describe the place. She wondered whether it had been built to keep the peasants out, or the monks in. It was more like a fortress than a place of worship, and she realized she'd been spoilt by the wonder and lightness she'd felt in the Sagrada Familia.

It certainly was impressive, however, and she and Roberto wandered around the extensive grounds, exploring small alleys, and walking up steps, until eventually Tess was moved enough to bring out her pad and sit and draw for a while, when they found a secluded little shrine. Roberto, seeming content to let her sketch, perched himself on a low wall and watched her work.

Tess, absorbed in her craft, wasn't aware of his gaze until she'd finished and looked up at him, catching his eye. His expression was inscrutable, but he smiled readily enough when she put her things away and walked towards him.

'Look,' he said, leading her to a break in the foliage on the opposite side of the path to the shrine.

Tess looked. The view of the valley below and the mountains around was spectacular, but she realized what Roberto really wanted her to see was the bank of cloud creeping over the tumbling peaks behind the monastery and slipping silently down the side of the mountain.

'The weather can change quickly up here,' he told her, and they stood in silence for a while, Roberto staring into the distance, and Tess watching Roberto. He looked thoughtful and a little troubled, and she wondered what was going through his mind. She dearly wanted to ask, but felt it would be intruding, so she reached for his hand and squeezed his fingers instead. Slowly, very slowly, he turned to her, and for a second she wondered if she had been too forward, but then he squeezed her hand in return and a slow smile lit his face, sending little tingles down her spine. His fingers caressed the back of her hand, and, as she gazed up at him, she had the insane hope that he would kiss her.

'Would you like to see La Moreneta?' he asked suddenly, letting go of her hand, and the moment was gone. 'It means "the little dark one" in Catalan, and it seems a shame to come all this way without seeing her,' he added.

'What is it?' she asked.

'Santa Maria de Montserrat is the patron saint of Catalonia,' he explained, in tour guide mode once more. 'It is thought that the statue of her and the Christ child which she has in her arms was carved in the twelfth century. She is called "the little dark one", because she is one of the Black Madonnas. It is said that the abbey where she sits is the location of the Holy Grail. There will be a queue to see her, but now you are here…' He shrugged.

'Of course I want to see her,' Tess declared.

'There's one thing you should remember – don't kiss her.'

'Excuse me?'

'Many people kiss her feet, but I wouldn't recommend it. Not if you want to be able to run the marathon, and you might not even be well enough to go home next week, if you catch something really nasty.'

'About that,' she began, as they made their way inside the abbey. 'I wish I didn't have to go.' There, she'd said it. 'I've fallen in love with Barcelona and I really don't want to go home.' Then she added in a much quieter voice, 'I'll miss you, too.'

He whispered back, 'I will miss you, too. More than you can imagine.'

Oh, my, that was just what she needed to hear. As unfeasible as it was, the sentiment behind the words made Tess glow with happiness. He felt the same way, and Tess didn't care if she didn't see one more painting, as long as she could spend the rest of her time in Barcelona with the man she loved.

She *what, now*? The thought had taken her by surprise – did she really think that?

She did, she realized. She had come to care for this man far more than any other man she'd ever met.

Now she was going to have to find a way to live with it.

Oh, damn and blast!

A little on the sombre side after that internal revelation, Tess waited quietly by Roberto's side as they queued to see the Black Madonna, shuffling a few steps forward every now and again. And every now and again, her arm would brush against his and she would bite her lip and wonder how she was going to deal with life without him in it. And every now and again he would look down at her, speculation and concern in his eyes.

The interior of the abbey was more like what Tess had been expecting, and she tried to keep her mind off Roberto by admiring its ornate splendour. Burnished gold was the predominant colour, and as they slowly moved across the abbey and up a set of stairs towards the gallery which housed the statue, Tess found herself comparing the solemnity of this church to the light-heartedness of Gaudi's, and comparing the happiness she had felt in the Sagrada Familia to the sadness she was feeling now. Her surroundings seemed appropriate to her mood somehow.

And there she was, the Black Madonna. The statue was certainly awe-inspiring and almost decadent, the sense of history and religious power it exuded leaving Tess oddly moved as she air-kissed the lady's feet, getting a sense of the history and religious power that the statue exuded.

Lunch was a late affair, taken in a tiny taverna in an equally tiny village. They sat outside on the pavement, Tess wearing her fleece but enjoying the sun anyway. They shared a pot of *fabada asturiana*, which Roberto told her was a rich, warm bean stew, mopping it up with chunks of the freshest bread Tess had ever eaten. A salad, also to share, accompanied the dish, and Tess thought there was something quite romantic about eating out of the same earthenware pot, their spoons dipping in and out and forking up bright red tomatoes and glossy leaves of spinach from their shared plate. Especially since they had to sit close together in order to share their meal.

A group of elderly gentlemen on the table next to them played dominoes, smoked little cigarettes, and drank *leche de pantera*, which Roberto insisted Tess try when she asked what it was, because it looked suspiciously like milk. She sipped hers gingerly, not really tasting the milk but certainly tasting the gin and cinnamon that Roberto told her was in it. The men cheered and raised their own glasses, laughing at her when she pulled a face.

And for a while, Tess felt completely at home and at ease in this tiny village in the middle of nowhere, sharing a meal in the sun with a handsome, thoughtful man at her side.

The handsome, thoughtful man took her to the village church next. It was possibly even smaller than the taverna.

Whitewashed inside and out, it had a tiny bell tower housing a single, gleaming bell.

Roberto stopped to speak to a hunched old lady dressed from head to foot in black and sporting a bright, flowery headscarf. Tess let the words wash over her as she explored the little building, with its simple yet moving altar, and eight rows of dark, polished wooden pews either side of the aisle. An unadorned carving of Christ on the cross hung behind the altar and a crudely-worked stained-glass window above it allowed light to stream in.

Tess felt a tremendous sense of peace as she slid into a pew and bowed her head. Not at all religious, she could nevertheless appreciate the atmosphere and simple beauty of this little church.

She saw Roberto slip the old woman some euros and asked him about it once they were outside.

'They need money to help with the repairs,' he explained, 'and to pay the man who tends to the graveyard behind.'

When Tess went to pull her purse out of her bag, Roberto stopped her. 'I have made a donation for both of us,' he said. 'Now, shall we drive back, and think about dinner?'

'Dinner! Really? We've only just had lunch.' Admittedly, it was a very late lunch, and it was now nearly five o'clock.

'I was thinking of dropping you off so you can relax a bit then I can pick you up at nine? Will you be hungry by then?'

Tess found that she was, although the drive back to Barcelona in Roberto's death-trap of a car didn't do anything to help. But she was surprisingly peckish when he collected her later, this time on foot, and took her to a little place serving Thai food, where they ate and drank, and talked and laughed, until the wee small hours.

With each hour Tess spent with Roberto, she realized she was falling harder and faster for him. And it filled her with dismay and wonder at the same time.

When Roberto saw her back to the hotel, pulled her close, and wrapped his arms around her, Tess felt as though she could stay there for ever, breathing in the heady mixture of man and cologne, and feeling totally and utterly at home in his embrace.

When he released her, with the familiar kiss on her forehead, Tess's heart filled with a love she had no idea how to bear.

Two Days to Race Day

Tess spent the morning, or what was left of it, after having woken up rather late, at the Picasso museum. She was on her own because Roberto had informed her that he couldn't see her until that evening, and she felt quite sorry for him having to work after such a late night the night before. At least she'd been able to wake when she was ready and enjoy her usual breakfast, before heading into the centre of the city.

She had always been slightly underwhelmed by Picasso's work, and nothing she saw served to change her mind. The museum was situated right in the heart of the Gothic Quarter, which she was normally enchanted with, and was housed in a wonderful old building, complete with medieval arches and stone staircases, and balconies and galleries, and all the things she normally adored... but the great man's work? Pft! She couldn't have cared less.

Feeling rather alarmed by her attitude, Tess left the museum and wandered into an area she had yet to explore while she tried to analyse what was wrong.

She didn't feel much better when she arrived at the conclusion that it was the lack of Roberto that had taken the shine off things today. She had become so used to having him by her side, her constant companion, that she found she missed him sorely.

She still felt the same when she turned onto La Rambla, Barcelona's famous street. Unlike the Gothic Quarter, La Rambla had a distinctly cosmopolitan feel. Everywhere she looked there were bars, cafes and stalls selling a variety of touristy items, with the lovely smells of coffee and cooking enticing her to stop and eat, and people bustling to and fro. The sheer busyness of it was overwhelming, and as she strolled down the wide, tree-lined road she heard so many different languages that she lost count.

Feeling hungry, she decided she would eat at the next place she came across. She wanted to sit outside, watch the world go by, and take her time over lunch. It was just a pity a certain man couldn't join her.

Las Tapas Sabrosas? Hmm. The restaurant's tables were almost all taken, and that was always a good sign. She had really enjoyed the tapas she'd eaten on the day she'd met Roberto (*but was that more to do with the man than the food?* a treacherous inner voice asked) that she decided she'd have them again. She sat at one of the few free tables, trying to ignore the slight feeling of disloyalty at not eating tapas at Roberto's restaurant, and looked around for a waiter. White shirt and black trousers or jeans seemed to be the obligatory uniform, and she spotted one, catching his eye.

'*Sí, señorita?*'

'The menu, please, oh, and a glass of mineral water, no ice.'

'No menu.'

Was this a Barcelona thing? She'd assumed it was only Las Tapas Picantes which refused to tell people what they were about to eat, yet she'd spotted the familiar boards and notices outside other restaurants. Maybe it was a tapas thing?

'I bring you the dishes of the day,' the waiter offered, with a disinterested air. She got the feeling he was telling her she could take it or leave it.

Bemused, she said, 'Yes, please,' then retrieved her phone from the depths of her bag whilst she waited for her food to appear.

She texted Emma.

Eating tapas.

You had that the other day.

So? I'm having it again. I liked it.

She'd also enjoyed the company but didn't tell her sister that.

What was the Picasso museum like – lol

Tess rolled her eyes, but there was no way she would ever tell her sister that she actually agreed with her. After the magnificence of Gaudi, in Tess's humble opinion, she thought Picasso was a poor relation.

Good. Got hungry.

Going for a run later? I think you should.

Ran the other evening!

Tess protested, whilst knowing her sister was right. She really did need to fit another one in. The race was only a couple of days away and it was important that she kept her fitness levels up. After all, it *was* the reason she was here.

Her stomach did a slow roll. Why, oh why, had she agreed to do such a thing? The fleeting thought that she could *say* she'd run it and go sightseeing instead passed briefly though Tess's mind, but she knew her conscience would never let her do such a thing. Then there was also the problem of the whole world being able to track her progress in all its live disappointing-ness, so she'd never get away with such blatant deceit. Which reminded her – she had to register tomorrow and collect her race bag with her number and tracker tag, not forgetting the free T-shirt that every entrant was entitled to. Luckily, she could register early in the morning, then get on with her day. There was so much still to see, and she'd barely scratched the surface of the city. She shoved the hope that Roberto would be with her to one side.

'*Gracias*,' she said, as her drink was placed in front of her.

Taking a sip, she sat back to watch the world go by, sunglasses on, basking in the sun. *I could get very used to this*, she thought, imagining herself working in the mornings (painting, that is, not any other type of work), going out for a spot of leisurely lunch, then flitting back to her artist's garret for a siesta before dabbling with her paints once more in the afternoons. Somehow, doing that in England didn't have the same appeal. For one, it was unusual to get two days in a row when the weather made eating lunch outside possible, and for another, England, or the part of the country where she lived, simply wasn't set up for al fresco dining. The only people who braved sitting on the pavement were those who wanted a cigarette with their coffee. Besides, there was a distinct lack of pretty squares and wide boulevards in Worcester – though you could sit by the river if you didn't mind getting splashed by excited children running through the little fountains, or being hissed at by the swans.

She wasn't sure what made her glance over her shoulder towards the interior of the restaurant; maybe it was a sixth sense, or perhaps a sound had alerted her, but what she saw brought a frown to her face. Taking her sunglasses off, she squinted to get a better look, peering into the relative gloom.

Surely that wasn't… was it? It was!

Roberto was side-on to her, his suit jacket slung over the back of his chair. He was deep in conversation with an older man, and totally oblivious to her scrutiny.

Tess wondered if she should go over and say hello, or do something else to attract his attention. She was about to stand up and walk over to him when Roberto and the other man got to their feet. Roberto wore an expression she'd never seen on his face before: almost sullen and rather cross. The older man looked annoyed too and kept shaking his head whenever Roberto spoke. Then the man threw his hands up in the air in despair and began to turn away, before turning back, picking up a large envelope from the table and shoving it at Roberto. Roberto took it, glanced inside, then shook his head and tried to give it back. The other man stepped away, speaking rapidly; Tess understood something of the tone, even if she didn't understand what was being said. The older bloke sounded demanding and a little imperious, as if he was telling Roberto what to do.

Roberto, his expression closed and hard, nodded once, picked up his jacket and put it on, before stuffing the envelope into the inside pocket. The other man clapped him on the shoulder, and she clearly saw Roberto flinch. He actually looked annoyed at the contact.

Before she had a chance to gather her thoughts, Roberto was walking towards the front of the restaurant. For some reason which she couldn't put her finger on, Tess wasn't sure that she wanted him to notice her. Making a snap decision, she dropped her napkin and bent to retrieve it, not resurfacing from under the table until she was certain he had gone.

She caught sight of him again as she sat up, seeing him getting quickly into a sleek black car – the same car she had seen him driving once before as she sat in the open-topped bus. She hadn't believed it was him at the time, but she realized now that it must have been.

Within seconds he'd pulled out into the stream of traffic and shot away, and Tess watched until he'd disappeared from view. Then she leaned back in her seat and took another sip of her drink, wishing her glass contained something stronger.

She narrowed her eyes. There was something not quite right about the whole thing, and she considered what she knew about him – which wasn't very much at all, ticking the facts off on her fingers: he was a waiter; he shared an apartment with a bloke called Diego; he drove an old banger.

Then there was what she didn't know, and that was quite a considerable amount.

A thought occurred to her – he hadn't seemed too familiar with the old car on the way to Montserrat, though he had got better at driving it as the day went on. At the time she'd thought maybe he was nervous at having her in the car with him, but he clearly didn't seem to suffer the same problem with the vehicle he'd just got into. There hadn't seemed to be the same degree of fiddling around with the controls – he'd simply climbed into it and driven off.

Then there were his clothes and his watch. Everything he wore looked expensive, and yes, they might be fake – she clearly recalled how she'd assumed the watch was – but…

Where am I going with this? she asked herself, and found she didn't have an answer. But, thinking back over the past few days, she felt in her heart that something wasn't quite right, that there was something he wasn't telling her.

On the day they met he had insisted on providing her with dishes no one else in the restaurant had been offered, and, not only that, but he had joined her for lunch, then took off to show her around the city without any apparent concern that he was bunking off work. Maybe he had some time owing to him, and that was fine, but it occurred to her that he hardly ever seemed to be in work, and was certainly rarely in work when she would have expected a waiter to be.

Yet another thought occurred to her – maybe he was the manager…

But that wouldn't explain why he had been coming out of one of the most expensive apartment blocks in the city – she was certain now that it had definitely been him. Nor how he was driving a car which was probably worth more than everything she owned (which, to be fair, wasn't a great deal), and neither did it explain why he was having clandestine meetings with men who gave him fat, brown envelopes and didn't look happy about it.

OK, Tess, slow down, she told herself. There might be a totally reasonable explanation. But the thought nagged at her all the same: there was something shady going on.

'Oh, thank you,' she said, as the waiter placed a selection of tapas in front of her. 'Excuse me, but could I ask you about the man who just left? The man in the suit who was sitting over there.' She pointed behind her.

'What do you want to know?'

'His name is Roberto?'

'Roberto, *sí*.'

She sighed. At least he'd told her the truth about his name. 'Is he… er… what does he do?'

'Do?'

'Yes, where does he work? Erm…' Tess stopped when she saw the waiter's face – it was pinched and closed-mouthed.

'I think you better ask him,' was all the man said, before turning on his heel and stalking off.

Seconds later she saw him talking to the same older man who Roberto had been sitting with, and jerking his head in her direction. Both men stared at her, the older man with an expression of hostility on his face.

Tess tried to focus on her meal, but her appetite had disappeared. She wished she'd never said anything now, and, as she picked at the dishes, she felt the older man's gaze on the back of her head.

Feeling uncomfortable, she paid, leaving most of her meal on the plate. Once she was away from the restaurant, she hurried into the maze of streets in the Gothic Quarter as quickly as possible, wanting to leave the man and his stares as far behind as possible.

For a while, she wandered without any direction or purpose, feeling rather out of sorts, and not even the narrow streets with their allure could lift her mood. She didn't want to do any more sightseeing and neither did she have the urge to dip into any of the interesting shops, and she certainly wasn't in the right frame of mind to whip out her sketchbook, so she settled for a hot chocolate and *churros*, dipping the sweet pastry into her drink and feeling rather naughty as the sugar replaced the proper meal she hadn't managed to eat earlier.

Over her snack, she worried at the problem before deciding that she must give Roberto the chance to explain himself. It was silly to jump to conclusions. Feeling better about the situation, she made her way back to her hotel, and went for a run.

—

Dear lord, but that was hard, Tess thought, tottering through the lobby, panting like a steam train, sweat trickling down her back. When she got back to her room, she threw herself into one of the easy chairs and closed her eyes.

All the walking certainly hadn't compensated for all the food she'd eaten over the past few days, and she'd clearly lost a bit of fitness. Though she'd enjoyed her run and knew she'd feel better after it (honest, she would, she told herself… *just give me a minute to recover*), the thought of taking part in a marathon filled her with more dread than it usually did.

More familiar with the city now, she'd taken a similar route as when Roberto had accompanied her, though she had got slightly lost and had ended up running past the Olympic stadium and taking an unfamiliar route down off Montjuïc.

Time to check in with Emma.

Just went for a run.

Good. How are you feeling?

Fantastic!

Tess crossed her fingers.

Her phone rang.

Gotta go, phone call.

She ended the conversation with her sister.

'Hello?' She knew her tone was a little frosty, but she couldn't help it.

'I missed you today.' It was Roberto – she felt a tingle from her head to her toes when she heard him speak. 'Let me take you to dinner,' he said.

'Aren't you working tonight?'

'No.'

'You weren't working this afternoon, either, were you?' Damn. She hadn't meant to say that, but she desperately wanted there to be a logical explanation.

'I was.'

'I saw you in La Rambla, in a tapas restaurant, with an older man. You seemed to be arguing…'

'Ah.' A pause, then his smooth voice flowed down the line like melted chocolate. 'I was running errands for the owner. He has a chain of tapas bars. If you see a restaurant with "Las Tapas" then another word after it, it is Miguel who owns it. He has four restaurants in Barcelona alone, and several more in other cities.'

'What about the car?'

'What car?'

'I saw you driving a big black thing with tinted windows.'

He chuckled. 'She belongs to Miguel, my er… boss. She is nice, no? Miguel asked me to take some papers to Sitges to be signed. Sitges is a town further down the coast, about forty-five minutes away. He is opening a tapas bar there and… the, er… how do you say… *el abogado…*' He paused.

'Estate agent?' Tess suggested.

'No, legal… er…'

'Solicitor?'

'*Sí!* Solicitor. Miguel wanted me to take the papers today and he gave me his car to drive.'

Ah, a simple explanation after all, and Tess was mightily relieved to hear it, though she thought she might have upset him a bit by being so cool when she answered the call. His English had become less fluent, and she noticed that he sometimes did that when he was embarrassed or upset. Bless him!

'So, dinner?' he repeated. When she agreed, he added, 'By the way, you might want to wear a dress,' before ending the call, leaving her to wonder what he had planned.

When he arrived to pick her up, Tess saw that he was wearing a suit in a dark grey, which fitted him as if it had been made for him, with a pristine, white, open-necked shirt underneath. And it was his boss's car he was driving, not his own.

As he hurried around to the passenger seat to open the door for her, she was relieved she'd brought a nice dress with her. She almost hadn't bothered to pack it, but she'd folded her faithful little black fitted number with the lace sleeves into her suitcase at the very last minute – just in case.

Before she slid into the car, she gave the vehicle the once-over.

'Where's your car?' she asked.

'M… Miguel said to keep this for today and bring it back later. It is much better than—' He hesitated for a fraction of a second, then shrugged. 'This is much nicer.'

Tess agreed. She walked around the car, admiring its gleaming lines, and wondered if it was new. It was difficult to tell because Spanish number plates didn't seem to show the car's year of manufacture, and with this one sporting the plate '4000 RPM', she was pretty sure the 4000 didn't have anything to do with the year it came off the production line. Though when she slid into the luxury of the leather seat and smelled that new-car smell and saw how pristine it was inside, she guessed it must be quite new.

As Roberto switched the engine on, the whole dashboard lit up, leaving Tess fervently hoping that he knew what all the displays and gadgets were for. There appeared to be more dials and gauges than the International Space Station, and the interior was probably roomier, too. She leant back against the headrest and inhaled the rich leather smell.

Roberto appeared more confident driving this than he had been when driving his own car, and Tess guessed it was probably because his old banger wasn't as safe or as reliable as it should have been. She watched as he handled the beast of a machine with a certain nonchalance, running expertly up and down the gears, and negotiating the heavy traffic with ease.

'Where are we going?' she asked.

'I thought you might like to see the harbour. There are two or three cruise ships in port, and a little walk before dinner would be nice.'

'I'd like that. I haven't had a chance to see it yet.'

'The biggest yacht in the world docked last night,' he told her. 'She is magnificent. I believe she is owned by a Russian.' He let out a sigh. 'I cannot imagine being that rich.'

'Neither can I, and I'm not sure I'd want to be,' Tess replied.

'You don't want to have lots of money?'

'Of course I want money, but that's only because life is a struggle without it. I'm not greedy – I just want enough to live on, and enough to pay for a few treats now and again, like a nice holiday, or to be able to afford to go out for a meal occasionally. But what I'd really like is to earn enough from my painting not to have to work in the pub or in my parents' launderette.'

'You work in a pub? That's a bar, isn't it?' he asked, giving her a swift glance as they waited for a set of lights to change.

'Sort of.' She laughed. 'Pubs aren't like any of the bars here. An English pub is an entirely different creature altogether.'

'And you serve drinks?'

'Yes, I'm a barmaid. I do three nights a week at the moment, but when I go back I'm going to see if I can cut it down to two, or maybe one. I'm gradually getting more and more illustration work, and though it's not guaranteed it *is* increasing.'

'What about the laundrette? Do you wash clothes?'

'Not exactly. My parents own a laundry service. They take in linens, towels, uniforms, and so on, from various hotels and restaurants in Worcester. They've been doing it for years, and both Emma and I used to help out as we were growing up. I'm not sure how much help we were actually giving, but the small wage they paid us was welcome.'

'You will give up the laundry soon, too?'

'Fingers crossed, yes.' Tess wasn't particularly superstitious, but she crossed her fingers anyway.

'That's good.'

Conversation ceased for a while as Roberto hunted for a parking space, before finding one and driving into it. When they got out of the car, he caught hold of her hand and they made a dash for the opposite side of the busy main road, laughing as they ran. She fully expected him to let go of her when they reached the other side, but he didn't. Instead, his fingers caressed the back of her hand, sending little shivers up her arm, then he gave her hand a squeeze and she glanced at him.

He was smiling down at her; as she smiled back, she skipped a few steps and he laughed at her antics, but she felt so happy and carefree, and content. Yes, that was the word – content. She was in a beautiful city, with the sun on her hair, and in the company of a gorgeous man – what more could she ask for?

The Passeig de Joan de Borbó was a wide street with trees down the length of it, with bars, shops and restaurants on the one side, the blue waters of the harbour on the other. Tess and Roberto strolled hand in hand, admiring the boats, and Roberto pointed things out which he thought might interest her.

Tess oohed and aahed at the various vessels moored in the harbour; when they came to the longest yacht ever built, she was impressed to say the least, even though it didn't really appeal to her.

'It's big all right, but I'm not too keen,' she said.

'You don't like it?' Roberto asked, his eyes searching her face.

'Yes and no. I like the sleekness of it, but I don't like the showoffiness of it.'

'"Showoffiness"?'

'It's too flash, too "in your face".'

'Ah, this must be the English reserve I've heard so much about,' Roberto teased.

'Maybe, but to me it seems too big, too self-important.'

'The man who owns it is very important, at least in terms of wealth. But I agree, I don't like it either.'

They rounded the corner of the vast jetty into a world of smaller craft, and Tess smiled. 'This is more like it.' She gestured to a modest white boat with the name *Miranda* painted on the side. 'It's big enough, but it isn't stupidly big. I like this one,' she announced.

'One day I will buy it for you,' Roberto promised, solemnly, and she giggled.

'I'd prefer a studio,' she joked. 'Painting on a boat might be a bit tricky.'

'A studio it is!' he said grandly. 'I will buy you the biggest and best studio in all Barcelona.' He was smiling, but a cloud passed over his face. 'You may have to wait a while,' he added.

Tess fell silent. 'A while' was going to be never, because she only had a few more days left in this lovely city, then it was back to drizzly old England. She wasn't looking forward to it at all, and wished he hadn't reminded her just how little time she had left here, in this wonderful city.

With this wonderful man.

'Now it is time for dinner,' Roberto said, filling the sudden lull in the conversation. Tess wondered if his thoughts had been travelling along similar lines, or if his remark had been one of the throwaway variety.

The restaurant was not what she had been expecting. Until then, she and Roberto had eaten in small places that served good food but weren't ridiculously expensive. Unlike this one. Right on the waterfront, it clearly catered to the kind of people who could afford one of those sparkling white boats out there.

She gulped when an officious waiter took her jacket, showed them to a table, and placed a menu in her hands. There was no way she could afford this, not if she wanted to eat for the rest of her stay. In fact, if they had a meal here, she might have to live off beans on toast for the remainder of the month when she returned home.

'My treat,' Roberto said, when Tess, wide-eyed and horrified, put the menu on the table and opened her mouth to insist they leave.

'No way,' she hissed. 'You know how I feel about you paying for me.'

He rolled his eyes. 'What is the world coming to when a man can't take a beautiful woman out to dinner?'

'I'm not saying you can't take me out to dinner! You can – just not here.'

'You don't like it?' He glanced around and frowned.

'I don't like the prices. See that?' She jabbed a finger at one of the main courses. 'Seventy-six euros for a bit of… whatever it is.' She waved a hand in the air, having no idea what the dish was, but feeling certain it must be overpriced.

He sighed. 'I didn't want to tell you, but this is work,' he admitted.

'Work?'

'Sí. My… *jefe*, my boss, Miguel, is thinking of buying this place. He is well known here and I am not, so he asked me to come here to… how do you say? Check it out.'

'Ah. Work.'

'Is that OK? Are you angry?'

'Of course I'm not angry.'

'I wanted to be with you this evening, and I have to work, so I killed two birds with one hand. I'm sorry for not telling you sooner.'

Tess suppressed a giggle. Roberto could be so funny. He looked so anxious, too, that she wanted to leap over the table and kiss the worry off his face.

'I understand,' she said. 'Thank Miguel, won't you, for allowing you to bring me along. But I still have no idea what could cost seventy-six euros.'

'That,' he replied, craning his neck to see what she was referring to as she picked up her menu again and opened it, 'is the cheek of a cow.'

'A what? Eww. No thank you! What else have they got?'

Roberto translated the menu for her while they ordered drinks and waited for them to arrive. He seemed very much at ease, but Tess kept glancing around, as if she expected the manager to identify them as intruders and tell them to leave. She wished she was wearing something a little more glamorous, but at least she wasn't wearing jeans, and she was thankful that Roberto had given her the heads-up.

When she took a sip of the chilled white wine which their waiter had placed reverently on the table, she guessed it probably cost more than every scrap of clothing she had on.

'Do you do this often?' she asked.

Roberto narrowed his eyes a fraction. 'Do what?'

'Spy on other restaurants?'

He threw his head back and laughed, and Tess noticed how several women on a nearby table, all of them chic and beautiful, were watching him discreetly. He didn't look at all out place here, unlike her; he looked as though he dined in restaurants like this every day of the week, and he seemed relaxed, confident and fully at ease. Tess, on the other hand, was on edge, scared she'd make a fool of herself, and felt like the proverbial fish out of water.

'Yes,' he said. 'Sometimes. It is always good to know what the competition is doing.'

'I wouldn't have thought tapas bars were in competition with a place like this,' Tess pointed out.

'They aren't. Miguel owns many restaurants, and the tapas chain is only a small part of his business.'

It sounds like this Miguel has his fingers in all kinds of pies, Tess thought, but she found she still couldn't shake the feeling that something wasn't quite right about the whole situation, or Roberto's role. She trusted him, of course she did – but she was still sure there was something he wasn't telling her.

The feeling intensified when the maître d' sauntered over to their table.

At first, Tess thought, 'This is it, this is where we are told to leave', because quite clearly, she looked as though she couldn't afford so much as a coffee in a place like this, but the maître d' greeted Roberto with enthusiasm, although when Roberto said something in rapid Spanish, the other man lost some of his friendliness. Tess also noted another odd thing – when Roberto smiled at the maître d', it didn't quite reach his eyes. Instead, they seemed to hold some kind of warning, but then the expression was gone so quickly that she wondered if she'd imagined it.

The other man turned to Tess. 'And this young lady is…?' he asked, bowing slightly to her.

'Tess Barton,' Roberto answered.

'Nice to meet you, Miss Barton.'

'Nice to meet you, too.'

'I am Adolfo. If you need anything, anything at all, please ask.' Another little bow. His English was impeccable, but when he turned to Roberto he spoke in Spanish once more, which Tess thought was a little rude. She'd expect that kind of behaviour in the Spit and Sawdust, but not in such an upmarket place as this appeared to be.

Tess listened hard, but after thinking that Adolfo had just asked Roberto if she spoke Spanish, she gave up trying to translate. They spoke so fast, she had no hope of keeping up even if her language skills had been better, because the words seem to run into one continuous stream.

'What was that all about?' Tess asked, when Adolfo left.

Roberto shrugged. 'It is nothing. He is surprised to see me here, that is all.'

'Is your cover blown?'

'My what?'

'Does he know who you are?'

'Yes, he does.'

'Then your cover is blown. He knows you're here to spy.'

'Ah, I see. No, I told him I'm here to dine with a special lady who deserves the best. Flattery always works with Adolfo.'

'He didn't seem too pleased to see you.'

'He's always like that.'

Tess wasn't convinced, but she let it go. It wasn't any of her business. Anyway, she intended to enjoy herself tonight, especially since neither she nor Roberto were paying for it.

And enjoy the evening she did!

The service was attentive and discreet, the food was delicious (though she still considered it overpriced and a little pretentious), and the wine flowed, though maybe a little too freely on her part, as Roberto only had the one glass because he was driving, and Tess drank most of the contents of the rather delicious bottle all by herself.

Even the frequent glances from the table of women she'd noticed earlier didn't bother her. Roberto was a handsome man, and over the past couple of days she'd often observed women giving him appreciative looks. But he was with her and not them, so they could look all they wanted.

As the evening wore on, Tess relaxed considerably – though that might have had something to do with all the free-flowing wine. Halfway through her third glass, she refused Roberto's suggestion that he order another bottle. At this point she was pleasantly mellow but not yet tipsy, though that could soon alter if she drank any more.

She felt remarkably grown-up and quite adult for a change, and silently thanked her parents for teaching her which knife and fork to use, and to not put her elbows on the table. She felt she'd conducted herself pretty well. At least she'd not shown herself up. Roberto had impeccable table manners, and she didn't want to think she'd let herself down.

Full, but not uncomfortably so, Tess willingly agreed to a short stroll to work off all the delicious food.

'Was everything to your satisfaction, *señorita*?' Adolfo appeared at their table.

'It was lovely, thanks.' She wobbled a little on her unaccustomed high-heeled sandals. 'Oops! Sorry.' She blushed furiously, not wanting the maître d' to think she'd had too much to drink.

Adolfo didn't bat an eyelid. 'Roberto tells me you are from England, and this is your first time in Barcelona?'

'Yes, that's right. It won't be my last, though – I've fallen in love with your city.'

Adolfo's eyebrows shot up like a pair of energetic caterpillars. He looked from her to Roberto and back again. 'No doubt you have. It is easy to fall in love, is it not?'

Though Tess smiled in response, she sensed there was an undercurrent to the other man's words. Was he trying to warn her off Roberto? Surely not; it was probably the language barrier.

The maître d' snapped his fingers and her jacket appeared as if by magic, held by a waiter, who stood near the door. 'I have a feeling I will see you again, Miss Barton,' Adolfo said, giving her yet another tiny bow.

'I hope so, and thank you, the meal was lovely.' Tess walked towards the door, Roberto following, but when she reached the man holding her coat, she realized Roberto wasn't behind her. He had stopped at the table with the ogling women sitting at it, and was speaking to one of them. Another was chatting on her phone, but when she caught Tess watching she gave her a dirty look.

Tess blinked. What on earth had she done to deserve that?

Roberto's expression was closed, his mouth a straight line. Whatever they were talking about, he didn't look happy. He took a step away, and one of the girls, model-thin with large dark eyes and a sheet of shimmering black hair which fell to her waist, caught hold of his sleeve and held him back.

Roberto shook his head, and gestured towards Tess.

Tess watched the scene, half in and half out of her jacket, and wondered what was going on.

'It is nothing,' Roberto said, when Tess asked as he finally caught up with her, and ushered her out of the door.

'It was quite clearly something,' Tess persisted.

'OK, if you must know, they wanted me to join them. Of course, I refused. I told them I was out for the evening with you.' Roberto put his arm around her. 'One of them is an old friend of my eldest sister. I haven't seen her in a while and I think she may have wanted to catch up.'

Tess had a feeling there had been a little more to the conversation than catching up, because neither Roberto's face nor his body language had been that friendly. The phrase 'icily polite' popped into her head, and she got the impression that one of them might have been hitting on him.

But what if they had been? Tess was in no position to object. Roberto wasn't hers and he never would be. In a few short days she would return home, and he'd soon forget the odd English girl who loved to draw.

'What are you thinking?' he asked, taking her hand in his. 'You're very quiet. Speak to me, Tess.'

She sighed. 'It's nothing. I'm just a bit sad at the thought of going home.'

His hand tightened in hers. 'I'm sad, too, but I don't want to let it spoil the time we have left.'

Neither do I, she thought, and when he stopped and tugged on her arm until she turned to face him, she thought he might kiss her and she closed her eyes, waiting with a fluttering heart for the touch of his lips on hers.

'*Disculpa*, Roberto.'

Roberto froze.

Tess opened her eyes, aware that someone was standing directly behind her, a female someone who didn't sound at all happy.

Roberto gently extricated himself from their embrace, but he kept an arm around Tess's waist, as she turned to face the newcomer.

'Ana-Sofía,' he said, his voice slightly hoarse. He cleared his throat. 'What do you want?' Tess heard a hint of irritation in his tone.

Ana-Sofía was about Tess's age, dark and exotic to Tess's pale and interesting (though Tess had never felt less interesting in her life). The woman's thick, black hair was caught up at the back of her head in a chignon, with some strands left loose to curl artfully about her immaculately made-up face. She had perfect skin, smoky eyes… but if those eyelashes were real, Tess would eat her sweaty trainers. Even with a coat protecting the woman from the slightly chilly evening March air, Tess could see that this unwelcome intruder was slim. She was tall too, nearly as tall as Roberto, though the impossibly high heels she wore added several inches to her height. Diamond studs (*probably fake*, Tess thought, sourly) glittered in her ears, and a necklace shone at her throat. Tess concluded that if you consulted a dictionary, under the word "sophistication" it would say "see *Ana-Sofía*".

'What do you want?' Roberto repeated in English, and frowned when Ana-Sofía replied in rather fast and very annoyed-sounding Spanish. She looked ready to spit flames, gesticulating constantly, and Tess was pretty certain the gestures were aimed at her. The snarly looks certainly were, but Tess stared impassively back, which seemed to annoy the woman further.

This must be an ex-girlfriend, Tess guessed, thinking that Roberto and Ana-Sofía must have had some kind of relationship for the woman to be so annoyed. The question was, did they still have one? Judging by the amount of unintelligible vitriol spewing from the woman's mouth, they possibly still did.

Tess didn't want anything to do with it, if that was the case.

'*Has terminado?*' Roberto asked, when the woman paused for breath.

'No, I have not finished!' she spat in English. She took a step closer to Tess. 'He does not want you. He will see it soon, but I see it now – you are a gold-digger. You do not fool me.'

Tess blinked. What on earth was this woman on about!

'Ana,' Roberto growled, and the hair on Tess's neck rose. If Ana-Sofía had been a man, Tess thought Roberto might have let fly a punch or two. She felt the tension thrumming through him. He was furious, and he didn't care if Ana-Sofía knew it.

The other woman recoiled, but she soon regrouped and began shouting at him again, throwing her hands in the air. No ring, Tess noticed. That was something – at least he wasn't married to her, or engaged. *An ex, then. Probably.* Tess hoped to goodness that Ana-Sofía wasn't still his girlfriend.

Roberto abruptly let go of Tess and took a step towards Ana, then just as abruptly, he turned on his heel, grabbed Tess's arm and stomped off, with Tess almost running beside him to keep up. She looked over her shoulder at the other woman, but Ana-Sofía made no move to follow them. She stood there, a picture of defiance, and lifted her chin, glaring back at Tess. Tess hastily looked away.

'Are you still seeing her?' she puffed. 'Stop, please, I've got to stop.' Her sandals weren't meant for running in.

Roberto slowed and turned to Tess. 'I am sorry, I wasn't thinking. Are you OK?' he asked, and she was thankful that his voice no longer held any hint of annoyance.

Tess shrugged. Her answer depended on his. 'Are you still seeing her? And who is she, anyway? Your girlfriend? And what did she mean when she called me a "gold-digger"?'

Roberto slung an arm around her shoulders and held her close. Tess stood rigidly, anger sweeping through her.

He kissed the top of Tess's outraged head, and said, 'She is nothing to me, but she would like to be. And as for calling you a "gold-digger", she probably heard it on a TV show.'

Tess found it hard to believe that Ana was nothing to Roberto. Look at the woman – she was gorgeous! How could any man in their right mind not be attracted to her?

'I don't believe you,' she said.

'It's true.' He kissed her hair again. 'She watches the Kardashians—'

'I mean,' she interrupted, 'I don't believe that she is nothing to you.'

Roberto tilted Tess's chin up. 'She is not. I mean it. She may be beautiful, but she is not a nice person. She is spoilt, like a princess. She has always got what she wants, and it annoys her that I'm not interested in her.'

Tess frowned, trying to work out the dynamics. 'And that's the only reason for her shouting at you?' she asked, incredulously.

'It is complicated,' he began, then stopped as Tess tried to pull away. 'Not complicated, like Facebook complicated,' he amended, quickly. 'Complicated because our parents are friends and they have always hoped we would one day get married.'

Tess finally broke free. 'She is your *fiancée*?' she cried.

'No, you're not listening to me. She is nothing to me, not my fiancée, not my girlfriend. I don't like her, and even if I hadn't met you I would never marry her, not even to make my parents happy. You make me happy, Tess. *You!*'

That took the proverbial wind out of her sails. 'I do?'

'You do.'

'I still don't understand why she was shouting at you.'

Roberto gripped her arms. 'Because she wants to be with me.'

'Does she love you?' Tess was starting to feel almost sorry for the woman; she was beginning to feel an affinity with her. Tess was already half in love with Roberto, and the thought of him being indifferent to her was devastating.

'Probably not. But I am one of the few people in her life who has said no to her, so it makes her want me all the more. Can you imagine a marriage based on that?' He shuddered. 'I want marriage to be about love, total and utter love. I will settle for nothing less.'

Tess shivered. He was staring at her so intensely that she thought she might fall into his eyes and drown.

'It is getting cold and late. I'll take you back to the hotel,' he said, misinterpreting the shiver.

–

When Roberto pulled onto the kerb, and he had given her the usual kiss on the forehead, Tess got out of the car, without a backward glance, and hurried to her room, too full of conflicting emotions to want to linger.

Had he been about to kiss her? She thought so, and she'd been ready for it – would have welcomed it – but the arrival of Ana-Sofía had ended it before it had begun.

But the one emotion that kept her awake far into the night was jealousy. Ana-Sofía was beautiful and fiery, and clearly thought she had some kind of claim on Roberto even though he denied it. They obviously had some kind of history, and Tess was wracked with jealousy because of it.

The second emotion preventing her from sleeping was love.

Tess was horribly in love with Roberto, and she had no idea what to do about it.

One Day to Race Day

After a restless night, Tess woke feeling sluggish and out of sorts. But, after breakfast and three cups of coffee, she began to perk up a little, and she perked up a great deal more when she saw what was waiting for her outside the Fira de Barcelona when she went to register for the race.

The large open area around the exposition centre was awash with people, many of them with suitcases or rucksacks, and all of them looking fitter and more race-ready than Tess felt she would ever be. It was enough to make her question her commitment to tomorrow's race.

The run yesterday evening came back to haunt her. She'd puffed and panted like a steam engine in dire need of a service, and today her knees were a little stiff. How the hell was she going to run a marathon tomorrow? She gulped and almost turned around.

There were only two things that kept her from backing out: the fear of letting Emma and everyone else down, and Ella. *I'm doing this for you, Ell*, she mouthed silently as she joined the long, snaking queue that stretched all the way from the inside of the exposition centre and right around the massive open space in front of it. *Just how many people are entered in this race anyway?* There must have been thousands.

Her heart sank; she'd be here for hours. She sent a text to Emma asking her if she knew how many people had entered the marathon.

Emma texted back:

> About 30k.

Tess sent her a photo of the hundreds of excited race-entrants.

> Blimey! Have they all turned up at once?
> You can register up until 8pm tonight, you
> know.

> I'm in the queue already. It seems to be
> moving quite fast.

And it was. There was a constant shuffling forward, and Tess was already nearly halfway to the entrance.

Then her phone rang. Tess had a feeling she knew who it was, before even looking at the screen.

It wasn't Roberto, however, and disappointment washed over her as she dealt with an enquiry about a commission, although it did serve to take her mind off both the race and Roberto long enough for her to reach the end of the queue and have her bag checked, then be ushered through the doors into the exposition centre. Tess made some notes and promised to contact the client in the next few days (she was going to have to do some hard work when she got home to reach this particular deadline), at the same time as finding the right registration desk, signing her name, and receiving her race pack.

She ended the call and looked inside the bag. Her number and the tracker tag she had to wear on her trainer were the main things she needed and, satisfied that both were present, she took a couple of quick photos of the exhibition hall and sent them to Emma, along with her race number.

There was no going back now.

The hairs on her neck prickled with terror and excitement in equal amounts. *She was going to run a marathon.* Up until this moment, it hadn't seemed real. Even when she had arrived in Barcelona, she had been able to kid herself that this was nothing more than a lovely holiday in a beautiful foreign city. But seeing all these people having their photos taken next to a blown-up map of the route, or buying all kinds of running gear, or collecting their free T-shirts (she was determined to get hers and vowed to wear it with pride when she got home, to show that she'd taken part in the marathon, regardless of how poorly she'd do on the actual day), it suddenly became very real indeed.

Idly, she wandered around the various stalls, picking up vests and shorts, and eying up the multi-coloured trainers with envy, while recoiling at the price tags on everything. She watched people on static running machines having their gait analysed; she ate a sample of an energy bar and bought a couple, just in case, though she had brought some with her from home; and she took numerous photos and sent them off to her sister. But all the while her mind was on last night, and how she had felt about Roberto.

As soon as she was out in the fresh air once more, with the highly charged atmosphere of pre-race excitement behind her, her phone pinged. It was a text from Emma.

Given your race number to Mum and Dad.
Going to their house tomorrow with Declan
to track you.

Great. Now the whole family could see her snail's pace progress. Tess hoped she would be able to complete the race within the time set. She had only six hours to get around the course, as six hours was the cut-off time – any longer than that and you were disqualified from the race. The time seemed terribly short. Yikes!

She also felt a little cross – there she'd be, sweating herself into an unattractive blob, with every part of her in agony, and the rest of her family would be tucking into roast beef with all the trimmings and watching the little dot which represented Tess crawling around the city.

How are your spots?

Tess asked Emma, trying not to think about the race any more for a moment.

Mostly scabbed over. Only a couple of new
ones coming out now, thank God.

Damn. No chance of Emma catching a last-minute flight and joining her, then. Tess was truly on her own.

Stop feeling sorry for yourself, she thought, *and get on with the rest of today*. Aside from ensuring that she had a good carb meal and an early night, the rest of the day was hers to do with as she pleased, and she knew exactly what she wanted to do with some of it.

Descending into the depths of the metro once again, Tess navigated her way to the Plaça de Catalunya and El Corte Inglés.

She didn't want the shopping centre – she was after the department store of the same name. It was huge, and from what she could see, it sold everything from pins to elephants (as her mum used to say). But it didn't sell the very thing she wanted, and after trailing around the store for half an hour, she gave up and left.

Wondering where to try next and deciding Google might be able to help, she had only just entered her password into her phone when it rang, making her jump.

Her 'hello' was a little breathless and slightly apprehensive. After the rather unsatisfactory end to the evening last night and her subsequent realisation that Roberto meant a whole lot more to her than he should, Tess was a little nervous.

'I want to see you,' he said without preamble, and her heart did a flip.

'I have to buy a veil for Emma,' she said, wanting to see him too, but not sure if he'd enjoy trailing around wedding shops with her – if she knew where any were, that is.

'Would you mind if I came with you?' he asked, and she let out a breath she wasn't aware she'd been holding. That sounded wonderful, and she frowned at the way her treacherous heart did another little flip, this time from excitement and anticipation.

Trying to keep the mood light and not reveal too much of how she was feeling, she said, 'Only if you can find me a wedding shop to visit. I've just been in El Corte Inglés and they don't stock anything weddingy at all.'

'I'm sure I can come up with something,' he said. 'Wait by the monument to Francesc Macià – it's a big, modernist sculpture that looks like upside-down steps on a pyramid. I will meet you there in one half hour.'

Tess bought a coffee and made her way to the opposite side of the *plaça*. Plonking herself down on the low wall surrounding the monument, she waited for him to appear.

It didn't take long. She spotted him from some distance away and watched him stride confidently towards her, his eyes scanning the faces of all the young women he passed, not pausing on any of them until he saw her. When he spotted her, his smile crinkled the corners of his eyes and Tess simply couldn't help smiling back, but his face sobered quickly when he reached her side.

'Do you want to talk about it?' he asked, after giving her a peck on each cheek.

'Talk about what?'

'Yesterday. I think you are still angry with me.'

'I'm not angry,' she said, 'though I would be if I found out you were lying to me.'

'Lying to you?'

Was it her imagination, or had Roberto suddenly become very still?

'I don't like playing the other woman,' she stated, 'and if you really are having a relationship with Ana-Sofía, I don't want to be the one to come between you.' Then she watched his reaction carefully.

He showed no hint of remorse or guilt. In fact, the only thing emanating from him was relief – or was she imagining that, too?

'I meant it when I said Ana-Sofía is nothing to me,' he replied. 'We are not in a relationship, we never have been, and we never will be. To be honest, I haven't had a girlfriend for a nearly a year. Until now.' His stare was intense, and she could feel herself falling into it.

Until now? What did that mean? That *she* was his girlfriend? The thought made her shiver all over. 'Your girlfriend?' she asked. 'Is that what I am?'

And, being honest, did she want to be?

From her point of view, the answer was clear. Yes. And no.

'If you want to be,' Roberto said.

'Roberto, I…' she hesitated, and he was quick to jump in.

'It's OK if you don't. I understand. You are beautiful and intelligent, and there is probably someone in England waiting for you.'

'No, there isn't anyone,' she said. 'If there was, I wouldn't be with you now.'

'*Bien*, this is what I thought, but I wanted to make sure.'

He started walking and she fell into step alongside him. 'I'm going home on Tuesday,' she said. 'So how can we be in a relationship?'

Roberto smiled. 'If we want it enough we will make it happen.'

What he was hinting at was wonderful, and it was fantastic that he thought about her in that way, but it was impossible. Rather than get into a useless discussion about distance, flights, the cost of those flights, Tess changed the subject.

'Is it always this sunny in Barcelona?' she asked, feeling the warmth on her face and luxuriating in it once more. It wasn't quite lying-on-a-sun-lounger-and-then-cooling-off-in-the-sea weather, but it was certainly warm enough to sit at a pavement cafe, watching the world go by, without having to wear a duffle coat.

'The weather has been good for a couple of weeks,' he responded, and she was grateful that he let the other matter go. 'March is usually cooler than this, and it can rain. But not today. Today it is beautiful, no?'

He caught her hand in his own, and his fingers caressed her skin, sending little shivers up her arm, then he squeezed her hand, and she glanced at him. He was smiling down at her, and she smiled back. Bugger the future and going home! She'd deal with that when the time came and not a moment before.

Tess's eyes popped out on stalks and her mouth went dry. How much? For a bit of lace? Never! She should have known – she'd read somewhere that if something didn't have a price on and you had to ask, then you probably couldn't afford it. And she most definitely couldn't afford *this*.

She gazed about, helplessly. Maybe the assistant had shown her the most expensive item and this was some kind of weird sales tactic, so that any others she was shown would seem reasonable by comparison?

Roberto and Tess were sitting on a white leather sofa, with a couple of coffees on a table in front of them. The room was plush and sumptuous, and there wasn't a wedding dress in sight. But there were three huge fitting rooms (empty at the moment), and Roberto had appeared to have done some serious talking just to get them in through the door.

'You are supposed to make an appointment,' he told Tess, by way of explanation. 'It is only because they are between brides and you are only wanting a veil that they agreed to see us.'

Blimey! Fancy having to make an appointment just to have a gander at a dress or two, Tess thought. She clearly had a great deal to learn about weddings, and she was suddenly very pleased indeed that Emma had taken their mother with her for her various fittings, instead of dragging Tess along.

She gingerly touched the veil the sales assistant was holding out to her. It really was very beautiful, in just the right shade of ivory that Emma wanted. It was delicate and simple, and exquisitely detailed, designed to be draped over the back of the head and sit there without a tiara or a comb or anything like that holding it in place.

Emma would absolutely adore it. But Emma was never going to set eyes on it, because there was no way on earth Tess was going to buy it. She didn't have that much money left, and even if she raided her bank account, she wouldn't be able to pay nearly a thousand euros.

Bloody hell! Weddings were very, very spendy indeed!

'Is there anything any cheaper?' Tess hissed at Roberto, out of the corner of her mouth. 'Like, below the one hundred euro mark?' Even then, Tess was pushing the boat out, but she'd budgeted for that amount and knew she could afford it. Just about.

Roberto spoke to the sales assistant, who frowned slightly and shook her head. He spoke again, and this time the woman smiled and nodded, sending Tess a professional smile.

'Is there anything,' Tess asked, 'or should we try somewhere else?' She'd had a funny feeling she was about to rocketed out of her comfort zone when Roberto had led her towards the Avinguda Diagonal, and she'd been proved right. 'Why did you pick this place, anyway?'

'My sister recommended it.'

'Your sister?' He'd mentioned last night that he had a sister, but he'd not said anything else about her.

'I asked her where was a good place, and she said here,' he explained.

'You asked your sister?'

'Who else would I ask?' He seemed genuinely perplexed.

'I thought you might have just known. You seem to know everything else.'

Roberto laughed. 'But not about wedding veils or where to buy them, so I asked Ginia. She was married last year, so I thought she'd know more than Lula.'

'Who's Lula?'

'My other sister. I have two. Lula is the oldest, and her wedding was a long time ago, but Ginia married last June, so I thought she was best to ask.'

'You've got two sisters?' Tess seemed to be stuck on this nugget of information and was having trouble getting past it. Roberto hadn't mentioned his family much in all the time they'd been together; Tess thought it was a bloke thing, this not giving away much personal information: Declan hadn't been very forthcoming either – whenever she'd spoken to him and asked about his mother, all he ever said was, 'Fine, thanks.' If it wasn't for Emma, Tess would never have known the woman was a top hairdresser who had recently won one of the most prestigious awards in the hairdressing world. These little bits of personal information never seemed to matter as much to men, Tess concluded.

Come to think of it, she *had* asked Roberto the odd question about his family and his home life, but he never seemed to answer, always turning the conversation onto a different subject, or—

'*Señorita?*' The sales assistant was in front of her, holding out another exquisite creation. Ivory again, except this one wasn't as long, but it was just as beautiful.

'She says it is all made by hand,' Roberto translated. 'Spanish lace, in the old tradition, but with a modern design. See the pearls around the front?'

The sales assistant swept her hand gracefully along the edge of the lace.

'It's gorgeous,' Tess said, then whispered to Roberto, 'How much?'

'Ninety-nine euros,' Roberto replied promptly.

'How come it's so cheap?'

Roberto spoke to the sales assistant. 'No one wants it because the fashion is for long veils, ones that trail across the floor,' he translated.

This one was hip length, and Tess studied it anxiously, wondering if Emma would prefer a longer one.

She decided to text her mother – maybe she would know.

> In wedding shop. Want to buy a veil for Emma. Long or short?

Crossing her fingers that her mother would pick up the text sooner rather than later, Tess examined the fabric again. It was gorgeous – she could just see Emma wearing it.

> How short is short? Try it on for me and send me a photo.

'How long would you say it is?' she asked Roberto. 'Mum wants me to try it on and send her a photo.'

'Good idea!'

Tess was led across the room and seated in a white chair in front of an old-fashioned dressing table. As she stared at her (rather scruffy) reflection in the pristine mirror, the sales assistant expertly swept Tess's hair up and twisted it into a loose bun at the back of her neck. Somehow, the woman had managed to leave soft wisps curling around around her face, framing it perfectly. Tess promptly decided that once they had finished photographing the veil, she was going to ask if she could leave the pins in so Tess could wear her hair like this for the rest of the day.

With great care, the other woman placed the veil on Tess's head, the simple act of having the bun keeping it from slipping for the moment.

Wow. Tess was transformed. She didn't think she'd ever seen herself look so lovely. No wonder brides went for all this white, lacy stuff if it did wonders like this.

She was about to turn in her chair to speak to Roberto, when her eyes met his in the glass, and she gasped. His expression looked so full of love and longing, it took her breath away. Tess stared at him, unable to look away, drowning in his dark-chocolate eyes. Then the assistant moved, blocking Tess's view, and she drew in a shaky breath.

Yet when she stood up to face him, she thought she must have imagined it – Roberto was his normal, friendly self, with no hint of the emotion she could have sworn she'd seen.

–

Parcel paid for and wrapped in layer upon layer of tissue paper and placed reverently inside a white box with a satin ribbon and bow, the veil looked a hundred times more expensive than it was, and Tess was very pleased with the purchase indeed. Afterwards, they'd had a stroll past Casa Batlló and had made their way to Las Tapas Picantes for a late lunch.

'This time I *do* recommend the tapas of the day,' Roberto said, as he pulled a chair out for her. 'I think you will like it, and I have opened a bottle of champagne. I think you will like that, too.' He lifted her hand to his lips, and kissed the back of it.

The waiters cheered, and Roberto threw them a dirty look. 'Take no notice. They are *estupido*.' He said the last word loud enough for them to hear.

'Why are they cheering?' Tess wanted to know.

'They have never seen me like this with a woman, and they are making fun.'

Her smile grew wider. 'Never?'

'Never.'

The glances and remarks continued throughout the meal, but Roberto bore it with good grace, and he even slung a comment or two back at them. Not for the first time, Tess wished she'd made more of an attempt to learn the language.

'Did you know they'd be like this?' she asked, refusing a second glass of champagne – the last thing she needed tomorrow was a hangover, even a hint of one.

Roberto did that lovely shrug of his. 'Maybe.'

'We could have gone somewhere else,' she suggested.

'There is a reason I brought you here,' he began, excitement in his eyes, then he stopped as the door opened. Tess took one look at his expression and guessed who it was before she'd even glanced over her shoulder to check.

Ana-Sofía stalked in like she owned the place, oozing elegance and self-confidence. She blew a kiss to one of the waiters behind the bar – who did a good impression of a statue, as he froze in the middle of wiping a glass, his mouth open. Only his eyes moved as they flicked between Tess, Roberto and Ana.

She made a beeline for Roberto, and, to Tess's dismay, the other woman leant over him and kissed him on the lips. Tess let out a gasp, and even as Roberto was pushing Ana away, she was scrambling to her feet.

'I… um…' A sob escaped her, and she stumbled towards the door.

Roberto leapt from his chair, and elbowed Ana-Sofía to one side. Tess noticed that the other woman had a very smug look on her face indeed. 'Tess, don't go,' he called, following her to the door.

'I have to. It's obvious now,' she said, anguish in her voice.

'What is, Tess? Speak to me!'

'You and her.'

'There is no "me and Ana"! I've told you, there never has been and there never will be.'

'Try telling that to *her*.' Tess jerked her head towards Ana, who had picked up Roberto's glass and was running her finger seductively around the rim, her eyes focused on the pair of them and a twisted smile on her lips.

Tess flung herself away and staggered forward, escape the only thing on her mind. She couldn't remain here another second. Roberto mightn't be able to see it, but Tess could: he and Ana were made for each other. They had the same confidence (though in Ana it was more akin to arrogance), the same easy style… hell, even their looks complemented each other. Both were tall, dark and attractive, and they went well together.

'Tess, I beg you, please don't go. I will come with you,' Roberto cried, before sending a stream of angry Spanish at the other woman.

'Stay, you belong with her,' Tess cried.

Roberto grabbed her arm and swung her around. Tess careered into his chest and let out an "Oomph!" of surprise.

'No, I do not. I belong with *you*,' he said emphatically. 'We are meant to be, and I won't let Ana or anyone else come between us.' Keeping a firm hold on Tess, his arms encircling her, he swivelled around until he faced Ana-Sofia and shot off a few words.

The other woman sneered.

'You have no manners,' Roberto responded in English. 'I try to introduce you to my girlfriend, and this is how you behave.'

'She is not your girlfriend,' Ana retorted in English. 'You only met a few days ago. I know, I have been asking around. And she lives in England – too far for a booty call, even for you.'

Tess felt Roberto flinch, then his whole body tensed. What he said next, Tess didn't understand because he spoke in Spanish, but she did see the shock and incredulity in the other woman's eyes.

Ana gathered herself to her full height (which was considerable, given the spiky stilettos she had on), and took a deep breath, before stalking slowly towards the door. Tess shrank back a little as Ana came closer.

'You are a fool if you think he will stay with you. He won't.' She looked at Roberto. 'Have your fun, get the little English girl out of your system. But know this, Roberto, *mi amor*, I will not wait forever.' With that she swept out of the restaurant, a cloud of perfume wafting behind her.

Tess sagged against Roberto, close to tears. He held her close, stroking her hair until she regained her composure.

'What did you say to her to make her so mad?' Tess asked, when she felt able to speak.

'She was mad already,' Roberto said. 'She became worse when I told her…' He stopped. 'Wait, let me show you instead.'

Tess hesitated; she wasn't sure how much she could take this evening.

'Do you trust me?' he asked.

He'd asked that very same thing of her before, and she had trusted him then. She had to trust him now, so she nodded.

Roberto slipped his hand into hers and led her into the street. They had only taken two steps to the left when he halted.

'I want you to think seriously about this,' he said. 'I have, and I would like you to say yes, but you have to be sure it is what you want.'

Oh, no, was he going to propose to her? Surely not!

He put his hand in his pocket, and Tess's heart somersaulted. This was going too fast, too soon, she wasn't ready for—

A bunch of keys.

Tess stared at them blankly as Roberto searched for the right one and unlocked a door beside them. The dark, weathered wood blended into the stone, and there was nothing remarkable about it – it was a door like so many others in the Gothic Quarter.

Bewildered, she shook her head. She had no idea what was going on unless – was he taking her to his place? No, that wasn't it, because he'd told her he lived near the university and she knew that was a few miles from the city centre.

He pushed the door open to reveal narrow steps leading straight up, and indicated that she should go ahead of him. When he flicked a switch, the dim interior was transformed into black and white marble steps, with a shiny brass banister running up the side. The staircase was old but spotlessly clean.

'This building is nearly six hundred years old,' he was saying, as he followed her. 'Imagine how many feet have climbed these stairs.'

Tess didn't want to imagine anything; she wanted to know where he was taking her, and why.

'Wait,' he said, and inserted another key from the small bunch into a door on the first landing they came to. He pushed it open and stood back to let Tess pass.

'What?' she began, walking into a small hallway and gazing around.

'It has only one bedroom, but it will do, I hope.'

'Are you thinking of moving?' she asked. 'This is lovely.'

Four doors led off the hallway, the one on her left being the living room, which was spacious, if a little sparsely furnished. Floor-length curtains drifted slightly in the breeze from a pair of open French windows and the little balcony beyond. She could easily imagine sitting out there on a summer's evening, watching the world pass by on the street below, the enticing aroma of food wafting up from the tapas bar, a glass of wine in her hand…

'There is a kitchen in this room here, the bathroom is here, and this is the bedroom,' he said. 'Both the bedroom and the bathroom look out onto a small courtyard.'

Tess leaned out of the window for a better look.

'Well?' Roberto demanded, after watching her explore.

'I love it!' She was glad he'd brought her here because now, when she was back in England and trying to picture him, she would imagine him in this flat, getting dressed for work, or relaxing with a beer at the end of a long day. It was really handy for his job too, being right above the restaurant – though maybe for him it would be a bad thing, being so close!

Some of the tension left Roberto at her words. 'I hoped you would. So, will you consider it?'

'Consider what?'

'Living here.'

'Wait, what? Say that again?' Tess was concentrating so hard on committing every detail to memory that she must have misheard him.

'Would you live here?' he asked.

Oh, he wanted her opinion before he decided whether to take the apartment or not. 'In a heartbeat!' she cried. 'It's gorgeous, and I know it's only got the one bedroom, but I assume Diego isn't moving with you, so that's not really a problem, is it?'

'Why would Diego want to move in?' Roberto looked baffled.

'Well, he's your flatmate, but I fully understand why you'd want a place of your own, especially one this nice.'

'*Me* live here? No, I meant *you*.'

'*Me?*'

'Yes, you. This is your apartment. If you want it.'

'But I have an apartment in Worcester.' Tess frowned, not sure what Roberto was trying to say.

He came closer and put his hands on her shoulders. 'You can give it up. Move to Barcelona. You don't have to leave here.' His unspoken 'You don't have to leave *me*' hung in the air between them.

'But... but...' Tess searched the room, as if the answer to her confusion lay in one of the corners. 'I can't! What about my jobs? My painting? My family?' She paused for breath. 'How much is this place, anyway? I bet I won't be able to afford it.'

'You said you wanted to stay here, that you would love to live in Barcelona. I am making it so that you can.'

'Yes, but saying you'd like to live in the place you go on holiday to isn't the same as actually doing it, is it?' she protested. Yes, she'd fallen in love with Barcelona, and she'd also fallen in love with Roberto, but...

'It can be.' He sounded certain.

'I can't, Roberto! My life is in the UK. I can't just leave my family or my friends. And what about my jobs? My work?'

He sighed, put his arms around her and kissed her on the nose. 'Please, Tess, think about it.' A look of sadness crept into his eyes. 'I don't want to lose you, and I'm afraid I will when you return to your own life. I think you will forget me.'

'Never,' she whispered, then cleared her throat and said, a little louder. 'I will be back, I promise.'

'When? Next week? Next month? In the summer?'

Tess shook her head, not knowing how to answer. She'd be back when she could afford it, and she had no idea when that would be. 'I don't know,' she admitted quietly, very close to tears once more.

'*Exactamente!* This is what I worry about – that you will not come back.'

Tess hadn't bargained on this. The thought of carrying on their relationship had crossed her mind more than once, but she'd always pushed it away because she didn't think it was feasible, or that he'd want to. Now he'd gone and thrown all this at her, and she had no clue what she should do.

She'd love to stay, of course she would, but she was well aware that living there would be very different from visiting.

Or would it?

Most of her work – she put the bar and the laundry to one side for a moment – was done by phone, internet and post, so the location wasn't that much of an issue. But her whole life was in England – she couldn't just up sticks and leave. Emma, for one, would be appalled, and she dreaded to think what her parents' reaction would be.

No, as lovely as the idea was, she simply couldn't do it. Anyway, it was too big a decision to make on the spur of the moment. Going home would give her some perspective on her feelings and the opportunity to consider whether she could actually do this, whether she had the courage to turn her whole life upside down, or whether she'd simply got caught up in the moment and had let her feelings run away with her.

She was conscious of Roberto's arms still around her waist, his mouth on her hair, and his warmth and solidity. For a second, Tess didn't know how she was ever going to leave. But real life intruded, as it so often does, and she knew she had to go back home. As wonderful as his suggestion was, it was nothing but a pipe dream. She didn't earn enough from her painting yet to pay the bills in

Worcester, and Barcelona was bound to be considerably more expensive. She had no idea what the rent on an apartment like this would be, but she was pretty certain she couldn't afford it. Talk about becoming a starving artist in an attic!

'If it is money you are worried about, what if I could get you a job?' Roberto suggested, and Tess was disconcerted to have him read her mind so easily.

'I don't speak Spanish,' she pointed out.

Another of his classic shrugs. 'It is of no matter – if I can find you a job, would you consider it?'

'Yes, no, oh… I don't know! It's all rather sudden. I don't think I can just give up my flat and move to Barcelona at the drop of a hat.' She leaned back to squint at him, as a thought occurred to her. 'What about you. Where will you be living?' Was he planning on them living together? Because, if so, he hadn't mentioned it, and she wasn't sure she was ready for that, either. This was all moving much too fast!

'The apartment will be yours, not mine. If, in time, we both wish it and it is right, then maybe we will live together.'

Tess took a step back, freeing herself from his embrace. 'You're saying you want me to turn my whole life upside down, but you're not sure this' – she gestured to the pair of them with her finger – 'is *right*?'

'Oh, *I* am certain,' he said, never taking his eyes from hers. 'But *you* are not.' He ran his tongue nervously across his lips. 'You don't have to give everything up,' he explained. 'Not until you are sure. Stay here, for a week, two weeks, a month. Just try it. If you don't like it…' He looked away, and she wondered if he meant to say, 'If you don't want to be with me enough to stay', but he finished with, '... you can always go back home. This is not about us, Tess, me and you. It is about *you* – your dreams, your life. I want you to be happy and I think you can be happy, living in this city you've come to love.' He looked up and away, staring over the top of her head and into space. 'I thought it is what you wanted,' he added softly.

'I don't know,' she replied, and he must have heard the heartache and anguish in her voice, because when he looked down at her again he smiled, and his own voice was sad when he said, 'It is OK, I understand. It is a big thing and there is much to consider. Go home, think about my offer – the apartment will still be here, if you change your mind.' With a visible effort, he pasted a smile on his lips, and with the prick of unshed tears in her eyes and a lump in her throat, all Tess could do was nod.

'I will drive you back to your hotel now, if that is what you want,' he said. 'But will you agree to have dinner with me again, this evening? There is something I want to show you this evening before we eat, something I think you will enjoy. Is that OK?'

She hated that he sounded so uncertain, so unsure of himself. The confidence she associated with him had gone, and underneath was a much softer, more vulnerable and less sure of himself Roberto.

'OK, but what do you want to show me?' she asked, biting her lip. *Please, not something else to try to persuade me to stay*, she prayed, *because I don't know how much more I can take.*

'The fountains,' he explained.

'What fountains?'

'The ones I want to show you. They light up, but only in the dark. Shall I pick you up at eight?'

'Ah, I see. Then, thank you. I'll be ready.'

They drove back to Tess's hotel in silence.

All the while Tess was showering, and getting dressed and putting on some make-up, the only thing she could think about was living there, in this glorious city, and being so near to the man she loved.

Roberto was waiting for her in the hotel lobby, lounging against a pillar, arms crossed, watching the lift. Tess had used the stairs, so she was able to walk across reception without him noticing her, and she took the opportunity to study him. He really was quite gorgeous, with his white T-shirt, faded jeans, black jacket and black hair still glistening from an obviously very recent shower. How he had managed to get from there to his place and back again, and found the time for a shower, was beyond her.

Unexpectedly, he straightened up and turned around, smiling broadly, his eyes twinkling and, as she got nearer, she realized that she was reflected in a mirrored column right in front of him. He must have seen her staring at him.

'Hi,' he said, and Tess coloured a little, but she soon forgot her embarrassment when he led her quickly outside and onto the main road. A swift dart down the underpass and out the other side brought them onto an avenue lined with smaller fountains which led to the far larger and much more impressive ones in front of the Museu Nacional d'Art de Catalunya.

People thronged the open space and a sense of anticipation and excitement filled the air. At first the water arching into the sky from the many jets was the usual white colour, lit by sunken spotlights, and though night hadn't completely fallen it was dark enough for the effect to be quite magical, especially when the breeze carried a fine mist across some of the spectators.

'Carles Buigas designed it in 1929 for the Great Universal Exhibition,' he told her, as they made their way through the crowd, searching for the best spot. 'Apparently there are over four thousand five hundred lights, and the pool holds about three million litres of water.'

Then the music started and the show began, and everyone turned towards the fountain, which had an array of colours shooting through it. Tess held her breath, mesmerized, as the shapes danced and flowed in front of her eyes. Then there was not just one fountain, but many, and all of them displaying changing chameleon colours and rainbow hues, the water arching and pulsing in time to the music.

For half an hour they watched the hypnotic jets of water stream into the sky, but, as Tess stared at the mesmerizing scene in front of her, she was always very aware of the man standing next to her, his arm touching hers.

Dinner was a quiet affair, slightly melancholy. Despite Tess's intention of simply living for the moment and enjoying the time she had left in Barcelona, that had been before Roberto had planted the seed in her mind that she could actually live there permanently, that she could make this city her home.

Roberto was respectful of her mood, and instead of trying to persuade her that she should stay, he asked her about her family instead.

'Tell me about Emma,' he said, over the largest shrimps Tess had ever seen in her life. Not that she had much of an appetite, but she knew she had to eat, otherwise there was a strong possibility she would run out of energy halfway around the course tomorrow.

'I think I've told you this before,' she began, squirting lemon juice onto her plate. 'Emma is three years younger than me, really pretty, really intelligent, and getting married to a lovely guy called Declan.'

'And you also told me she had a twin, that you had another sister,' he said, softly. 'Do you ever recover from something like that?'

'I honestly don't think you do,' Tess said. 'You learn to live with it, that's all. Mum and Dad had to keep it together for me and Emma but, looking back, I think they really struggled. Emma fared the worst, though. She was so little, and I'm not sure she really understood what dying meant until it actually happened to Ella. I remember how we used to go the hospital to visit Ella and see the same faces over and over again, until one day one of those faces wouldn't be there any more.' Tess put her fork down and stared into the distance. 'Usually it was because they had passed away, or were spending their last days at home, but sometimes, just sometimes, a lucky one would go home because they were in remission.'

Roberto reached across the table, put his hand over hers and squeezed.

She smiled at him, grateful for his sympathy. 'I don't think Emma knew what death was, didn't understand the finality of it until it happened. I don't think any of us did. I remember crawling into bed with her, night after night, because she was inconsolable, and I didn't want Mum to see her crying because it would set Mum off, and I simply couldn't bear it.'

'You felt you had to comfort them?' he asked, his soft eyes full of emotion.

Tess nodded. 'Mum and Dad were hurting so much.' She blinked at the sudden tears. 'And Emma? It was like she'd lost half of herself. It was awful.' She paused and added quietly, 'Sometimes it still is.'

'I'm sorry, Tess, I didn't want to upset you.'

'You haven't, and I think it's good that you reminded me why I'm running tomorrow. I'll be thinking of Ella all the way, and I know she'll be watching me and cheering me on. I just wish Emma was running it with me.'

'She will be – in here.' Roberto touched her chest gently. 'Just like Ella is in here.' He smiled lovingly at her. 'But tell me, *querida*, who was comforting you?'

It took Tess a very long time to fall asleep that night. She had too many emotions and thoughts eddying through her mind.

And one of them was why Roberto had called her 'my darling'.

Race Day

Tess felt sick. Along with pre-race nerves, she'd slept badly again, for the second night in a row, this time because she couldn't stop thinking of Roberto's offer. She knew he meant well and had really gone out of his way to make the decision as straightforward and as easy for her as possible, as far as the practicalities were concerned. But Tess's inhibitions were too deep to be eased by a flat and the possibility of a job. She was still no nearer to getting her head around the idea of leaving England and everyone she knew and loved. She understood all too well that the family had lost one member already, and she was very aware that moving so far away might have a negative impact on her parents and her sister.

Tess seriously thought she was going to throw up. Her stomach churned, her palms were sweaty and she wondered if she was having palpitations, because her heart was thudding so hard and fast that anyone who checked her pulse right now would think she was already running the race. *I'm not ready for this, not one little bit*, she thought, as she attached the tracking device to the laces of one of her trainers. *I'm going to make a total fool of myself*, she worried, as she pinned her number on her running vest.

She was still feeling the same way as she forced a croissant down her throat and slurped her coffee.

Tess sent her sister a text.

I hate you, Emma.

No, you don't. You'll have a great time.

I won't. And I do hate you.

Good luck.

I'm gonna need it.

'Yeah, I wish you were here, too,' Tess muttered into her coffee cup. 'Preferably instead of me.' Why, oh why had she agreed to do this? She wasn't sporty; she'd never been picked first for the netball team – some days she was lucky if she was picked at all, and she'd never felt the urge to cycle anywhere, or to go for a jog or a swim. Her idea of a session at the local gym was a soak in the hot tub and a wilt in the sauna, with absolutely no exercise involved whatsoever.

And here she was, preparing to run 26 miles. It sounded even worse in kilometres – 42! Grrr!!

The only thing stopping her from backing out was the thought of all the money Emma had so conscientiously raised (of course Tess had done her share of fundraising, but it wasn't nearly as much as Emma's contribution), and that she'd have to give it all back.

And Ella. The image of her sister smiling out from the specially-made T-shirt was the other reason. After all, Tess was doing this for her, in memory of her, and if Ella could see her now she'd be laughing her socks off. She'd also be cheering Tess on, and Tess smiled softly at the thought.

With breakfast finished, Tess had yet another nervous wee (the thought of needing to go halfway around the course filled her with dread), then headed out of the hotel in the direction of the start line.

Goodness gracious me! Tess had never seen so much Lycra in one place!

Thousands of runners thronged the Plaça Espanya and thousands more people had come to see their friends and loved ones off. Tess weaved through the crowds, working her way down the Avinguda de la Reina Maria Cristina, past the now-still fountains which lined the wide boulevard, and on towards one of the cordoned-off areas behind the start line. Her race number was printed on yellow paper, indicating that she needed to go the yellow area; to stagger the start times, the runners were separated by anticipated race times – those who were likely to finish in the quickest times were allowed to start first. Tess was two-thirds of the way back, and even then she thought Emma was being ambitious, having declared on the entry form that they would run the marathon in four hours. Being at the very end of the line may have been a more appropriate starting position for Tess.

With half an hour to go and feeling more nervous than she had ever felt in her life, Tess looked for a place to wait. Not wanting to be in the thick of it until she needed to be, she trotted up some steps and onto a walkway above the road. Pausing when she reached the middle, she looked down. Runners were gathering on the road below, a sea of multicoloured tops and shorts, with the occasional shark costume or Batman outfit to liven things up. Thank goodness Emma hadn't suggested they dress up. Tess was going to have enough trouble hauling herself through Barcelona's streets as it was, without being hindered by a heavy, hot Mr Blobby suit, or by being the back end of a pantomime horse.

The far side of the bridge reached across to the large open space with that magical fountain playing in its centre; it looked very different in broad daylight, especially with so much activity going on. She eyed a stall selling coffees and pastries, her mouth dry, but common sense got the better of her, and she took a swig of water instead. She intended to ditch the bottle before the race started, and rely on grabbing a drink from one of the many drinks stations along the way, although she did notice that some runners were wearing elaborate hydration systems so that they didn't have to divert to the side of the road for water.

Seeing loads of entrants warming up by jogging slowly or doing leg stretches, Tess thought she ought to do the same, so she lifted one leg behind her, grabbed her toes and gently pulled her heel into her bottom. Then she did the same with the other leg.

Feeling more like a runner and less like an observer, she did some hopping and jumping on the spot, then ran a few paces, repeating the process until she became worried that she risked using all her energy on the warm-up and leaving none for the actual race itself. Instead, she found a spare piece of wall and sat on it, swinging her legs, trying to focus on her breathing. But, all too soon, the marshals began calling for the runners to take their places. Tess hopped off her wall and took a shortcut down the banking which lined the road, taking her cue from other runners wearing the same coloured numbers.

This was it. She was doing it! She was about to run her very first marathon, and excitement finally overrode nerves as she became caught up in the atmosphere. She was jammed in with thousands of others as they waited their turn to cross the start line, and she felt an odd mixture of being part of something much bigger than herself, while at the same time feeling more alone than she had ever been in her life. She wished she had someone to cheer her on, but many others seemed to be alone, too. One of the women next to her smiled and gave her a thumbs-up.

Freddie Mercury's 'Barcelona' blared out of the loud-speakers, and a roar went up as the first of the runners set off. A few minutes later Tess's group, which was at least a couple of thousand strong, if not more, was ushered forward, until gradually she inched nearer and nearer the inflatable arch that signified the start of the race.

Then they were off, music blasting in her ears, being constantly bumped and jostled by her fellow runners, until the arch loomed overhead and she was through and out the other side, and running as though her life depended on it.

After a few hundred yards she settled down to a more sustainable pace, her legs moving in a steady rhythm, her breathing even, and she found she was actually enjoying herself. The long straight road was lined with spectators, cheering and waving, and Tess, with nothing hurting (yet), felt on top of the world.

She passed the one-kilometre marker with ease, and the two-kilometre one, then checked her watch. She'd only taken eight minutes. Really? Wow, that meant she was on track to complete the marathon in… she did a quick mental calculation… *under two hours.*

That can't be right, she realized. If it was, it meant she was flat-out sprinting, and she certainly wasn't going that fast.

A hairpin bend brought Tess close to the three-kilometre marker, and suddenly she understood what was wrong. She'd been looking at the kilometre signs and thinking they were in miles, so she'd not run three miles, she'd actually run (another mental calculation) roughly one and two-thirds.

Damn it! But it did make more sense. Nine-minute miles were more like it, not the four-minute ones she'd just calculated. Gosh, if she could do a mile in four minutes, she'd be the fastest marathon runner in the world.

Chuckling to herself despite the momentary dismay, she veered to the side of the road, grabbed a cup of water from the water station and drank it down, determined not to become dehydrated. The sun was up, and though it was only just coming up to eight in the morning it was already warmer than she was used to. Her training runs back home had all taken place between October and March, when the weather was normally dull, wet and chilly, and not bright, warm and sunny as it was in Barcelona.

Sweat beaded her forehead and trickled nastily down her back as she ran past Camp Nou, Barcelona's famous football stadium, but she still felt strong, and the runners had thinned out a little so there was more space to manoeuvre. If she concentrated hard, she could pretend she was out with Emma, pounding the streets of Worcester, and that this was a normal Sunday morning run. She tried not to think of the 30-odd kilometres still to come, and instead checked them off one at a time.

Each street looked similar to the one before, and she was soon lost and wishing she'd paid more attention to the blown-up map of the course in the exhibition centre where she'd registered, but by the eleventh kilometre she found herself running down a more familiar road. Ahead, in the distance, was the Museu Nacional d'Art de Catalunya yet again and, if she wasn't mistaken, her hotel was down the next road on the left. She was almost back at the start of the race, and the urge to quietly slip away and disappear into the coolness of her hotel room was almost overwhelming.

But she was past the turn-off before she could act on her impulse, and there was another long, straight road ahead. She found herself grabbing a handful of jelly babies from the next station and washing them down with a cup of water, then she was running towards the 16-kilometre point and waving at the crowds around the Sagrada Familia with Queen's 'Don't Stop Me Now' blaring in her ears from her iPod.

She felt as though she could do this forever, that she could run to the end of the world and back, and she was doing it not just for Ella, and not for Emma either, but she was doing it for herself too, and she felt marvellous.

She felt dreadful. Her legs were as heavy as a sack of potatoes, her back ached, and her feet were in bits. She couldn't breathe properly either. Gone was her previously smooth in-out rhythm, and in its place was a sort of strangled, panting gasp.

Nothing helped. Not her music, nor the crowds, and the other runners passing her made her want to cry. She was at the 28-kilometre mark (she had no idea what that was in miles, and was too tired to try to work it out), and, to add to her misery, she'd just run up a really long road which doubled back on itself, so she had the agony of watching the runners who were further along in the race than her run past her on the opposite side of the road. She was almost in tears when she came to the double-back bend and had to run the full length of that blasted road all over again. Whoever designed the route was a sadistic bastard who should be sent to hell and made to run up and down this stretch of road for eternity. Then he would know what it felt like.

She hated him (it had to be a bloke, she thought, with no logical reason), and she hated her sister too, for the stupid idea of entering the marathon in the first place and for blackmailing her into running it. She also hated Emma for catching chickenpox (*I bet she did it on purpose*, Tess fumed silently), and who was now probably sitting in their parents' house watching their mother calmly preparing Sunday lunch. Tess hated chickenpox for its very existence. She hated her parents for not insisting that Tess shouldn't be allowed to come here on her own. And she even hated Barcelona for putting the event on in the first place. She wished all those other damn runners would stop running past her, and she wished all those annoying spectators would stop cheering and bloody well go home. Hadn't they got anything better to do on a Sunday morning, like wash the car, play golf or take the kids swimming?

And she'd heard the same songs twice now, because the shuffle facility on her iPod was intent on torturing her, as if she wasn't being tortured enough already.

The 32-kilometre mark saw Tess dragging her feet along a road with the city on her right and the coast on her left, cursing everyone and everything she could think of.

'You can do it,' someone shouted.

Tess ignored it. She was sick of people shouting encouragement. She didn't need encouragement. What she needed was to get these damn trainers off her feet, to have a shower and then a lie-down, and never to have to run anywhere again. Ever. Not even for a bus. She'd get a taxi—

Now, that was a thought. A taxi. She could go straight to her hotel and sod the race. If crossing the finish line was that important, then she'd get the taxi to drop her off at—

'Tess, you are doing good.'

No, I'm sodding not, she thought at the unseen shouter. *I'm going slower than a tortoise on a slow day, I hurt all over, and I'll be lucky if I finish before this time tomorrow. Now, bugger off and leave me alone.*

'Keep going, Tess. You can do it.'

She aimed a glare in the general direction of the voice, which was just behind her, yet somehow keeping pace with her, and she frowned. If it was keeping pace with her, then that meant her speed was only a little faster than a stroll, and, anyway, how did he know her name? She glanced over her shoulder. A man was jogging just beside her, and not just any man either...

'Roberto,' she croaked, through a dry throat and even drier lips.

'Here.' He lengthened his stride, came alongside, and handed her a bottle of water.

Tess gulped it thirstily. When she gave it back to him, it was with narrowed eyes and a jutting chin. 'What do you think you're doing?' she asked.

'Keeping you company.'

'I don't need company,' she growled. 'What I need is for this to stop.'

'It will – in another nine kilometres.'

'No, now.'

'You can do this, Tess. You know you can.'

'Oh, bugger off.'

'I do not know this "bugger off".' He was looking at her with concern. 'Ah, I see, you want me to go away?'

'Yes, I want everyone to go away and leave me alone.'

'I'm not going anywhere, except to the finish line with you.'

'How can you? You aren't entered in the marathon.'

'That doesn't stop me running by your side.'

'Well, it should.' She really didn't need him to see her in this state. Romantic love under the Spanish sun? Ha! There was her nothing romantic about her own particular Romeo taking one look at her red, sweating face and doing a runner himself – in the opposite direction. Look at her – she was a mess, and a tired, tearful, grumpy mess at that.

'I am not leaving you. If your sister was here, she wouldn't leave you, either,' Roberto insisted.

Yeah? Don't bet on it, Tess thought. Emma was too competitive for her own good. She would probably have finished the damned race by now and be drinking champagne out of her trainer, or whatever it was you did to celebrate the end of 26 miles – sorry, 42 kilometres – of hell.

'See, you have completed another one,' Roberto pointed out, as they passed the 33 sign. 'Only nine more to go.'

'How did you find me?' Tess gasped. She should really conserve her breath, but hey-ho, if talking to Roberto helped to take her mind off this never-ending Satan's run, then so be it.

'I waited for you,' he said.

'Since when?'

'Since the race started.'

'Why here? Why not at the start? Or halfway?'

'Because I have friends who have run *la maratón*, and they all tell me that around twenty-five to thirty kilometres is when you hit the wall.'

'The wall?'

'Yes, that's when your body has nothing left to give but your mind tells it to keep going anyway. This is the bad part, just here. I know you don't have your sister to keep you going, so I'm here instead.'

That was really quite sweet of him, really it was. And despite her aches and pains, and the terrible weariness, Tess wished she'd taken the time to put some mascara on.

Oh, don't be silly, she told herself. Any make-up would have been sweated off her face long ago, and if he could stand to see her like this then he was seeing her at her worst and he hadn't run away yet. That was something, at least.

She gave him a tiny, half-hearted smile, and he grinned back at her.

'That is my woman!' he cried, and Tess frowned for a second, until she realized he meant to say, 'That's my girl!'

Another left-hand turn, and the course swung away from the seafront to plunge back into the heart of the city.

'The zoo, it is over there,' Roberto said, jerking his head to the left. 'I will take you some time,' he added. Tess knew he was trying to distract her and she was grateful for it.

And half a kilometre further, he said: 'See that? Barcelona has her very own Arc de Triomf. Not as spectacular as the one in Paris, they say, but I don't care. It is ours.'

They left the Arc and its beautiful open avenue behind, and entered a more commercial style of street with shops and banks. Tess's mood began to drop again. Would this damned thing never end?

'Can we stop? Please, just make it stop,' she pleaded, almost crying with the effort of putting one foot in front of the other.

'Tell me about your sister again,' Roberto demanded.

'Emma?'

'No, Ella, the one you run this race for.'

'I've told you everything,' she protested.

'You haven't told me how you felt, how it affected you. You told me about everyone else, but not you.'

'How do you think it bloody well affected me?' Tess yelled, speeding up as much as she could (which wasn't very much at all). She wished the damned man would go away so she could stop thinking about Ella.

'You tell me,' Roberto countered.

'Go away.'

'No, I can't.'

'Well, shut up, then.'

'I can't do that, either. Tell me, Tess. And you didn't answer my question last night – who comforted you?'

'Shut up!'

'Who, Tess? Who?'

Unable to take any more, Tess screamed, 'No one, OK! No one!'

She felt his hand on her shoulder and shrugged it off, angrily.

'I guessed so,' he said, keeping pace with her easily as she staggered slightly erratically. She wasn't sure if it was exhaustion, anger or grief that was responsible, but whenever Roberto tried to steady her, she glared furiously at him until he backed off.

'I think you had much on your shoulders,' he said. 'Both your own sorrow and that of your sister. I think you took it upon yourself to try to comfort her, even when you were hurting so badly, too. Forgive me if I am wrong, but I believe you tried to become the twin your sister lost. It was too much for someone so young.'

Tess stared back at him, her mouth open even further than it was already. This man had just summed up exactly how she felt. 'I was – *am* – three years older than Emma. I had to be strong for her,' she said, tears gathering in the corner of her eyes again. She dashed them away angrily.

'It is OK to cry,' Roberto said.

'No, it's not.'

He stopped suddenly and grabbed her arm, spinning her round to face him. Tess was so worked up, she didn't notice that they had stopped running. '*It is*,' he insisted. 'Did you cry when she died?'

'Of course, I did! I—'

Tess paused. No, she hadn't, not really, she realized. She had done then exactly what she was doing now. Whenever tears threatened, she had held them back, brushed them away. Emma had shed enough tears for the both of them, and her little sister had relied on her so much that Tess couldn't let her down, she'd had to stay strong for her. Their parents had been in pieces and hadn't been much use, so it had been up to Tess to be the calm one, to be the strong one, to help her sister cope with her unimaginable grief. But when had she dealt with her own? Never, that's when. She had buried it deep and had got on with her life, helping Emma and her parents come to terms with Ella's loss, but she had been so busy helping her family that she had been unable to help herself. And now Roberto was bringing it all out in the open at the worst possible time. *How could he?*

The threatened tears spilled over, running in torrents down her cheeks.

'This is good; it will help you heal,' Roberto said. 'But not now – later. Now you have a race to finish, and you are running it for her. There will be time for tears later, when you have crossed the finish line.' He gestured at the laughing, young girl on her T-shirt, and Tess pulled it away from her stomach and peered at the upside-down image of her sister.

'For Ella,' she said.

'For Ella, and for *you*.'

Gathering what little strength she had left, with Roberto by her side to provide a life raft for her determination, Tess ran like she had never run before. There was nothing left in the tank, she was running on empty, yet still she ran. Her face was a mask of pain, and her heart hurt even more than her legs and her feet, yet still she ran.

The silence stretched out between them, and all those things both said and unsaid were louder than the crowds lining the road, encouraging her silently. Every so often Roberto reached out to touch her shoulder, spurring her on, and she sucked the strength out of him, drawing his energy and determination into her heart and soul and using it to keep her body going.

At 39 kilometres, the sea was once more on their left. She couldn't see it, but she could smell it and taste the salt on her lips – or was it her own tears and sweat which added such piquancy to those final few kilometres?

'Two more to go,' Roberto said, as they swung away from the sea once more. 'You're nearly there, *mi amor*, nearly at the end,' he added.

Sure enough, bit by bit, the crowds grew thicker and barriers appeared on either side of the course, funnelling the runners towards the finish.

'I can't do it,' Tess croaked, almost slowing to a walk. The last few kilometres were uphill, the gradient not steep, but the gradual pull at the end of so many arduous miles was totally sadistic.

'You can, and you will.' Roberto slung her arm around his shoulders and supported some of her weight for a few paces, until shame made her shake him off.

'I have to do this on my own,' she insisted.

'No, Tess, you do not. Not any more.'

She staggered forward. 'I have to, don't you see? This is the only thing I can do for Ella.'

'*Vale*,' he said in Spanish. 'OK.' He backed off a little. 'I understand, but know this – you do not have to carry the burden of grief on your own. You have a family. You all share your pain equally.'

What made Roberto so bloody wise? Of course she had a family, and of course they all grieved. What did *he* know about it?

Sudden anger kept her going. *Just one more kilometre left, one more, that's all.* Then she could stop, and forget the effing marathon had even taken place.

Almost abruptly, they were at the roundabout she knew so well, and were running alongside the fountains. The crowd was cheering, and music boomed in her ears. Then she was under the blow-up arch and through the finish line and sinking to her knees in relief and exultation.

She'd done it. She'd really done it. Twenty-six miles all in one go.

Tess sat on the tarmac, tears pouring down her face, and someone put a foil sheet around her shoulders and patted her on the back. She felt euphoric and jubilant for a whole minute, but then an overwhelming grief surged over her. *Ella, poor Ella*, she thought, seeing her sister's cute little face in her mind, looking so like Emma's yet so much her own. And, with a grateful gladdening of her heart, Tess realized that whenever she thought of Ella, it wasn't the little girl ravaged by a dreadful disease that she saw, but a happy, smiling girl, full of life and laughter.

'For you, Ella,' she sobbed. 'I love you, little girl. I love you, sister, wherever you are. Sleep tight.'

Tess felt a touch on her arm, and she looked up. But no one was close enough to her to be responsible for that feather-light touch.

And it couldn't have been Roberto either, because Roberto had disappeared.

—

He was waiting for her on the other side of the roundabout, perched on the low wall surrounding the park. He looked cool, fresh and enigmatic, and Tess couldn't read his expression.

'I thought you'd gone home,' she said, hobbling stiffly towards him, still clutching her foil sheet about her like a shawl.

'I wasn't part of the race, so I slipped away at the end,' he said. 'But I am here now.'

'So you are.'

'How do you feel?' He hopped off the wall and took her arm.

'I'm not sure. I don't think my body has caught up with itself.' She gave him a wry smile. 'I'm pretty sure I'll pay for this later, but for now all I feel is a bit let down.' She saw his quizzical expression. 'Deflated, like it's an anticlimax.'

'Have you spoken to your family? To Emma?'

'Not yet.'

'I will help you to your hotel, then you must call them. They will be very proud of you, and you should be proud of yourself, too.'

She was, but for now the only thing she felt was drained, both physically and emotionally. All she wanted to do was to have a nice cup of tea and a shower, followed by a lie-down. A very long lie-down. Possibly for the next few weeks.

'You need a shower and a bath,' Roberto announced, after claiming her key card from reception and escorting her to her room. 'Call your family. I will run you a bath.'

A shower and a bath? She must have heard incorrectly. Not sure that a bath was a terribly good idea, she reached for her phone, suddenly desperate to speak to her family.

'Mum?' Tess's voice cracked slightly, and she hoped her mother didn't notice.

'Oh, darling, we're all so proud of you!'

Tess heard her father yelling, 'Go girl!' in the background, and the sound of Emma squealing. She held the phone away from her ear and winced.

'How was it?' her mother was asking, when Tess risked perforating her eardrums by putting the phone back to her ear once more.

'Not too bad,' she said, and to her surprise she found it to be true. At the time it had been awful, but with the perspective of only just a little more than an hour between her staggering lurch over the finish line and now, the horror of the race was beginning to dim a little. And though Tess had no intention of ever running another marathon again, she suspected when the aches and pains had worn off, she might – just might – be *tempted* to do it again.

Her mind was rambling, and Tess blamed it on the exhaustion. 'I'll speak to you later, Mum,' she promised. 'I've got to go and have a shower. I'm all sweaty and horrible.'

She was ending the call when Roberto emerged from the bathroom. 'Your bath is full,' he said, and he held the door open for her.

'What I want is a shower,' Tess protested.

'I agree. Shower first, then a hot bath. It will ease your muscles.'

'Oh, OK.' It made sense, and, after closing the bathroom door behind her and having a quick shower, Tess eased herself into the scalding water. Her thighs and calves let out a sigh. Lord, but that felt good. Her feet throbbed, and she had yet to inspect them for the blisters she knew were there, but it was a good throb, a healing throb, as though the blood was circulating once more, puffing out flesh which had been ground to a pulp from those many, many steps she had taken over the course of the race. She bet she'd more than managed her recommended 10,000 steps a day that day! She had probably done enough to keep her going until Christmas.

She heard the bedroom door close softly and a pang shot through her. Roberto must have thought it best to leave her to her own devices, but he could at least have said goodbye before he went. Leaning her head against the edge of the bath (Roberto had thoughtfully rolled up a small towel up for the purpose – so sweet of him!), Tess went over the events of the day.

She had known it was going to be tough, but she hadn't anticipated it being as tough as it had been. Her last few training runs with Emma had skirted around the 22-mile mark, and at the time the thought of running an additional four and a bit miles hadn't daunted her. But the reality of those extra four miles had proved to be a whole different ball game. Besides, she'd probably gone off too fast, caught up in the excitement of the event, and had burned out sooner than she'd anticipated. Then there was the actual course itself. She was certain that her unfamiliarity with it, and the fact that she was in a strange city, had affected her mindset. She'd been in more of a holiday mood than a running-a-marathon mood ever since she'd arrived, and this had shown in her running.

Still, she had done it, and she gave herself a mental pat on the back. Six months ago, the thought of entering a marathon hadn't even crossed her mind. She'd never once considered it, not even when the highlights of the London marathon had been shown on the news. She could honestly say she had never thought, "I'd like to do that", as she'd watched the emotional, tired and sweaty runners cross the line.

Yet she *had* done it.

Roberto was right – she should be proud of herself. She also needed to thank him, because without his support she probably would have given up at the 30-kilometre mark. He was the only thing that had kept her going.

Her eyes closed and her limbs loosened as she relaxed further, allowing her thoughts to drift to Ella. She often thought about her lost sister, but she realized that since Ella's death she'd only remembered the good stuff. That was something her family seemed to do as a unit, and although it was better to remember Ella as healthy and happy, Tess suspected that Roberto was probably right: Tess hadn't given herself the chance to grieve for Ella properly, and he'd also been right in saying that Tess had thought that her role was as the strong one in the family. And that she still did.

When she examined what he'd forced her to admit, and what he'd said, she found she agreed with him. All the time during Ella's illness and after her death, Tess had subconsciously felt that she needed to be the strong one, to be there for Ella. And, deep down, Tess recognized that she hadn't felt as though she had the right to mourn as much as the rest of the family. Tess had lost a sibling, but her parents had lost a child and Emma had lost a twin. It was like Tess had been playing a game of grieving Top Trumps, with none of the others aware they'd been playing, yet they'd all trumped her soundly without any of them being conscious of it.

It was time she faced this.

As Tess lay in her cooling bath, her fingers and toes wrinkling from the water, she finally allowed herself to mourn: for Ella, for Emma, for her parents – but most of all, for herself. She realized for the first time in over a decade that she was just as entitled to her emotions as the rest of the family, and she let them out and howled her grief to the world. She also understood it was time to live her life the way *she* wanted. If Ella's death had taught her anything – and the lesson was long overdue – it was that life was very short and so very precious, and it had to be lived to the full.

When Tess eventually climbed out of the bath – it took her three goes at it – she felt cleansed, free almost, as if a weight she'd not even been aware that she had been carrying had lifted from her heart. Wrapping a towel around herself, she hobbled into the bedroom to make a hot drink.

'Oh, hello,' she said, surprised and a little embarrassed to see Roberto. He had probably heard her howling away, lying in the bath.

Roberto was making tea, English tea, studiously pouring boiling water over the teabag. He smiled at her, but his eyes were wary. He was still in his running gear, but he'd been busy while she'd been washing her sorrows away, she saw, when she noticed the bed. He'd spread a towel over it, placed a pillow at the foot end, and a bottle of massage oil next to it.

Oh!

He saw her looking. 'I have made tea,' he said, adding the milk and passing her the cup. 'Drink it first, then I will massage your legs.'

Oh my! The tingle went all the way to her toes. Though to be fair, they were probably tingling because she'd spent roughly five hours pounding them into raw meat, and another thirty minutes immersing them in scalding water. Tess was actually pleasantly surprised that she could feel them at all.

Tess took a few sips, the hot liquid reviving her instantly (there was little that a cup of tea couldn't help with, her mother claimed), and she eyed the towel with a mixture of excitement and trepidation.

Was a massage the only thing on offer, or did he have plans to take things further? More to the point, would she let him?

After all, he hadn't even kissed her yet.

'Lie down,' he instructed, and Tess took a step closer to the bed, wondering what she should do with the towel she was wearing. She glanced at him anxiously.

'Keep the towel on,' he suggested, when she made a tentative move to discard it. 'I want to work on your legs.'

Tess secured it more firmly around her boobs, then lay down on her front, where she could hear him but couldn't see him. The anticipation of his hands on her skin was excruciating. The bed dipped as he sat by her feet, and she tensed when he pushed the long, fluffy towel up her legs to expose the tops of her thighs – and he chuckled at her sharp intake of breath when he tucked the fabric around her, protecting her modesty.

He popped the cap on the bottle of oil, and she heard him squirt some into his hand. Then she waited, breath held, to feel his fingers on her skin, letting out a sigh when he finally touched her.

Lightly at first, he slid his palms up and down her thighs, giving her time to get used to the sensation of his hands on her body, and she gradually relaxed. He must have sensed some of the tension leaking out of her, because his strokes became firmer as he worked his fingers deeper into her muscles.

'Ow!' she cried.

'Do you want me to stop?'

'No, no, don't stop.'

'I don't want to hurt you.'

'But I want you to.'

'Excuse me?' His voice was full of laughter.

'It hurts, but in a nice way. Oh, ow!'

He had the most wonderful hands in the world. The muscles in her thigh were almost crying, but she meant it when she said the pain was a good pain; she could feel her left leg unknotting as he worked on it, though she kept having to bite back whimpers of pain.

Moving to her calf, he made her cry out again. 'Bloody hell, that hurts!' she yelped, her voice muffled by the pillow – she wasn't entirely sure whether he'd put it there to support her head, or if she was meant to bite down on it.

He dug his fingers right into the calf muscle and even underneath it, running his thumb along the bone until she was almost sobbing. She had no idea calves could hurt so much, or be so knotted.

Aware she sounded as though she was being tortured, Tess buried her head further into the pillow and tried to control her whimpering, but by the time he moved to her foot, her howls were so loud she hoped the rooms either side of hers were empty, because if anyone was listening they would think she was being murdered.

And Roberto had only worked on one leg – he had another one to go!

By the time he'd finished, Tess was totally and utterly drained. When he used a spare towel to rub the excess oil from her skin, she didn't even have enough energy left to wonder what he was going to do next.

The brush of his lips on the back of her neck was so light that she wondered if she'd imagined it, but when he kissed her between her shoulder blades, she knew she hadn't.

This was it – they were going to make love. Languidly, she turned over and squirmed onto her back. When she saw the expression on his face, it nearly stole her breath. His eyes were darker than she'd ever seen them, and his lips were parted. He looked as if he wanted to eat her, inch by glorious inch. She closed her eyes and waited for the inevitable.

This man made her feel like she was the most precious, beautiful woman in the world. And life was for living, right? No more hiding in the shadows, no more "what ifs". If this was all they had, and they never saw each other again, then so be it. No one else had to know except her, and as long as she was happy with it, that was all that mattered.

She waited, and she waited.

Then she opened her eyes.

Roberto was wiping his oily hands with a tissue, uncertainty crossing his face. 'You need to rest,' he said.

No, no, what I need is you, she wanted to say, but she saw that the desire had left his eyes, and Tess couldn't bring herself to beg.

She sat up and he tugged at the sheet on the bed, drawing it back.

'Get in, and rest,' he instructed, and she did as she was told, knowing he was right – again. She was deathly tired, and though the massage had eased some of the ache from her muscles, she realized just how wiped out she was. A huge yawn took her by surprise.

With another yawn, she crawled up the bed, hanging on to her towel for dear life, then she slipped between the cool sheets and knew no more.

—

The smell of coffee flooded her nose and she licked her lips thirstily. Gosh, she felt awful – like she'd been run over by a truck. Everything ached, including her eyeballs. Was she ill—?

No, wait… it started to come back – the rush of adrenalin at the start, the endless miles, the long straight roads, the urge to stop, to throw in the towel, to—

Talking of towels, she seemed to recall that at some point Roberto had sensually massaged her legs whilst she'd been wrapped in one. She felt underneath her. Not a dream then, because the towel was still there.

Coffee? *Roberto!*

Forcing her reluctant eyes open – though Tess already had an idea of what she'd see – she looked straight into the eyes of the man who had saved her bacon. Without him, she never would have finished the race. She had some other things to be grateful to him for, too, but she didn't want to go there right now.

What she wanted to do was to drink a well dry.

'Water?' she croaked, making a pathetic attempt to sit up.

Roberto had changed out of his running gear, and was sporting a pair of chinos and an open-necked shirt. His hair was damp, and Tess realized he must have gone back to his own place to shower and change.

He folded the newspaper he had been reading and put it on the small table, then got to his feet and walked over to the minibar.

Cold water. Gimme, gimme, Tess thought thirstily, holding out her hands and making a grabby motion.

He poured her a glass and gave it to her.

She drank it down and held the empty vessel out, expecting it to be refilled.

Roberto shook his head. 'No, not yet. Let your stomach get used to it. I don't want to have to clean up...' He made retching noises.

Tess cleared her throat. 'Sick,' she supplied, feeling the water seeping into every cell. 'What day is it?'

'It is still Sunday.' Roberto checked his watch. 'Five thirty in the afternoon. How are you feeling?'

'Bleh.' She'd only been asleep for a few hours and she could probably do with more, if she was honest, but she was so thirsty.

His lips twitched. 'Are you still speaking English?'

'Uh huh.' She nodded. 'More?' She held out her glass again.

This time he filled it almost to the brim. 'Drink slowly. You are dehydrated. After this, I will make you coffee.'

She sipped, staring at him over the rim of the glass. As she started to revive, she was becoming acutely conscious that she didn't have a scrap of make-up on, and her hair was probably a tangled mess. She just hoped that Roberto could get past the hideousness that was post-marathon Tess.

With a groan, she stretched her legs out one at a time, muscles and joints letting her know they weren't amused at what she'd done to them.

Roberto averted his gaze and set about boiling the kettle and making her the promised coffee. Mission accomplished, he placed the steaming cup on the bedside table and picked up his keys.

'Where are you going?' she asked.

'To leave you to get dressed. I will come back for you later. Six thirty?' And with that, he was out of the door, and she was left listening to his receding footsteps as he strode down the corridor.

Thankful that she had some time and privacy to make herself look presentable, and noticing that she was starting to feel hungry, Tess was eager to get ready for dinner. But first, she had to get out of bed. As she tried to get her reluctant legs to work, she realized she was stiffer than a broom handle. It took her ten minutes to ease her achey body from the bed to the bathroom, but with each step she took, movement became that much easier. Her ankles weren't too keen on bending and her knees protested, but it was the muscles in her thighs which were causing her the most discomfort. She did a few careful stretches and gradually they loosened, until she began to feel less like a ninety-year-old with a bad case of arthritis – she vowed to be more sympathetic the next time her grandparents complained of aching joints – and more like herself again.

By the time six thirty came, Tess was feeling almost normal-ish. She'd drunk the rest of the two-litre bottle of water from the minibar and had made another cup of the awful instant coffee; she'd washed her hair, dried it, had pinned it up off the back of her neck, and had applied a smidge of make-up. She'd put on a flowing skirt, a pretty T-shirt and topped it all with a cardi, before grabbing a jacket just in case, and she finally felt able to face the world. As long as she didn't make any sudden moves and wasn't expected to walk more than a few feet, she felt confident she could manage dinner without falling over.

As she waited for six thirty she couldn't believe how kind and thoughtful Roberto had been, or that they'd only met a week or so ago. How many men would run the last quarter of a marathon, provide a massage, and stay with her afterwards to make sure she was OK? If someone had asked her a few days ago how she felt about a man who she hardly knew watching her while she slept, she would have been creeped out. But the thought of Roberto quietly slipping off to shower and change, then returning to sit in the chair to read his paper, hadn't concerned her in the slightest. In fact, she was comforted by the thought that he cared.

More to the point, he hadn't made a single move on her. He'd behaved like a perfect gentleman, and now the man in question was on the other end of her mobile, asking her to come down to the lobby whenever she was ready.

She was halfway out of the door before he'd hung up, and she would have been even faster if her legs had worked properly. Her ankles still didn't like bending and the big muscles in her thighs were making themselves known, but she hobbled to the lift (no stairs for her today) as fast as she could.

'You look better,' Roberto said, coming forward to greet her, his hands outstretched to take hers.

'I feel better,' she confirmed, as he enfolded her into a hug. She breathed in the scent of him. It felt so right being in his arms that she let out a little sigh of disappointment when he pulled back slightly.

His face was inches from hers as he stared into her eyes, as if to make sure she wasn't lying and that she really was as OK as she claimed to be. Tess stared back, and with each second that passed she fell deeper into his gaze, until the only thing in the world was him and those dark, dark depths.

At first, the touch of his lips was barely there, as light and as soft as silk, but then she let out the gentlest of sighs and her own lips parted. Flinging caution to the wind, Tess let herself go, falling into the moment, and the kiss deepened, sending shivers right through her. She was aware she was trembling slightly, but she couldn't seem to stop.

Her soft whimper of dismay when he dragged his mouth from hers and drew back made him chuckle, and a cough from behind the reception desk brought Tess back to the present. Oh hell, she'd almost jumped Roberto right in the middle of the hotel's lobby. What must he think of her? She fanned her face with her hands and laughed self-consciously. It had been a long time since a man had had the kind of effect on her to almost make her lose control in public. If anyone actually ever had…

'Let's eat,' Roberto said, his voice hoarse. 'I'm taking you somewhere special, and I hope you'll like it.'

Maybe having something to eat was a good idea; she needed time to reflect a little, time to gain some control and perspective. She knew her face was glowing, and she bit her lip in chagrin. She was acting like a girl experiencing her first kiss. But what a kiss it had been!

'Where are you taking me?' Tess asked, as she folded herself stiffly into the passenger seat of the sleek black number (thank God Roberto wasn't driving his own rust bucket) and buckled her seat belt. By now she was familiar enough with the city to know that they were heading out of it, rather than into its heart, as Roberto started to drive.

'A little place in the hills. The food, it is—' He paused and brought bunched fingers to his lips and kissed the tips. '*Magnifico*. You will enjoy it.'

This time she enjoyed the journey more, having not felt the need to grab onto anything – she shuddered to think of Roberto driving his own car back down these steep and twisting roads in the dark. Before long, and without any cursing, he was pulling up in front of what looked like a modest old farmhouse, not a restaurant.

Tess was intrigued. This didn't seem like the sort of place many tourists would frequent, and she looked forward to some authentic Spanish cooking.

'*Abuela? Soy Roberto, y he traido a alguien,*' Roberto called, as he pushed open the door and walked straight into what looked like someone's living room.

Tess hung back, uncertainly. This wasn't what she'd been expecting at all, but a wonderful smell of garlic and herbs filled the air, so she guessed some cooking must be taking place. She just hoped they hadn't barged in uninvited on a random family's supper.

An old woman, her face creased with wrinkles, bustled into the room. No more than four foot six, she was as tall as she was round, and wore an eye-catching array of patterned skirt, patterned blouse and a pinny with huge sunflowers on it. But her expression was warm, her eyes crinkling up until they almost disappeared into the folds of her skin, while a wide grin, which showed off several missing teeth, lit up her face.

The little old lady was the epitome of what Tess thought a granny should look like.

She moved towards Tess, holding out her arms, and enfolded her into a hug. Then the old lady stepped back a little before reaching up to cup Tess's face with surprisingly strong, gnarled hands.

A flurry of Spanish ensued, and from the tone and by the way Roberto either shook his head or nodded, Tess guessed the old lady was asking the questions and Roberto was providing the answers. Whatever passed between them, Tess sensed she was welcome and that maybe she had passed some test, for when the old lady finally let go of Tess's face, her smile was so wide it almost split the little wrinkled face in two.

'This is Celestina, my father's mother,' Roberto said, wrapping an arm around the old woman's shoulders and giving her an affectionate squeeze.

Grandmother? Was Roberto really introducing her to his family so soon? Tess mentally paused for a second, before coming to the conclusion that this was probably simple hospitality on Roberto's part. He wanted to show her some traditional Spanish home cooking, and he must think that his grandmother was the best person for that.

Her tummy gurgled loudly, and Celestina laughed, reaching forward to pat Tess on the stomach, whilst firing a string of words at her.

Roberto translated. 'Abuela thinks you need more fat on you. She says you are too skinny.' He said something to his grandmother and translated again. 'I told her you have just run *la maratón*, and this is why you are so thin and hungry.'

Her? Thin? Hardly! She wasn't plump any more, but she certainly wasn't thin, either. But she was most definitely hungry!

Roberto took her jacket whilst Celestina retreated to the kitchen. Tess sat on an old, blanket-covered sofa, listening to the cooking noises emanating from the other room, as Roberto laid the table and opened a bottle of wine.

While Tess sipped, letting the berry flavours settle on her tongue, she looked about her. The house hadn't appeared very big from the outside, but the living room was actually quite spacious, if somewhat old-fashioned. The stone-tiled floor sported a couple of rugs, and on top of those sat a sofa and a pair of comfy chairs, all covered with bright throws. The walls were whitewashed, and the furniture was heavy, dark and very solid. Knick-knacks were in abundance, and a small painting of the Virgin Mary sat on a sideboard at the other end of the room, surrounded by candles.

Roberto noticed her interest. 'Abuela is a good Catholic,' he explained. 'She goes to mass and says prayers to the Holy Mother every day. She is also one of the best cooks in Catalonia,' he added, proudly.

He was right, Tess realized, when she was invited to sit at the solid, scrubbed table. The food was delicious. Much of the conversation flowing around her was in a foreign language, so Tess was able to concentrate more on her meal, except when Roberto translated.

In between mouthfuls of scrumptious pork with red pepper and almond sauce, Tess was quizzed about where she lived, what work she did, and what her family was like. It was actually quite nice that Roberto translated his grandmother's questions and her own replies, when he could simply answer them all himself, and leave Tess out of the conversation completely. She was struck again by just how considerate and thoughtful he was.

'*Sí, muy hermosa,*' Celestina cried, clapping her hands together and following it up with a stream of Spanish, when Tess – via Roberto – told the old lady that she had a younger sister.

Tess looked at Roberto.

'Abuela says my sisters are very beautiful, but they have yet to give her *bisnietos* – great-grandchildren. She tells them to hurry, because she might die tomorrow.'

Tess was shocked. 'Is your grandmother ill?'

'No,' Roberto laughed. 'She is' – he waved his hands in the air – 'dramatic.' He reached across the table, covering his grandmother's tiny hand in one of his much larger ones. 'Abuela will live for a long time, but she is convinced that women should have children early, before their...' He paused as his grandmother spoke, then grimaced. 'She says, before their eggs go bad,' he finished, with a tolerant shake of his head and a wry smile.

Celestina spoke again, pointing at Tess and patting her own stomach.

'Oh, no more for me, thanks, I'm full. It was delicious!' Tess said.

Roberto looked away, and Celestina jabbered at him again. 'That was not what she was saying,' he said eventually, clearly embarrassed. 'Abuela told me to say that you need to find yourself a husband and have babies before it's too late. I'm sorry, but she is old and her views on life and marriage are, too.'

When Celestina spoke again, Roberto blushed.

'What did she say?' Tess asked, bemused. She had never seen Roberto so disconcerted before – it was quite sweet.

'Please, this is not from me, I don't say this,' Roberto said. 'This is from my grandmother. *Vale, vale*, OK, OK,' he said to Celestina, as she pointed to him then to Tess and flapped her hands at her grandson.

'She thinks you are lovely, and that I should marry you,' Roberto said, biting his lip, though whether it was from mortification, or because he was trying not to laugh, Tess couldn't tell.

After a pause, during which Celestina smiled widely and nodded her head, Roberto said, 'Take it as a compliment. In the past she hasn't thought anyone was good enough for me.'

Tess's mind swirled like water going down a drain, thoughts following swiftly one after the other. An image of Ana-Sofía popped into her head, but she pushed it away. Then she said the second thing that came into her head, but as the words left her lips she could have kicked herself.

'I'm not good enough,' she said. She lived a thousand miles away, came from a different culture, couldn't speak Spanish, and was as far from the passionate, beautiful and elegant Ana-Sofía as she could possibly get.

'My grandmother thinks you are. She thinks the reason I brought you here is for her to give her approval.'

'But have you explained to her that we only met a week ago?' Tess protested.

'I did, and she says it doesn't matter, that love doesn't depend on time. She chooses to ignore the fact that we haven't known each other for long, and Abuela is very good at ignoring what she doesn't like.'

'But… but…' Tess spluttered.

'Abuela is old, and her beliefs are, too. I told her I wanted to show a visitor what proper cooking is, in a proper home, but she thinks I have another reason for bringing you here.'

'Have you?' Tess asked quietly.

Roberto smiled sadly, and Tess's heart did a little flip-flop. 'Maybe. I brought you to meet my grandmother because I like you, and I very much want you to stay in Barcelona.'

Lordy, but this was suddenly becoming rather heavy and intense, and slightly uncomfortable, even if their audience of one was unable to understand a single word they were saying.

'I like you too, Roberto,' Tess admitted, 'but I go home in two days.'

'I know, and I have told Abuela this, also.' He turned back to his grandmother and gave her another pat on the hand.

There was something very touching about the way Roberto behaved with the old lady. As far as Tess could tell (the language barrier was a bit of a hindrance), Roberto wasn't condescending or patronising. He radiated love and warmth towards his grandmother, and was quick to include the old woman in the three-way conversation. He also insisted on doing the dishes, which Tess thought was quite cute, considering the chore was probably one he did in work every day.

Leaving Tess alone with Celestina, he carried the plates into the kitchen, after waving away Tess's offer to help.

'You talk to Abuela,' he said. Although how much talking Tess could do was debatable, so she resorted to pointing at things and smiling instead.

'This is pretty,' she said, pointing to the vase full of blue flowers in the centre of the table.

Celestina didn't appear to be at all interested in flowers: instead of answering Tess, the old woman leaned forward and made a grab for Tess's hand. 'Roberto, he good boy, *muy bueno*. He love *tu*.'

'Eh?' Tess resisted the urge to snatch her hand back.

Celestina nodded wildly. 'He love...' She pointed at Tess. 'I see. I—?' She pointed to her head and then her heart. 'Here,' she said. 'I see.'

Tess's heart lurched. Did he really love her, or was it just wishful thinking on his grandmother's part? A part of her, a very large part indeed, hoped that Roberto did in fact love her. But it was a bittersweet hope. What good was it to love her when she was leaving in two days? It was bad enough that she loved him, but now it appeared that he too was soon to be as miserable as she knew she was about to be.

The pair of them said their goodbyes, and Tess felt like a total fraud when Celestina wrapped her in a hug and then patted her cheek. Roberto kissed his grandmother's lined face, pulling the old lady close, and whispered into her hair. Celestina smiled and nodded, and finally, they were out of the door and into the car.

All the way back, Tess was lost in her thoughts, unsure what to do. She so desperately wanted to remain in this beautiful city: she had fallen completely in love with it. Barcelona had everything: awe-inspiring architecture, a medieval heart, swish shops, a stunning harbour, a sweeping beach, the mountains, the café culture – what wasn't there to love? She could seriously see herself living there, painting, working, and immersing herself in everything the city had to offer.

And then there was Roberto. He was making it easier for her dream to become a reality by his thoughtfulness. A ready-made apartment, the possibility of a job to tide her over until her painting was established... In some ways, her life there wouldn't be much different from back home. But, in other ways, it would be totally transformed.

And there was still the *problem* of Roberto. Her thoughts kept circling back to him, but how could they not, when she was as much in love with him as she was with his city?

The question was: was he in love with her, too, as his grandmother had suggested, or was he simply being a nice person? She was pretty sure he was attracted to her, but being attracted wasn't the same as being in love, was it? And if he didn't have the same feelings for her as she had for him, would she be able to stay there knowing they would never be anything more than friends?

She tried to take Roberto out of the picture, to consider the option without letting her feelings get in the way, but it was impossible. And if someone had asked her, before she had left England, if she would live in Barcelona, she guessed she would have had the same dilemma. Could she take the plunge and move to a foreign city, and leave everything and everyone behind? Was she strong enough?

She had no answer to that.

Before she knew it, the car was pulling into the kerb, and they were outside her hotel. Roberto cut the engine and gave her a cautious glance. 'You aren't annoyed that I took you to visit my grandmother?' he asked. Tess could see the worry in his eyes.

'No, it was fantastic. Thank you,' she replied. 'Your grandmother is lovely and you're right, she's a wonderful cook.'

'It has been a nice evening, no?'

'Yes.'

'Then I am happy,' he said, and he kissed her until she was breathless.

And to her surprise, when he walked her to the hotel's doors, Tess realized she was happy, too. In fact, she was far *too* happy, and that wasn't exactly making her decision any easier.

–

Exhausted but unable to settle because of all the thoughts spinning around in her head, Tess made a cup of tea, changed into her night things, and lay on the bed, propping herself up with several pillows. Then she picked up her phone and started to scroll.

She'd received loads of texts and had missed a couple of calls, but she'd deliberately put her phone on silent earlier, not wanting their meal to be interrupted, so now she set to work replying to family and friends, and smiling as she read the messages of congratulations.

One of them was from Carol, the editor she had worked with on the adult fairy tale book.

> How did you do? Did you make it around the course in under six hours?

Tess texted back:

Not bad – four hours, fifty-seven.

It was quite late in the evening, and she didn't expect a reply, so was surprised when her phone pinged a reply.

That's good for a first time out. How are you feeling?

Ha! Good question! Physically, she was both better and worse than she had anticipated. She wasn't hurting as much as she thought she would be (which was probably due to Roberto's care), but although she was totally and utterly exhausted, her brain was whirling around at ninety miles an hour, keeping her very firmly awake.

Emotionally, she was a wreck, and a whole gamut of feelings were still cascading through her mind – elation that she had completed the marathon, regret that Emma hadn't been by her side, and sorrow that she'd had to run it at all (if Ella had still been alive, the subject of running a marathon for charity may never had raised its head).

And then there was Roberto. Again.

Every thought, every emotion, circled back to him and how she felt about him, and his suggestion that she stay in Barcelona. Bless him, he really thought he was trying to make the decision easier for her, when in reality he had made things ten times harder. Without anywhere to live, she wouldn't even have entertained the idea; it would have been a pipe dream, nothing more. But Roberto had suddenly made it a real possibility.

And then there were her feelings for Roberto. Could she go back home and walk away from the man she loved?

She texted back:

Shattered. Can't sleep tho.

Planning on doing any more?

Not a chance!

Tess was certain. Though she did feel empowered by the fact that she'd done something that she would have considered impossible a few months ago – which was why she was caught in such a dilemma now. Before the marathon she probably wouldn't have had the courage to even think about doing… what she was thinking about doing. But, post-marathon, she felt she could do anything, that nothing was beyond her. Part of it was the realisation that back in October she had thought that for her to run a marathon was an impossibility. The other part was the realisation that she had her own life to lead, and that Emma did, too. She didn't have to be there for her sister so much any more. Emma was getting on with her life, living it the way she wanted. Now it was time for Tess to do the same.

I have another commission for you.

Carol's text stated, breaking into her thoughts.

I'll email you the details.

That's wonderful. I'll start it when I get back home.

When I get back home. The words made her heart sink. Yes, she was missing her family, but…

She desperately wanted to talk to someone, but that someone couldn't be her parents – not at this hour, at least, and they were too emotionally invested in her returning home to give her impartial advice. Nor could it be Emma, for much the same reason. Though Tess might have realized it was time she let go a little, she wasn't sure her sister would feel the same way. No, Emma wouldn't be the best person to seek advice from.

Tess spotted a text from Faye and a missed call, and she checked the time. It was late, but Faye might be up. Rather than calling and risk waking her friend, Tess sent a text.

Are you awake? If not, don't worry, I'll call you tomorrow.

She had no sooner pressed 'Send' when her phone rang.

'Well done, you!' Faye cried as soon as Tess answered. 'I'm so proud of you! I knew you could do it.'

'Thanks.'

Faye picked up on Tess's tone immediately. 'What's wrong?'

'Nothing's wrong,' Tess protested. 'Anyway, never mind me, how are you?'

'Still the same.' A deep sigh came down the phone. 'Hugh…?'

'I really don't want to talk about him right now.'

Tess heard the pain in her friend's voice. 'I'm here for you if you do. You know that, don't you?'

'I know, sweetie. Thank you.' Faye cleared her throat. 'Right, Tess, I know something's up, so you might as well tell me now, because I'll only winkle it out of you when you get home.'

Tess hesitated, then decided to come clean. After all, that was one of the reasons she was speaking to Faye, besides returning her friend's call. 'I've had an offer to stay in Barcelona,' she announced, then had to hold the phone away from her ear as Faye shrieked loudly.

'That's wonderful! How? Who? What— I mean, tell me about it!'

'I will if you stop shouting.' Tess couldn't help laughing.

Faye lowered her voice to a loud hiss. 'Of course, you're right. Shit! I nearly woke the bloody kids up.'

'How are my gorgeous godchildren?'

'You'll have to pop round to see them when you get back. *If* you get back,' Faye amended.

'Oh, I'll be back,' Tess said, doing a pathetic Arnie impersonation. 'I have to – I've got too many loose ends to tie up.'

'So, you're definitely staying in Barcelona, then?'

'That's the thing; I'm not sure.'

'Tell me all about it,' Faye said, and Tess did exactly that.

Unusually for Faye, she managed to remain silent as Tess told her friend about Roberto – how they met, what he did for a living, how she'd fallen for him, how kind and thoughtful he was, his offer of the apartment…

When Tess finally ran out of steam, Faye said, 'And the problem *is*—?'

'What if he doesn't feel the same way about me?'

'But what if he does?' Faye countered. 'Look, I'm not the best advocate for happily ever after, but you've got to seize the chance of love with both hands. So what if he just wants to be friends? You'll be no worse off being in Barcelona than if you come home, and at least you'll be in a fantastic city. Besides, if things don't work out, you can always get on a plane. It's not as if it's a life sentence, is it?'

'No, but…'

'I can tell you're scared, but Tess, you've got to take chances in life. And love is one of those things you simply have to take a chance on. There are no guarantees, but I will guarantee one thing.' Faye paused.

'What?'

'You'll regret it if you don't.'

Faye was right – Tess would regret it, and the last thing she wanted was to get to old age and think 'What if…?'

'Right then, send me a photo,' Faye demanded. 'What's his name again?'

'Roberto,' Tess said, thumbing through her photos for a nice picture of them both.

Faye sighed. 'Roberto *what*?'

'Roberto Pérez Montero.'

'That's a mouthful.'

Tess laughed. 'It's Spanish, you dolt! Anyway, why do you want to know?'

'Is he on Facebook?'

'I've no idea, I never thought to ask him. I don't use it much myself, to be honest.'

'You'll have to use it when you move to Barcelona,' Faye insisted. 'I want to live vicariously through you, so you'll have to post lots of photos. It's going to be so exciting!' Her friend let out another squeal.

'It's not going to be all that different,' Tess started to say, before Faye interrupted her.

'Of course it bloody well is!' she cried. 'Bugger, I didn't mean to shout, but I'm so used to having to speak louder than a pair of noisy kids in order to be heard that my volume button doesn't seem to be working. I hope I haven't woken one of the little blighters up. I'll see if I can friend him on Facebook, or follow him on Twitter. That way, I can see what you're getting up to, because you're hopeless at posting stuff on social media.'

Faye was right, Tess was hopeless at that sort of thing. 'Don't you go harassing the poor man,' she warned, with a laugh. 'I don't want my troll friend to scare him off.'

'Would I do such a thing?'

'Yes!'

'I've gotta go.' Faye let out a resigned sigh. 'Charlie's just woken up. Give me a call tomorrow, yeah, and let me know what you've decided. But be warned – I won't be happy if you decide to come home.'

Tess snuggled down and pulled the duvet up to her chin. Trust Faye to be all for the idea. She had always been the more adventurous of the two of them. But Tess valued her opinion and, deep down, she knew Faye was right.

Tess was going to take Roberto up on his offer.

'Ow, ow, ow,' Tess chanted, as she ordered her reluctant body out of bed and tried to ascertain the damage. She seriously wondered if she'd ever walk normally again when it took her a couple of minutes to limp to the bathroom. She'd slept in much later than usual, too, and was shocked to discover that it was almost midday.

A shower and a cup of tea helped, and by the time she was ready for breakfast, she was walking a little easier. She didn't look brilliant, but at least she was no longer shuffling around like a ninety-year-old.

Roberto had told her yesterday that he had to work today, therefore she didn't expect to see him until later. It was a disappointment, she had to admit, because she would have loved to have spent her last day in Barcelona with him, but at least she *was* seeing him.

Too stiff and sore to do much in the way of sightseeing – and, if she was being honest with herself, too tired anyway – she decided to walk the relatively short distance to the Museu Nacional d'Art de Catalunya, and sit in the sun on one of the terraces and watch the world go by. Despite her promise to visit the museum, she wasn't in the mood. Besides, there would be plenty of time for visiting all those places she hadn't yet managed to fit into her incredibly packed week, and she was really looking forward to having Roberto by her side when she did so.

She thought she might do some sketching instead – slow, leisurely strokes of the pencil, and not the frantic drawing which had driven her earlier sessions. Having all the time in the world made a whole lot of difference. Suddenly the pace of life seemed to slow.

Leaving the hotel, Tess decided that rather than the dash from one landmark to another, she would pass to the side of one of the two massive red-brick towers (she kept meaning to ask Roberto what they were) and wander down the Avinguda de la Reina Maria Cristina. The small fountains lining the wide road were still for the moment. Once over the little road bridge, she turned to the left and headed towards a stall selling drinks and snacks, and sat down at one of the tables to devour her *bocadillo* (she'd learned a new word – the first of many, if she intended to become fluent), and drink her coffee.

One baguette (*bocadillo* actually meant 'snack' but it also seemed to refer to baguettes) and two cups of strong coffee later, Tess still didn't feel like moving. And neither did she feel like drawing the fountain, nor the fairy-tale palace that housed the museum.

Instead she took out her pad and her charcoals, and began to draw from memory. It took a while to get the spark in his eyes just right, and his lips took a couple of attempts before she was happy with the shape of them and the hint of a smile, but when she'd finished and held the picture at arm's length, she was pleased to see she had captured perfectly the expression on Roberto's face when he had looked at her in the mirror in the bridal shop yesterday. And she hoped she could tell exactly what the expression was…

Love.

Smiling softly to herself, Tess fixed the drawing with her spray and leaned back in her chair, waiting for it to dry. She wanted to phone Roberto to tell him she'd made her decision, but as eager as she was to share the news, she really wanted to tell him face to face, to see his reaction. She also needed to tell him that she would be returning to England tomorrow. She *had* to – there were too many things to do, too many loose ends to tie up. And then there was Emma and her parents. She could hardly send them a text saying, "By the way, I'm not coming home", could she? This was a conversation she needed to have in person, no matter how difficult it might be. She had visions of all three of them trying to persuade her not to come back to Barcelona, that she was being silly, or irresponsible, or naïve, and she dreaded the tears (from her mother, at least) when she made them see how serious she was.

It wasn't going to be easy and she'd probably feel as guilty as hell for moving a thousand miles away, but this was her life and she had to live it the way she thought best. She wanted no regrets when she was older, and she had a feeling that if she allowed herself to be talked out of it, she would grow to resent those responsible.

So, tomorrow she had to go home, however much she didn't want to. The thought of not seeing Roberto, even for the few days it would take to sort her life out and arrange a flight back – who was she kidding, it would probably be more like a couple of weeks – filled her with an ache so deep she thought her heart might break.

And it was this intense emotion that made her see that she had made the right decision – imagine how much worse it would be if this truly was her last day and she was never to see him again? She didn't think she could survive it.

Tess treated herself to a hot chocolate and *churros*, feeling quite decadent as she sucked the liquid up through the pastry, and let life ebb and flow around her, enjoying the sensation of not having anything to do and nowhere to go. She felt cleansed, renewed and, in some strange, laid-back way, revitalized. And happy – really, really happy.

'I want to show you the beach, and I want to buy you an ice cream,' Roberto announced, when he picked her up later.

Tess laughed. 'Why an ice cream?'

'Because that's what you eat when you walk on the beach. Can you swim?' he asked suddenly.

'Yes, but I'm not going in the sea. It's not warm enough for that.'

'Not even to… how do you say… feet in?'

'Paddle. Maybe, we'll see.'

Roberto was driving the boss's car again, though they didn't go far in it. The beach was a ten-minute drive, and they parked in practically the same spot as when Roberto had taken her to the posh restaurant next to the harbour. They retraced their steps down the wide street with the boats on one side and shops on the other, but instead of turning around and walking back the same way, they kept going. Gradually, the buildings opened up into a promenade with the blue expanse of the Mediterranean on the left. And a beach.

The city by the sea certainly lived up to its name.

Tess was enchanted by the wide beach disappearing into the distance, and as soon as they stepped down onto the sand, she kicked off her pumps, delighting in the feel of the warm sand between her toes and the gentle, salty breeze ruffling her hair.

Despite her half-hearted protestations about it being too cold and the risk of getting wet, Tess allowed herself to be led to the water's edge where the small waves lapped, and she dipped her toes into the surf. The sea was rather on the chilly side, but her feet and ankles soon got used to it. The waves were actually more like wavelets, so neither of them got splashed too much, except for when Tess kicked water at Roberto, then ran off squealing when he tried to do the same to her.

She charged off down the beach at a rate of knots, giggling like a fool, Roberto hot on her heels. The sand squished between her toes, and she kicked up little spurts as she ran. He quickly caught her, grabbing her around the waist and pulling her into him, and she leaned against his chest, laughing too hard to stay upright, as he held her firm to stop her from collapsing into the sea.

'Shall I drop you?' he threatened, scooping her up into his arms and holding her tight.

'No, please, I'm sorry,' she cried, not meaning a word of it.

'You are a witch,' he said into her hair. 'You should be thrown into the water as punishment.'

'For what? Because your jeans are a bit wet? Aw, bless. Eek!!'

Roberto swung her around, almost but not quite releasing her. He was up to mid-calf in the waves, and if she fell now, she'd be soaked.

'For enchanting me, witch, that's why,' he said. Abruptly the playfulness was gone, and in its place was a serious face and a sombre tone. He stared intently into her eyes.

'I've enchanted you?' she repeated softly, lying quietly in his arms, her own wrapped around his neck and feeling the warmth of his skin. She played with the little hairs on the back of his neck, feeling their silkiness, and she breathed in the scent of him, her heart fluttering.

'You have, but I forgive you,' he murmured, and with infinite slowness he bent his head. His mouth claimed hers, softly at first, then growing more insistent as the kiss deepened, and when their lips parted, both of them were breathless.

'I love you, Tess,' he said, and her heart felt so full of love she thought she might burst.

He loved her! *He loved her!*

She thrummed with happiness. 'I love you, too,' she whispered, and when he kissed her again she melted into his embrace. It felt so right – *they* felt so right – and she knew she'd made the right decision.

'I'm going home tomorrow,' she said a little later. As the words left her mouth she felt Roberto's whole body tense and he took a deep breath.

'*But,*' she said, winding her arms around him even tighter and kissing his neck, 'only so that I can pack the rest of my things – my art stuff especially – and give notice on my flat and my jobs. And I also need to tell my parents, and Emma.'

'Oh, *mi amor*, I am so happy!' Roberto cried, and swung Tess around until she was giddy and giggling, and begging him to stop.

Finally, Roberto kissed her on the nose and put her down, Tess wobbling slightly, still feeling a little dizzy, but that might well have been from happiness. Without speaking, the love shining in his face saying more than any words ever could, he caught hold of her hand and led her up the beach, back towards the boardwalk. There, Roberto bought Tess the ice cream he'd promised (lemon for her, pistachio for him), and they sat on the edge of the walkway, letting the warm air dry their feet, arms around each other, watching the sun dip towards the horizon, the sky glowing yellow, purple and orange as the stars appeared one by one. It was the most romantic and wonderful evening of Tess's life.

Finally, after another hour spent sitting on the beach, despite how warm and lovely she felt inside, the temperature began to drop and Tess shivered.

'Ready for dinner?' Roberto asked, helping her to her feet.

Brushing sand off her behind and slipping her feet back into her pumps, Tess wondered if she should go back to the hotel and change first. She was hardly dressed for dinner, and she must look a sight with her hair all messed up and sand on her jeans, but when she suggested returning to the hotel, Roberto shook his head.

'You don't need to dress up tonight, not for where we are going,' he said, and instead of returning to the car as she assumed they would, he took her back into the depths of the Gothic Quarter.

The place had an entirely different atmosphere at night – the lights strung across the higher parts of the buildings twinkled like so many tiny stars, but the shadows were deeper, and though light and laughter spilled out onto the cobbles from the many bars and restaurants, and the shops that were still open, the whole area seemed even more *gothic* than it did in daylight. It was magical and thrilling, and she loved very part of it.

When they turned into the street where Roberto worked, Tess assumed they were going to eat at his restaurant, but to her surprise he led her past the entrance, then stopped.

'I wanted our last night together to be special,' he said, unlocking the same door he had unlocked two days before, and ushering her up the same flight of stairs. 'I wanted us to be alone, just you and me.' And she heard the hitch in his voice when he added, 'I thought this was goodbye.'

Her soul filled with love for this wonderful, lovely, considerate man, but he managed to surprise her again, and she gasped when she pushed open the door to the living room and saw what he had planned.

A small table, only big enough for two, sat in front of the balcony, a candle burning in its centre. More candles had been placed around the room and soft music came from a docked iPod. The table was laid with a white cloth, gleaming cutlery and sparkling glasses, and a bottle of red wine was already open.

'Bribery?' she asked.

'A little.' His smile was rueful. 'I thought that if I showed you that every night could be like this, then you might stay. Thank you, Tess, for loving me.'

He stepped towards her and she tilted her head ready for his kiss, but a knock on the door made her jump. Roberto must have been expecting it, for all he said was, 'Our food is here. *Bien.*'

He opened the door and a woman holding a large basket came in. She gave Tess a curious look as she walked past the open living room door and into the kitchen, and Tess heard the sounds of dishes clattering.

When the woman left, Roberto came in, carrying a couple of plates. 'Sit, eat, enjoy,' he instructed, so Tess sat and inhaled the aroma of the dish he placed in front of her.

'Padron peppers, deep fried in olive oil with sea salt,' he said, and she speared one with her fork and popped it in her mouth.

'Oh, yum,' she murmured, as the pepper melted on her tongue, releasing a sweet, salty heat. She ate another, and had soon cleared her plate and was ready for the next course.

While Roberto went to the kitchen to fetch it, Tess thought about the effort he had put into what he had thought was going to be their last evening together, and her heart soared. He had certainly pushed the boat out in the hope that he could change her mind about living in Barcelona. Although, she realized, as wonderful as this was, and as lovely of him to set it all up, the stark reality was that she'd probably be drinking water and living off bread and cheese every night – not wine, and what seemed to her to be à la carte cooking.

He returned with two more plates, and Tess's mouth watered.

'Poached chicken breast, with carrots, beluga lentils and chorizo,' he announced.

Tess tucked in with gusto; the flavours flooding her mouth were the tastes of Barcelona, and she wanted to savour every single one.

They ate in silence, not feeling the need to talk, noises filtering up from the narrow street below and music washing over them. Roberto was the perfect host, refilling her glass, and gazing into her eyes, showing her how much he loved her.

'There is something else,' he said, as the deliciously romantic meal drew to a close, and he returned from the kitchen with two cups of rich, aromatic coffee. 'If you want it, you have a job.'

'A job? What kind of a job?'

'Translation.'

'But I don't speak Spanish!'

'The translation is English to English.'

'I don't understand.'

He delved into the pocket of his jeans and his hand came out holding several pieces of paper. Giving them to her, he waited for her to read them. Tess scanned them quickly: one was a Spanish menu with the English translation underneath; another appeared to be some kind of press release for a company she'd never heard of; the third was a printout of an email. She studied the last one, carefully. Emma had forwarded her similar ones, to try to generate some enthusiasm in Tess. It was from the Barcelona marathon organizers, and she remembered how the pair of them had giggled at the very strange and oddly worded phrases. This one was no different: it had clearly been written by someone whose first language wasn't English, or maybe Google Translate had gone to town on it. Either way, the English was decidedly cringe-making.

'This is appalling,' she said, waving the pieces of paper.

'Can you write them properly?' he asked.

'Of course I can. See this here?' She pointed at random to a sentence and read, '"You can be gifting this to present, and it will be wrapped in paper pretty." It should read something like, "Gift-wrapping is available on request", or "If you wish to send this as a present, we can gift-wrap it for you."'

'Then you have a job!'

Tess wasn't convinced. 'Surely there are others who can do this?'

'Probably.'

'Then why me?'

'Because I asked, and they didn't. There are many companies, little and big, who could benefit from your services, and if you are still worried about paying the bills, there is always bar and restaurant work. I am sure Miguel will find something for you.'

'Oh, Roberto!' This was too much. She couldn't believe the lengths he'd gone to in order to try to persuade her to move to the city, the things he had arranged because he loved her. Her expression must have told him everything because he gathered her to him, crushing her to his chest, and they stood that way until Tess had soaked the front of his shirt with tears, and the faint noises from the street had lessened, and still he held her as though he would never let her go.

With a final kiss on her hair, Roberto released her. 'It is late. What time is your flight?'

'Ten thirty in the morning.'

He looked up and away, and Tess saw that his own eyes were damp. 'Can I drive you to the airport?' His voice broke, and Tess bit back a sob. Leaving him, even for a few days, was going to be sheer torture. She hadn't left yet, and already she couldn't wait to return.

'I'd love you to,' she said, though Emma had already planned the timings and the route to perfection. It would take an hour to get to the terminal, and Tess wanted to be there at least an hour and a half before the gate closed, which meant she'd have to check out of the hotel by seven thirty.

The whole going-home thing didn't seem real. When she tried to picture herself back in her little flat, all that came to mind was her artist's corner, and as she pictured it she realized that what she was really imagining was how her easels would look in the corner of this lovely living room, and how the light would stream through the French windows.

They took their time strolling back to the car, neither of them wanting the evening to end. In some ways, Tess was eager to shove her clothes into her little suitcase and head to the airport, because the sooner she returned to England and sorted everything out, then the sooner she would be back in Barcelona, and in Roberto's arms once more.

When they kissed, as Roberto dropped her off at the hotel, it was as though they would never see one another again, and Tess clung to him as if she would never let him go.

But let him go she did. And, as soon as she reached her room, she started packing. As she rolled up jeans and T-shirts, and laid out clean clothes for the morning, her stomach churned, both at the thought of leaving him at the airport, and at the thought of telling her family about him. The next few days were going to be a bit of an ordeal in more ways than one, she anticipated.

Damn it – her phone had died.

She'd been so wrapped up in Roberto that she hadn't even thought to look at it, and when she plugged it in, she saw she had several texts from Emma and a couple of missed calls: one from her mum, and one from Faye.

She did the dutiful daughter bit and rang her mother back first.

'Yes, I'll be careful, and no, I haven't forgotten where I parked the car,' she responded to her mum's warnings and worries about her impending flight. Then she texted Emma back.

Oh! She noticed that Faye had texted her, too:

CALL ME!!! URGENT!!

Tess, her heart in her mouth, rang Faye's number. *Please God, let the children be all right*, she prayed, as she waited for her friend to answer.

'What's wrong?' she cried, as soon as Faye picked up.

242

'Er… hi, Tess.'

'What is it?' she yelled. 'Tell me! Is it one of the children?'

'What? No, they're fine, honest. It's er… your fella,' Faye began.

'My fella? Eh?' What on earth was Faye on about? 'Do you mean Roberto?'

'Er… yeah. You did say he was a waiter in a tapas bar, didn't you?'

'Yes—?' Tess had no idea what was going on.

'What did you say his name was again?' Faye asked.

'Why?' Tess demanded.

'Look, I'm not sure, but I want to check something. Please, Tess, trust me for a minute.'

'Roberto Pérez Montero,' Tess said. 'But what's all this about?'

'Hang on a sec. I'm putting you on speaker.'

Tess heard the sounds of a computer keyboard, then silence, then a long, drawn out sigh. 'I'm sending you a link,' Faye said, and Tess waited anxiously for it to come through. She had no idea what was going on, but she had a really bad feeling about it, just the same.

A ping.

Tess examined the link before she clicked on it – a Wikipedia page. Frowning, she did as she was asked and followed it. And was totally unprepared for what she saw.

Roberto Pérez Montero appeared. *A* Roberto Pérez Montero – but Tess wasn't sure if it was *her* Roberto. The date of birth looked plausible but there wasn't a photograph. The only thing the brief couple of sentences told her was that this Roberto was the son of Miguel Pérez Hurtado, 'the Catalonian business magnate', and Valentina Montero Alvárez.

And that was it.

Miguel, as in Roberto's boss? Surely it was a coincidence? It must be – Faye had no idea how common both names were. It might be the Spanish equivalent of her Googling 'John Smith' and watching how many thousands of hits came up.

'So?' she said to Faye. 'It probably isn't him.'

'Wait, that's not all.'

Several more links came through and Tess clicked on them all. And suddenly her phone was filled with images of Roberto's handsome face. Sometimes he was on his own, sometimes he was with other people, and in some of them he was with women – beautiful women.

Every time she clicked and scrolled, a piece of her heart seemed to shrivel, because all too often Ana-bloody-Sofia's face was smack-bang next to his, looking into the lens with a beatific smile, or gazing up at Roberto adoringly. Tess thought her heart was going to shatter, it hurt so much seeing them together. They looked the perfect couple: both tall, both dark, both of them seriously good-looking.

'Tess?' Faye's voice was cautious. 'I'm sending you another one.'

Tess's eyes widened at a photo of Roberto and her on a Spanish gossip webpage. It must have been taken earlier that day, while they were on the beach. He was holding her in his arms, and they were kissing. It was a lovely photo of the pair of them, but it was the caption above it that turned Tess's heart to ice:

Has the Tapas Prince Found Himself a New Princess?

'He's famous, *really* famous,' Faye was saying, as Tess continued to stare blankly at the screen. 'Well, he is in Barcelona, anyway, and maybe in the whole of Spain.'

'He's not really a waiter, is he?' Tess whispered down the phone.

Faye said, 'No, love. He's the son of that Miguel Pérez Hurtado person, "the Catalonian business magnate". This Hurtado guy owns half the restaurants in Catalonia.'

'It says here,' Tess said woodenly, reading the page, 'that he's set to take over the family business, but has fallen out with his father and— hang on. There's a photo of the man I saw Roberto talking to in one of the tapas bars, I'm certain of it. It says here that he's Roberto's father.'

She let out a shaky breath. 'I should have known – I saw him coming out of one of the most expensive apartment buildings in Barcelona, and he's been driving this fantastic car, a Mercedes I think, but when I asked him about it, he said the apartment belonged to his boss, Miguel, and so did the car.'

'I suppose he's not strictly lying, if you can call your father your boss,' Faye pointed out, reasonably.

'I should have realized,' Tess repeated. 'I knew there was something dodgy about him. He dresses really well, and wears this gold watch, but I thought it was a fake and that his clothes were… oh, I don't know, copies or something, and he told me he lived with his friend Diego, and that he worked in the tapas bar below the apartment he'd found for me.'

She bit back a sob. 'I feel like such a fool. He probably owns the damned building, or at least, his family does. What did he see in me, eh? Did he enjoy making me look a total bloody idiot?' Tess was crying now, tears pouring down her face.

'I'm sure he didn't,' Faye tried to say, but Tess headed her off.

'What do you know about what his motives are?' she cried, then barked out a horrible laugh. 'Actually, I think you probably know more about him than I do.' She swiped a hand across her face angrily, dashing her tears away. 'I'm such an *idiot*.'

'No, you're not,' Faye said. 'You're in love, and from what you told me yesterday, so is he. He must have a perfectly good explanation for not telling you who he really is.'

'Maybe he's married,' Tess said, fresh tears trickling down her cheeks.

'Do you really think so?' Faye asked.

'I've no idea, but if he is I didn't know. I'd never do that to another woman.'

'I don't think he is,' Faye said. 'I don't think I read anything about a wife. There is one woman whose name keeps coming up, but he's definitely not married to her.'

'Not yet,' Tess said brokenly, staring at her phone again. 'She's called Ana-Sofía something or other.'

'Yes, that's her. Ana-Sofía Medina Sierra,' Faye said curiously. 'How did you know I was going to say her name?'

'Because we've met – twice – and the first time she accused me of being a gold-digger. Now I know what she meant. Roberto insists there's nothing between them, but she's awfully jealous and emotional for a woman he's not had a relationship with.'

Tess clambered off the bed and headed for the minibar and the little bottles of alcohol it contained. Opening the first one she came to she drank it straight down, then opened another.

Tess told her friend, 'The other night we went to some fancy, harbour-side restaurant, and I should have realized something was up then. I think I did know, but Roberto was so convincing. I bet it was his father's restaurant, because when we arrived the maître d' came over and Roberto started speaking to him in Spanish, even though the man spoke perfectly good English. Roberto must have been warning him not to spill the beans. Then there were these girls on another table, and they seemed to know him. He claimed that one of them was a friend of his sister's and I should have twigged then, because how would the sister of a waiter have a friend who could afford to eat in a place like that? Looking back, I bet they told Ana-Sofía we were there, because when we were outside she appeared. She had a bit of a go at Roberto and was shouting, and that's when she called me a gold-digger. I thought something had got lost in translation, but it hadn't, had it?'

Tess took a breath, and Faye dived in. 'According to this article in *¡HOLA!* magazine, there's speculation that Roberto is going to marry this Ana woman.' A pause, then, 'I'm so sorry, Tess.'

After numerous reassurances to Faye that she was going to be OK, Tess finally hung up.

Why, oh why, hadn't she thought to look up Roberto on the internet before now? She was a fairly computer-savvy person − after all, she'd set up her own website, admittedly with the help of an online service which did most of it for her − but for some reason it hadn't occurred to her to Google him. She'd been so wrapped up in him and her love for him, that she simply hadn't thought of it. She felt like a total idiot. He'd deceived her, lied to her, toyed with her feelings, and Tess thought her heart was going to break in two from the agony of it.

How could he have lied to her? And why? He'd done it so convincingly, too. God, but everyone she'd met when she had been with him probably knew who he was, except her. The waiters in 'his' tapas bar knew; the woman in the bridal shop must have known, considering Roberto's sister had bought her dress from there; Adolfo, the maître d', had clearly known – Tess's face flushed with embarrassment. The man must have thought her a right idiot. Roberto probably thought she was a right idiot too, not to realize. Tess felt a total and utter fool, as if Roberto had played her. Clearly he hadn't loved her enough to tell her the truth – if he actually loved her at all, that is.

Then there was the flat – what a pretence that was, she realized. It most likely belonged to his father, so what must his father think of her, being set up in some apartment as if she was Roberto's mistress? Was that all she was to Roberto – a bit on the side?

She turned her attention back to her phone and re-read the tag line on the photo of her and Roberto. *Tapas princess?* Ana-Sofía what's-her-name already looked and acted the part, and she and Roberto seemed perfect together. They looked perfect in every single photo Tess had seen them in. The stuff that was written about them didn't help Tess's mood, either. 'Apparently' (she did the air quotes in her head), they were destined to marry, to bring together two wealthy families. Roberto's father was in the restaurant business; Ana-Sofía's father was in shipping.

Tess's father owned a launderette. There was no way she could compete with that.

Ana-Sofía probably hadn't done a day's work in her life; Tess had been scrimping and saving since she'd left home. Ana-Sofía most likely had a maid to clear up after her; Tess kicked stuff under the bed and hoped she'd have time to deal with the mess tomorrow. Ana-Sofía probably didn't cook; neither did Tess much, so they had something in common at least, but when Tess was hungry she didn't snap her fingers and order something – she opened a tin, or fished a ready-meal out of the freezer. Occasionally she treated herself to sausage and chips from the chippy down the road, but that was only when she was feeling flush.

Ana-Sofía's haircuts probably cost more than Tess earned in a week, her clothes more than Tess earned in a month, and those studs in her ears had most certainly not been £3.99 diamanté ones from Topshop.

No, Tess thought, *Ana-Sofía is perfect for Roberto in every way.* They were the same people, they understood each other, they came from the same background.

Oh God, what was she going to do?

It was quite late, but Tess needed her dad. Not her mum – her *dad*. He'd know what to do, he always did. She listened to the phone in her parents' house ringing and almost hung up, realising at the last minute that she was only going to worry them, but just as her thumb hovered over the 'End Call' button, someone picked up.

It was her father and Tess blew out her cheeks when she heard his familiar voice. 'Dad?'

'Tess? Are you OK?'

'I'm fine,' she assured him, trying desperately to hold it together, not wanting to alarm him, and she heard his loud sigh of relief.

'Do you know what time it is? It's one in the morning!'

Tess let out a strangled hiccup. She'd been crying for the past hour, until her animal cries of distress had finally faded to hiccupping sobs.

'Have you been drinking?' her father demanded.

'No, I—' She gulped and cleared her throat, tears still perilously close to the surface.

'Have you been crying?' her dad demanded. 'What's wrong, Tess, tell me!'

'Everything,' Tess wailed.

'Have you been attacked? Where are you? Are you hurt? Tess! Speak to me.'

Tess smiled, despite her tears. 'I will if you'd let me get a word in edgeways,' she croaked, her throat sore.

'Well?'

'His name is Roberto,' she began, 'and I'm in love with him.'

Tess had kind of expected the stunned silence, though she hadn't expected it to go on for quite as long as it did. 'Dad? Dad? Are you still there?'

'I'm here, hang on.' There was some muffled talking and Tess heard her mother's voice in the background. 'I've told your mother it's nothing to worry about,' Dad said. 'She thought you'd been mugged or something.'

I have been mugged, Tess wanted to say, *and my most valuable possession has been stolen – my heart.*

Tess heard the sound of a flick as the kettle was switched on, then the sound of cupboard doors opening and closing, and she guessed her father was making himself a cup of tea.

'You've met someone.' It wasn't a question, but rather a statement. 'Your mother thought there was something going on, but I told her she was being silly. Looks like I was wrong. That explains why we've hardly heard a peep out of you for the past couple of days. Did he dump you, is that it?'

'No, I'm going to dump him.'

Just as soon as she got off the phone, Tess intended to send Roberto a text. She knew it wasn't a very nice way to end a relationship, but neither was finding out she was playing second fiddle to another woman. But she was desperate to hear a friendly voice first, to have someone to commiserate with her and tell her she was doing the right thing, and that everything would be all right, even if, deep down, she knew nothing would ever be really OK again.

'So, what's the drama about then, if you're going to give him the elbow?' her father wanted to know. 'You can't think that much of him, if you're planning on chucking him.'

'It isn't like that,' Tess tried to explain. 'He wants me to stay here with him—'

'Stay there? In Barcelona?' Her dad sounded outraged. 'Live with him, you mean?'

'No, I'd have my own apartment. He found one for me.'

'What do you mean, "he found one for me"? Where does *he* live?'

Tess sighed. 'He told me he shares a flat with some bloke called Diego, but I think he's really got an apartment in a building on a really expensive avenue.'

'What's he hiding?' Trust her father to get straight to the point.

'Nothing! He wants to give me some time and space, so we can get to know each other properly.'

'It all sounds a bit iffy to me,' her dad sniffed. 'And a bit sudden.' Tess heard his sudden gasp. 'Is he married? Is he trying to set you up as his mistress?'

Tess said, 'He isn't married.' *But there's someone lurking in the background who would like to be his wife, and I don't mean me.*

Tess shoved the idea out of her mind and brought her attention back to the conversation. 'I found out he's been lying to me,' she said, and went on to explain what had happened.

'That's it?' her father asked when she finished. 'He's been deceiving you about being well off? And why is that a problem?'

Tess heard him blowing noisily on his tea before taking a sip, and she smiled. The habit used to annoy the hell out of her when she lived at home, but now she found it strangely comforting.

'He lied to me,' she said.

'He must have had his reasons.'

'Yeah...' Tess replied uncertainly. 'But I can't for the life of me think what they are.'

'OK, let's try looking at things from his point of view. He's rich, yes?'

Tess nodded. 'Yes.'

'Good-looking?'

Her smile was sad. 'Really, really good-looking.'

'The rich bit alone would get women flocking around him,' her father pointed out, 'but throw in good looks, and I bet he's inundated with offers.'

Yeah, that was one of the problems... 'That's one of the things that worries me,' she said.

'You think he wouldn't stay faithful?'

'No.' She hesitated, wondering how best to put her feelings into words. 'He's got the pick of women,' she said, finally. 'Why would he want me?'

'Now you're just fishing for compliments!' Her dad laughed.

'I'm not! I'm serious. Why choose me?'

'Why not? Look, Tessy, I might be a bit biased here, but you're pretty, bright, fun, talented and intelligent. He'd be a fool not to want you.'

'I've seen tons of photos of him online and I'm so different to the women he's usually seen with,' Tess argued.

'Maybe that's why,' her father replied, astutely. 'You're not like every other woman he's met. You're different. You're *you*.'

'I suppose…' She still wasn't convinced.

'You say you love him. Does he love you?'

'He says he does.'

'Do you think he's lying about that, too?'

She shook her head. 'No, but—'

'But nothing. If you don't think he's lying, what's the problem?'

Tess didn't answer.

'You don't think you're good enough for him, do you?' her father said suddenly. 'Let me tell you something, Tess, you most certainly *are* good enough for him. You're good enough for any man, and if someone tells you different send them my way, and I'll put them straight. You're beautiful and – damn it, I'm not going through all your good points again, because it'll just make you big-headed, but you need to stop putting yourself down. Do what you feel is right for *you*, Tess, but if you love him and he loves you, then I say again, what's the problem? The money will only be a hindrance if you let it, and believe me, it can help smooth the way. It can't bring you happiness, but it sure can help. Your mother and I struggled for years, living hand to mouth – I don't want you to have to do the same, Tess, so don't let this come between you.'

Tess stared blankly at the wall as his words sank in. Her father had a point, she conceded. 'But there's still the problem of why he let me think he was a waiter,' she argued. 'Why didn't he just tell me the truth?'

'You'll have to ask him that, but looking at it from the outside, as I said before, I bet he has a lot of women wanting him just for his money, if he's as rich as you say he is. Maybe he's had enough of that and wants someone to love him for *who* he is, not for *what* he is, or for what he can buy them.'

Tess remembered the conversation they'd had when Roberto showed her the harbour where those incredibly expensive yachts had been moored, and how he had seemed surprised and a little pleased when she had said she didn't want to be rich. Maybe her dad had a point.

'What should I do?' she wailed.

'Whatever your heart tells you to do. Look, when push comes to shove, all you need is love, right? The Beatles said that, not me, by the way, in case you're interested.'

She rolled her eyes. 'What about you and Mum?'

'What about us, love?'

'How do you feel about me moving to Barcelona?'

'I'll miss you dreadfully, we all will, but you have to do what's right for you.'

'What if it doesn't work out?' Tess blew out a juddering breath.

'You can always come back home.'

'But I'll have nothing to come back to,' she protested.

'You will. You can move back in with your mum and me, and you'll still have your painting... so, what are you waiting for?'

'I want to move to Barcelona, I want to be with Roberto, but do you think it's too soon?'

'I proposed to your mother on our very first date,' her father admitted, suddenly.

'You did?'

'Yep. And she said "yes", too, but we carried on courting for a while before we told anyone else, especially our parents. We were worried they wouldn't understand, you see. If you feel this is the right decision for you, then do it, and if it's a mistake, then so be it, but you don't want to get to my age thinking, "What if?"'

'What about Mum?' She was the person Tess was most concerned about.

At that thought, Tess blinked away yet more tears, trying not to let them loose on the world. Her father was right, she knew it. So what if Roberto had deceived her? It was for a good reason, assuming her father's analysis was correct. And however awful she felt about moving a thousand miles away, she knew she couldn't live her life for her parents or her sister. She had to live it for herself.

'Leave your mum to me,' he promised. 'She'll be all right, and there are such things as aeroplanes, you know. Talking about planes, are you coming home tomorrow? Because I really think you should tell your mother in person.'

'I'm coming home,' Tess reassured him. 'I can't simply stay here – I've got too much to sort out, and then there are my paints and stuff.' She sniffed and wiped her damp eyes. 'Besides, even when I do leave, I'll be back for Emma's wedding.'

'Right then, now that's all sorted, I'm off to bed. I need my beauty sleep, you know.'

Tess smiled. 'I love you, Dad.'

'Love you too, Tessy.'

Tess was so thankful she'd spoken to her father. He'd given her some perspective, and some sound advice, just as she knew he would.

But there was one more thing she had to do before she went to bed – she had to speak to Roberto and tell him what she knew, and she wanted to give him a chance to explain himself before he arrived to take her to the airport. She had to speak to him tonight. As Faye and her father said, there must be a reason for what he'd done, and she hoped it was the reason her dad had suggested.

Tess picked her phone up once more, took a deep breath, then began to pace as she waited for the call to connect. There was no way she could sit still, with her nerves so on edge, and she realized her legs were shaking.

'Please answer, please,' she muttered, as the phone rang and rang. The ringing stopped.

'Roberto?' She knew she sounded anxious, but she couldn't help it.

'*Quién es?*' a female voice said.

'Um, do you speak English?'

'*Sí.*'

'Can I speak to Roberto, please?' Tess's heart was in her mouth. Why was some woman answering his phone? *OK, don't panic*, she told herself, *it could be one of his sisters, or— or who?*

'He is in the shower.'

For a heartbeat, Tess didn't know what to say, then she heard Roberto's voice in the background.

'*No es nadie, mi amor*,' the female voice replied, though it seemed the woman must have placed her hand over the phone, because her voice had become muffled and Tess heard the sound of high heels on marble or stone. Then the woman's voice became clearer as she called in English, 'I am coming,' before lowering her voice once more. 'Sorry, I promised to get Roberto a towel, and he is waiting for me. *Disculpe*, who did you say you were?'

'Um... it doesn't matter... I'll just... uh. Goodbye.' Tess ended the call and flung her phone as far away from her as she could, then collapsed into floods of tears.

The woman's voice had belonged to Ana-Sofia.

Tess's hand snaked into the packet of Minstrels. Who cared if she'd nearly finished a family-sized bag? And there was a large packet of crisps on the table with her name on it. That should see her through the next couple of hours, until she had to leave for the airport.

Here was another one, she saw, obsessively clicking on yet another photo of Roberto with Ana as she popped the chocolate into her mouth. There was something very satisfying about letting the sweet disc sit on her tongue for a while, before biting into the thin, crispy shell to reveal the softer chocolate inside. She was taking her time eating them – no one could accuse her of stuffing her face in hysterical abandon. She was actually being quite calm about the whole thing, she thought, if you ignored the tears trickling down her cheeks and plopping onto her chest. See, there he was, all smiley white teeth and tanned skin, with his arm around *her*.

Tess hunted for the date. Ah, not recent then, so that made her feel a teensy-weensy bit better. It was taken last

August – so far, she hadn't found anything more recent than late summer, of the two of them together. He'd had his arm around a few different women since then, but he hadn't been photographed lately with Ana-bloody-Sofía.

Tess chased the Minstrel down with a swallow of wine, and squinted at her glass. Half empty. From now on she was going to be a half-empty person, too. Like the wine bottle. Never mind, it would soon be totally empty, just like the way she felt right now.

Blearily, she turned her attention back to the screen. What was it Ana had said? '*No es Nadine*'? 'It's not Nadine.' Had Roberto been expecting someone named Nadine to phone, and if so, who was she? Tess tried to think back to the brief conversation with Ana-Sofía. It had seemed like the 'n' had been cut off, as if Ana had said 'naddy'. Actually, it had sounded like 'nathia', or 'nahthee-uh', with the emphasis on the 'nah'.

Tess typed 'nathia' into Google but the little translation man had nothing for her. 'Nathie, nathie,' she mouthed, and tried again. Nope, nothing, nada. Woah, wait a minute – she knew how nada was spelled, but she also knew that the 'd' was more of a 'th', albeit a soft one. Nadia, then? She typed again, but once more there was nothing, so she tried 'nadiu' and then 'nahdia', with no more success.

More gulps of wine, and now the bottle was definitely empty. Darn it all to hell! She'd call Reception and get them to send up some more.

'Hello? It's Tess. I need wine,' she said, hoarsely, her throat sore from crying so much.

'Sorry, *señorita*, but room service is *finite*. Ended.'

Bugger. She'd have to go out looking for some. She'd already been out once for supplies, because the stupid room service didn't do chocolate or crisps, and now she was forced to go out again. Stupid hotel!

Grabbing her key card and her purse but forgetting to put on any shoes, she staggered to the lift and leaned against the wall, wishing it would stop moving. Hang on, was it moving *because* it was a lift? Oh, yeah, so it was. Her giggle quickly turned into a sob.

'*Bist du OK?*' someone asked, as she almost fell out through the lift doors and onto the marble tiled floor of the reception area.

'Eh?' Tess stared up at a concerned-looking middle-aged man.

'Are you OK?' This time he spoke in English.

'Yeah, fine. Need another bottle.' She waved the empty one in the air. For some reason, she'd brought it out with her. 'Rio-ha. Rio-cha,' she tried to say.

The gentleman gave her a bemused look. 'Rioja?'

'Are you Spanish?' she asked him drunkenly.

'*Nein, Deutscher* – German.' He leaned forward to peer at her. 'Are you sure you are OK? You don't look it.'

'I'm fine. Need wine,' she said, and doubled over in a fit of giggles which quickly turned to sobs again. From her bent-over position, she could see the man's feet shuffling with embarrassment, and she bet he wished he hadn't stopped to ask.

'Are you staying at this hotel?' he asked.

Tess nodded.

'Perhaps you should return to your room?' he suggested, looking around the lobby and frowning.

'I'm not going anywhere until I've got more wine.' Tess slid down the wall. 'Do you speak Spanish?' she asked suddenly.

'*Ein bisschen*, a little,' the man admitted, scanning the empty reception desk.

'What does——?' Tess straightened up by sliding back up the wall. 'What does "no is nathee" mean?'

'Excuse me?'

'No es nathe-uh?' she attempted.

The German tried the phrase on for size, rolling it around in his mouth like a granny eating a boiled sweet. 'Sorry, I don't know, but I see a man who can help,' he said, and strode across the reception area so rapidly that Tess admired his turn of speed. The bloke couldn't wait to get away from her.

'I'll just stay here then, shall I?' Tess said to no one in particular. She swiped the back of her hand over her cheeks, before wiping the dampness off on her jeans. Bloody Roberto, making her cry. It was his fault she was like this. Him and bloody Ana-sodding-Sofia. *I hope they'll be happy together*, she thought sullenly, and promptly burst into tears again.

'Can I help you?'

Mr German had brought reinforcements in the form of one of the reception staff.

'I want wine,' she hiccupped through her sobbing.

'She says she is a guest here,' the German said.

'I will see her to her room,' the receptionist said, running his hand through his hair and rolling his eyes.

'I think she's had too much to drink,' the German added.

The other man got Tess facing the right direction for the lift and said, 'I think so, too.'

Tess let out a snort, halfway between a sob and a giggle, but she had something else on her mind, and said, 'No es nathe-eh.'

'It's no one?' the receptionist said, looking confused.

'What did you say?' Tess squinted at him. 'No one?'

'You just said, "It is no one".'

Ah, so that's what it meant. 'There was a "*mi amor*" bit too,' Tess said, 'but I already know what that means.'

"It's no one, my love." Yes, that's what Ana-Sofía had said. *Roberto thinks I'm no one.* Her heart did a nasty, slow roll in her chest. Ana had called him 'my love'. *She* was his love now, not Tess. It was clear from the too-much-information about sharing a shower with him that the woman must be sharing his bed, too.

He didn't love her, Tess – he couldn't, not when he was seeing Ana-Sofía – and certainly not the way she loved him, because her heart was breaking, and she didn't think it would ever mend.

Then Tess passed out on the floor.

Race Day + 2

'Tess!' Emma enveloped her in a hug as soon as Tess opened the door. 'I've missed you,' she cried. 'And I'm so proud of you!'

Tess smiled wanly back. 'Thanks. Missed you too.' She walked into her bedroom to finish her unpacking with Emma following behind, trying to keep her face averted, knowing her heartache must be written all over it.

'What's wrong?' Emma asked.

Yeah, that didn't work, did it? Tess thought, and turned to face her sister. 'I fell in love in Barcelona,' she began.

Emma laughed. 'I knew you'd love it! I just wish I could have been there with you.'

'Not *with* Barcelona – though I did that too – but *in* Barcelona. With a man called Roberto.'

'Oh.'

There was a very long silence, during which Tess lobbed dirty clothes into the laundry basket, and Emma looked shocked.

'Do you want to talk about it?' her sister asked, eventually.

'Not really.' Tess shrugged. She would have to explain what had happened at some point, but not now, not when it was still so raw.

She felt like something the cat had mauled and left for dead – her head was pounding, her stomach was in knots and her heart was broken. Tess admitted to herself that she was a mess.

She hadn't slept a wink all night, and though she felt deathly tired now, it was a weariness of the heart and soul as much as physical tiredness. She'd left the hotel shortly after the kind receptionist had checked the train times for her, and then escorted her back to her room.

Tess had arrived at the terminal early – very, very early. The last thing she had wanted to do was to bump into Roberto. Not that she thought he might follow her, but she couldn't be sure. She had sent him a text once she was through to the departure lounge, then she had turned her mobile off, and still hadn't switched it back on again. She'd called her parents and Emma from the landline once she got back to her flat, just to let them know she was safely home.

Home. Her flat hadn't felt like home since the minute she'd stepped back into it, and she had a feeling that it was going to take her a while to settle down again, to return to being the woman she had been before she'd visited the city by the sea – before she'd lost her heart. If she ever could, that is.

'I bought you a present,' Tess said to her sister, when she came across the beautifully wrapped box at the bottom of her case. She lifted it out and gave it to Emma.

'What is it?' Even though Tess could see that Emma was worried about her, her sister was still excited to receive a gift. And when she opened it and saw what was inside, her eyes filled with tears, and Tess was glad she'd bought her the wedding veil.

'It must have cost you a fortune,' Emma said, her face shining. 'It's beautiful! Oh, Tess, I hope you didn't spend too much – do you know how much Spanish lace costs? Oh, silly me, of course you do – you've bought some. And it's exquisite. I love it! Thank you, thank you, thank you!'

Emma leaned in for a hug, and Tess put her arms around her younger sister, trying not to remember Roberto's face in the mirror as Tess had modelled it.

Emma was saying: 'Let me give you the money for it – you can't afford this.'

Tess was affronted. 'It's a present,' she insisted, 'And, anyway, it was the last one they had in this style, so it was reduced.' Then a thought occurred to her, and instinct told her she was right. It hadn't been a sale item at all, had it? Roberto had somehow sorted something (and Tess wasn't sure what) with the sales assistant. He must have paid for most of it.

She shook her head, not knowing what to think, or how to feel. What she did know was that she needed to turn her phone back on and check her calls: she didn't want to risk missing a business call for the sake of not wanting to see Roberto's name on the screen.

She waited until Emma left before plucking up the courage to switch the darned thing back on. Immediately, she was inundated with notifications – mainly calls, and mainly from Roberto.

Without wanting to, but unable to help herself, she listened to the first voicemail.

'Tess? Turn your phone on – I'm outside. No matter, I'll come to your room.'

'Tess? Where are you? The hotel says you checked out hours ago. Tess?' This was followed by muttering in Spanish.

'I'm getting worried now. Please call me.'

'Call me. Please!'

She had 17 phone calls from him altogether – after the first few voice messages, Tess assumed he'd not bothered to leave her any more.

There was only one text, and when she read it, she had to clap her hand over her mouth to hold back her sobs.

I love you.

Although she wasn't hungry, Tess knew she had to eat. Having little in the fridge or the cupboards, she settled for a cheese and pickle sandwich, while trying to find some inspiration for her final illustration. Tess was trying to lose herself in her painting, and although the initial sketches for the book she'd been working on for the past five hours were almost finished, the last image simply didn't want to come, no matter how many times she read the text. It was about a nasty troll, who wasn't really nasty at all but had a dire reputation to uphold, and who was confronted by a little girl who wasn't in the least bit scared of him. The pair of them had lots of adventures, until the troll eventually turned over a new leaf, deciding it was better to help people than to hurt them. But he could still roar and shout when the occasion demanded. Oh, and he and the little girl became best friends.

I bet the little girl didn't grow up to marry the troll, though, Tess thought bitterly. Maybe she could write a sequel aimed at adults, where the little girl grows up and the troll runs off with another troll.

She took a desultory bite of her sandwich while standing at the kitchen counter, not bothering with niceties like a plate or sitting at the table to eat. She simply rested her bum against the counter and ate without tasting. It was fuel to stop her stomach rumbling and to make sure she didn't keel over, nothing more, nothing less.

However much she wanted it to be, this last illustration couldn't be as dark and twisted as the ones she'd just drawn. This one had to portray hope, and lessons learned, and fluffy-wuffy stuff to hammer home the message that we should all be nice to each other and treat each other with kindness. There had to be balance, and at the moment the illustrations were rather grim-heavy. Nice was what was needed, but Tess felt as far from nice as it was possible to get.

Maybe I could draw the troll having a tantrum, but looking out from the page and winking to show he doesn't mean it, Tess thought. No, that wasn't right… *OK, how about…?* No, not that either. She finished the last bite of sandwich and followed it with a glass of orange juice, then cleared her dinner things away and tried again. It was nearly ten o'clock by now and she'd worked non-stop since late afternoon, so if inspiration didn't strike soon, she'd call it a day. Besides, trying to draw to forget her misery simply hadn't worked, and though her phone had remained silent since that last text from Roberto telling her he loved her, she couldn't stop herself from checking the screen every few minutes.

She'd only just sat down at her desk again and picked up a pencil when the downstairs door buzzer went.

Who on earth could that be? She pressed the intercom button, expecting it to be her mother, or maybe her dad. She'd spoken to him briefly earlier, telling him she wouldn't be relocating to Barcelona, but she hadn't said much more than that, and he was bound to be curious to know what had gone wrong. It was a bit late for him to pop round, though…

'Hello?' she said into the machine.

No answer, not even static. The blasted thing must be broken again. She didn't know why she bothered with it. Nine times out of ten, she ended up having to traipse down the stairs and peer through the spyhole.

Which was exactly what she did this time.

But when she opened the door, it wasn't her father.

'Hello, Tess,' Roberto said.

Tess was speechless.

She stood, frozen to the spot with her mouth open, gaping at him. He waited for his presence to sink in, standing equally still – apart from his eyes: they were drinking her in, scouring the length of her, from her sock-clad feet to her messy bun. Tess couldn't help noticing that his eyes looked nervous, and hurt and confused.

'Hello,' Tess finally squeaked. Oh God, why couldn't she have found something more profound to say?

'Why?' was all he said, his voice hoarse. Then he stuffed his hands in the pockets of his cargos, hunched his shoulders, and stared at her.

'I know about you,' she said, after a too-long pause during which she tried to marshal her thoughts. The only thing running through her mind was, "He's here! He's really here!"

'You do? What do you know?' he asked, and she still couldn't accept that he was standing in front of her, so it took her another pause before she replied.

'Everything.'

'I can see that it bothers you. But, Tess, why didn't you talk to me first before running away? I could have explained…'

'I did. I tried to call you, but you didn't answer your phone,' she said. '*She* did. Ana-Sofia.'

'*Ana-Sofia?*'

'She said you were having a shower together. Or were just about to.'

Roberto jerked his head. 'We were not!' he cried indignantly. 'I have never had a shower with Ana.' Then he frowned. 'She told you *that*?'

'Yes.'

'When did she tell you this? Look, Tess, can I come in? I don't want the whole world to watch when I beg.'

Beg? What was he going to beg for? Deep down, Tess thought she knew, but she didn't want to believe he'd come all this way for her, just in case it wasn't true.

She moved to the side and ushered him in, closing the door behind him and hoping he didn't notice that she was trembling from head to foot.

'It is not as warm as Barcelona,' he said, following her up the stairs, and her memory of him doing exactly the same thing in the little apartment above Las Tapas Picantes was tempered with the inane thought that he'd travelled a thousand miles, and all he could talk about was the weather.

When he stepped inside her flat she saw his eyes dart around her living room and settle on her work-station, before checking out the rest.

'It is nice,' he said, politely.

'Not what you're used to,' she replied, and he had the grace to look sheepish.

'Please, sit down,' she said. 'Tea? Coffee?' Crikey, this was like talking to a complete stranger. She didn't wait for an answer, but dived into the kitchen, grabbing hold of the worktop with both hands and taking several deep breaths, wishing she had some alcohol in the house. Anything would do – wine, gin, absinthe…

Hearing a faint movement from the living room, she hurried to fill the kettle and spoon coffee into a couple of mugs. While she waited for the kettle to boil she tried to calm her heart rate down. Her pulse thudded in her ears and she was still shaking, so she leaned her elbows on the counter and put her head in her hands, wanting to hope he was there because he loved her, but not daring to, yet pleading it was true with every cell of her body.

When she'd seen him standing there, larger than life and twice as gorgeous, she'd wanted to throw herself into his arms. But he'd said he was there to beg, and she prayed fervently that he was going to beg for the same thing she was, and that he wasn't there to ask her to keep her mouth shut and not sell her story to the papers, or—

'Tess?'

She hadn't heard him enter the kitchen, and she jumped at the delicious velvety sound of his voice. Then she jumped again when he put a hand on her shoulder, only for him to snatch it away again at her reaction to his touch.

'Sorry, I didn't mean—' He halted.

Tess took a leap. Someone had to go first and what more did she have to lose? '… to break my heart?' she finished for him.

He looked away and shrugged. 'You broke mine.'

'Are you with her, Ana-Sofía?'

'Ana?' He seemed surprised. 'No, she is in Barcelona, I think.'

'I didn't mean did you bring her with you to England.'

'No, of course you didn't. I'm sorry, I'm very nervous.'

'Why?' Tess's voice cracked, and she cleared her throat.

'Of seeing you again.' Roberto paused, as if gathering his thoughts. 'To answer your question, no, I am not with Ana. I have never been with her. I have told you this several times.'

'So why did she say she was going to have a shower with you? After all, she *did* answer your phone.'

His eyes narrowed, and he looked into the corner of the room. 'What time did you call?' He took his phone out of his pocket and thumbed at the screen.

'I don't know, but it was really late. One thirtyish?'

'I don't have a call from you,' he said. He looked up at her. 'Ana must have deleted it.'

'You still haven't told me why she answered your phone in the first place,' Tess said.

'My parents were having dinner with Ana's parents, and after I left you at the hotel, I was too *emocionado*… too excited, to go back to my apartment, so I called by to tell them, my father especially, that I was in love. *Am* in love,' he amended. 'Ana was there. I didn't want her to be, but this is my parents' house, so...' He shrugged. 'I had a drink on the terrace while I waited for her and her family to leave. When Ana joined me, I was rude to her and got up as soon as she sat down. I wasn't in the mood to speak with her. I remember I left my phone on the table – that must be when you called.'

Tess knew Roberto wasn't telling the truth. 'She spoke to you, when I was talking to her,' she said, accusingly.

He thought for a second, then his face cleared. 'I remember shouting to her from the living room, because I thought I heard my phone ring, and she said it was no one, a sales call.'

'But—' But Tess didn't have any more questions. And her doubts were fast disappearing, too. The cow! Tess closed her eyes. Ana had set her up perfectly and Tess had fallen right into her trap.

When she opened them again, it was to find that Roberto was right in front of her, only inches away. She was close enough to smell his aftershave, mixed with the unique scent of him. His dark eyes were unfathomable, and for the first time Tess noticed the lines around them. He looked as though he was in pain. She knew that feeling all too well.

'Tess, I had to come. I had to know why you left so suddenly,' he said. 'And why you sent that text...' He blinked hard. 'I thought we had something special. I thought we were in love.' His voice broke on the last word, and he looked down at his feet.

'We did, we... oh, hell!' she cried. Her eyes filled with tears and she willed them not to fall.

'Do you still love me?' he asked, and his voice was full of anguish. 'I need to know.'

This was it; it was now or never, as the old song went. After all, if he'd gone to all this trouble to find her, he must still have some feelings for her.

'Yes,' she whispered. 'With all my heart.'

'Oh.'

Oh? Oh! Was that all he could say? She'd just laid her soul bare, and all he could say was "Oh"? Her tears made good on their threat and spilled over to trickle down her face.

'Is it so bad to love me?' he asked, softly.

'Yes, it damn well is!' she cried.

'You don't want to feel this way?'

'Would you? Look at me! It hurts. Loving you hurts, Roberto, and I wish I didn't feel this way, but I do. Satisfied?'

'I love you, too.'

'Oh.'

'See, it is not so easy.' His smile was small and uncertain, but the lines around his eyes weren't quite as pronounced.

'You. Love. *Me*.' Tess desperately wanted it to be true, but she had to make certain. Her poor heart couldn't take any more pain.

'I think I may have told you this before, too. Why don't you believe me?'

'I did, but then I found out who you really were and—'

'You decided I couldn't possibly love you?'

Tess nodded. 'And then there was Ana-Sofía…' she trailed off.

'You are an idiot.' His voice was filled with love, taking the sting out of his words.

'I know,' Tess whispered, as she swiped her sleeve across her face to mop up her tears. He loved her! Her heart swelled like a cresting wave and threatened to drown her in love.

'A beautiful, wonderful idiot,' he said, his body moving closer to hers, his arms slipping around her.

It was Tess's turn to smile. 'I know.'

'Can I kiss you?'

'You don't need to ask.' Tess tilted her head back and her lips parted.

'Not here.' His voice was thick with longing, and a raw hunger shone in his eyes. 'You have a bedroom, yes?'

'Yes, I have a bedroom.' Her breath caught as an answering longing shot through her. God, how she wanted this man. She vowed to hold him fast and never let him go, no matter what the future may hold.

He took a small step back and she almost groaned in despair, but her dismay turned to joy when he bent forward, scooped her into his arms, and said softly, 'Then let me show you just how much I love you.'

Tess melted into him. This was where she belonged, the only place she wanted to be, and when he took her to bed and showed her just how much he loved her, she knew he felt the same way as she did.

May

Weight: Who cares? I don't even own any scales.

'You are so clever.' Roberto's arms snaked around her from behind, and he rained soft kisses down on the back of her neck, making her shiver with sudden desire.

'Stop that,' she said. 'If you keep on, I'll never get this finished.'

"This" was Tess's gift to Emma and Declan – a portrait of her sister and her husband-to-be laughing and looking into each other's eyes, adoration on their faces. She hoped they would like it, but just in case, she'd bought them a more traditional gift to accompany it – a beautiful Tiffany-style lamp that Tess knew Emma would adore.

'Why do you need to finish it tonight? Surely it can wait?' He nibbled her ear.

It could, she supposed… But, no. This painting was in oils, and oil paint took a long time to harden. She wanted it totally dry before she risked wrapping it. But then again, what was one more day…?

'You're a bad man,' she said, pushing him away. She really had to get the painting done, and he was terribly naughty for trying to distract her.

'I can be good too, no?'

'No.'

'You'll change your mind when I show you something,' he said.

'What?'

'It's a surprise.'

'I haven't got time for surprises.'

'You'll have time for this one.'

Tess couldn't resist, and she allowed him to lead her out of the little apartment and down the stairs. As they strolled hand in hand down the street, Tess's heart swelled with love for this gorgeous man by her side. She still hadn't got over the shock of seeing him on her doorstep all those weeks ago, and sometimes she was scared to think of what her life might have been like then, if he hadn't come to England for her. After their emotional reunion (thinking about it still made her cry with happiness), they'd spent the next couple of days organising Tess's move to Barcelona. She'd taken him to meet her parents (well, she'd had to, hadn't she?) and Emma, and had even found the time to show him her city. Not that she could give him a great deal of information about it; in fact, it was Roberto who'd told her all about its history: he had been just as awed by the magnificent cathedral as Tess had been by the Sagrada Familia, and he had known almost as much about it, too!

'This tomb here is of King John,' he said during their visit, halting by the effigy of a man wearing a crown, his hands resting on his chest. He had walked to the foot of the tomb and read the plaque. 'It says here that he was born at Christmas in 1166 in the Tower of London, but I read somewhere that his birthplace was in Oxford.'

Roberto had looked genuinely perplexed and Tess had been forced to bite back a smile. He could be so earnest sometimes. 'I will have to check this later,' he said.

'You like history, don't you?' she asked, taking his hand and leading him to another tomb, this time of Prince Arthur, Henry VIII's older brother. His premature death had paved the way for England's most notorious king to take the throne and marry his widow, and so Protestant England had been born.

Trust Roberto to know all about that!

'My degree is in history,' he had said.

'You have a degree?' For some reason she'd assumed he'd worked in the family business from when he was quite young.

'Don't sound surprised.' He gave her a wounded look, followed by a sacrilegious kiss. 'My father wanted me to study business, but it doesn't stir my heart like history does.'

'It's a shame you never used it,' she mused.

Roberto took hold of her shoulders and turned her to face him, his expression suddenly serious. 'What would you say if I were to tell you that I might not be my father's son?'

'Pardon me?'

'My father, he wants me to follow in his steps, to take over the business, but this is something I cannot do.'

'Why not?' Not that she cared what Roberto did, as long as he was happy; she was simply curious. There was so much about this man she had yet to learn, and she was looking forward to every single discovery.

'It is his dream, not mine,' Roberto said simply. 'Whilst you were in Barcelona I had a series of interviews for a job with the Turisme de Barcelona.' He sounded a little apprehensive of her reaction, and cast several swift glances at her out of the corner of his eye. 'The tourist office,' he added, in case she hadn't understood.

So that's what he had been doing when he'd said he had business to attend to! 'Did you get it?' she asked.

He smiled shyly. 'I did. Is this OK?'

'Of course it's OK!' she cried, then lowered her voice when she realized she was in a church. 'Why wouldn't it be?'

'I won't be earning the same money as working for my father,' he said.

'Who cares about that? Money doesn't matter, not when we've got each other.'

Roberto leaned forward and kissed her on the nose, then he became serious once more. 'I don't want you to worry – I have enough money for us to live, more than enough, and the job, it pays well. But not enough to buy you a yacht,' he added, with a sly smile.

'I'm not worried,' she assured him, standing on tiptoe to kiss him on the end of *his* nose. In fact, in some ways she was relieved. She liked money, but too much of it made her uneasy. She hadn't been lying when she'd said she only wanted enough to live on and a bit extra. And who wanted a yacht anyway? She certainly didn't!

'I will sell my apartment, though,' he said. 'I'm not sure I can afford it.'

'The one you share with Diego?' she teased. 'Does Diego even exist?'

'He's real,' Roberto laughed, 'but no, I don't share with him.'

'And who did the old car belong to?'

'The chef in Las Tapas Picantes. The one who frowns a lot. That car is the worst thing I have ever driven.'

'I could tell,' she laughed. 'So, new job, eh? How do your parents feel about it?'

'My father is furious, though it is a very good job. He has threatened to cut me off; he says I am no longer his son.' Roberto looked surprisingly happy about it.

'You're not upset?' she asked.

'Not at all. Are you?'

Tess shook her head.

'He will, how do you say…? Come around. He barks worse than he bites, but for now, I am an orphan.' He threw his head back and laughed. 'Families, eh?'

Her family had taken the news of her impending move surprisingly well, and Tess guessed she had her dad to thank for that. Yes, there had been tears (hers, her mother's, Emma's – even her father's eyes had been suspiciously damp) but Roberto had charmed them as Tess knew he would, and they were delighted for her.

So, when she had found herself in Barcelona once more, tracking up and down the stairs leading to the apartment above Las Tapas Picantes, unloading her possessions, she had been as happy as if she was moving into a ten-bedroom mansion.

'I didn't think your father would agree to letting me live here,' she'd said at the time, when she realized that Miguel owned the whole building.

'He didn't, but he is scared of Abuela,' was Roberto's reply, and Tess had sent a silent "thank you" to Celestina, vowing to thank her properly the next time they met, which wasn't long after they'd moved in.

In fact, Tess had only recently met Roberto's parents, and she hadn't been looking forward to it, but they had been courteous and friendly. His mother, especially, had made a big effort to make her feel welcome – the roast beef dinner hadn't been as good as her own mother's, but Tess appreciated the gesture all the same. His father seemed to thaw a little as the evening progressed, but she couldn't help feeling that he blamed Tess for his son's rebellion.

Roberto cut into her thoughts. 'We're here,' he announced, after they had strolled right the way through the Gothic Quarter and out the other side. They were now on a road with fantastic views of the beach. 'Close your eyes.'

Tess did as she was told, wondering what on earth he was up to. She heard the jangle of a key and the click as it opened a lock. Maybe he had sold his Avinguda Diagonal apartment and had bought somewhere new? He took both her hands in his and guided her up a shallow step, then turned her around.

'You can open them now.'

Tess opened her eyes.

'Oh! Oh my!'

She certainly hadn't anticipated that! They were standing in the middle of a large, bright, open space, with white walls and white ceramic tiles on the floor. Sunlight streamed in through the huge widows, and Tess guessed the place might have been a shop in a former lifetime.

But it wasn't a shop now.

It was a studio.

Tess, hardly able to see through her tears of joy, stared at the easels, the stacks of blank canvases, the shelves holding brushes, and paints, and every other item she could ever possibly need. And that wasn't all – drying racks, a sink and worktops were all laid out in exactly the right position, and through an open door to the rear of the room, Tess could see an office, with a desk, complete with a computer and a scanner.

'There is a little kitchen and separate toilet behind the office,' Roberto said, watching her face.

'You've sold your apartment, haven't you?' she demanded.

Roberto chuckled, and she felt the rumble in her back as he stepped behind her and wrapped his arms around her waist, resting his chin on her head. 'I did.'

'And this is for me?' Tess was incredulous.

Another chuckle. 'Who else would it be for? It certainly isn't mine – I can't draw for chocolate.'

Tess let out a giggle. 'Toffee,' she laughed, blinking back those treacherous tears. But she was so happy, she could cry. Her very own studio – something she had always wanted.

But, wait…

'I can't afford this,' she began, but Roberto turned her to face him and stopped her protests with a kiss.

When they came up for air he said, 'You don't have to afford it. This is my gift to you.'

'I can't accept it,' she protested, 'it's too much.'

'Will it make it any easier for you to accept, if I say it is my wedding present to you?'

'Your *what*?'

Suddenly he was down on one knee and fumbling to open a small, black, velvet box. 'Will you marry me?' he asked.

Tess blinked back tears of joy and her heart soared with happiness. 'Yes, please! I love you, Roberto Pérez Montero.'

'I love you too, Tess Barton,' he replied softly, and Tess knew that she really was the luckiest woman in the world.